THE OMEN GIRL

THE OMEN GIRL

YUEH YANG

wattpad books **w**

wattpad books **W**

An imprint of Wattpad WEBTOON Book Group

Copyright © 2025 Yueh Yang

Content warning: death and minor violence

Published in Canada by Wattpad WEBTOON Book Group, a division of Wattpad WEBTOON Studios, Inc.

36 Wellington Street E., Suite 200, Toronto, ON M5E 1C7 Canada

www.wattpad.com

First Wattpad Books edition: October 2025

ISBN 978-1-99834-106-1(Trade Paper original)
ISBN 978-1-99834-183-2 (Hardcover edition)
ISBN 978-1-99834-129-0 (eBook edition)

Library and Archives Canada Cataloguing in Publication information is available upon request.

Printed and bound in Canada

1 3 5 7 9 10 8 6 4 2

Cover illustration by Sydney Bright
Typesetting by Delaney Anderson

To the ones who started the fires,
and the ones who put them out.

To the ones who stayed.

Thank you.

THE STARSONG LANGUAGE

BEGINNING FORMS

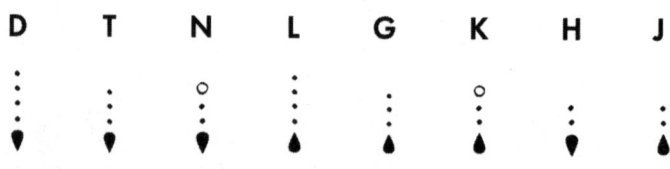

A   I   U   E   O   Y

B   P   M   F   V   W   R

D   T   N   L   G   K   H   J

Q   X   S   Z

MIDDLE FORMS

A	I	U	E	O	Y

B	P	M	F	V	W	R

D	T	N	L	G	K	H	J

Q	X	S	Z

ENDING FORMS

A   I   U   E   O   Y

B   P   M   F   V   W   R

D   T   N   L   G   K   H   J

Q   X   S   Z

STARSONG WORDS

Anvah
Humble to and
compassionate of
others' struggles
and shortcomings.

Ahavah
To seek someone's
well-being without
expecting anything
in return.

Enkrah
To manage one's
actions, thoughts,
and emotions.

Hrah
Adopting joy in the
coming future.

Rahv
To be loyal and
devoted and firm
in truth.

Sahd
A helping hand; a
blow to the head.

Sav
Of not giving in
to anger even in
the face of provo-
cation.

Sha
To be complete or
whole.

Tahv
Choosing goodness
over evil.

Beginning Form

A

Yir'agnia
Birdsong.

*The apostrophe denotes a
breath or a break in the sound.

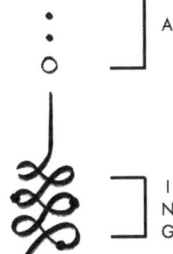

Middle Form — I N G

Ending Form — A

Beginning Form — R

Middle Form

I

Ending Form — Y

PROLOGUE

Against the canvas of the night sky, people turn into stars.

The city below is dim, its citizens hushed. Streaking above us and through the air are stars shaped like people, tearing past like fighter jets, hurtling away like a scream. Their skin is living liquid light, and stardust trails in their wake. The dust settles gold over my skin; it itches.

Father's hand is warm on my ankle. I'm sitting on his shoulders.

Look, he says. *Look, Sozo.*

I look, but the people are gone. They've dipped away into the dense geometry of the cityscape, and all is dark again.

Sozo, Mother says. She leans close to whisper. *If you win the Decade-Races, fly faster and better than anyone else, you'll win a wish, any wish.*

You'll win the right to anything you desire.

Do you understand, Sozo?

Yes, I lie, because I'm only four, and all I understand is the height of the world from my father's shoulders, and the warmth of my mother's hand on my back.

There's no need to understand races and wishes when I already have everything I need.

Against the canvas of a white, white wall, I am told to take off my clothes.

I'm lined up with other kids my age, six or seven years old. All our clothes are too big, our shoes too worn. Standing to my left is a girl, half a head taller with round blue eyes, and we look at each other. We're standing too far apart to hold hands, so all we can do is look at each other.

Men and women in blue police gear go down our line one by one to turn us and to check us, to look at us all over.

Listen up, they say. *There've been reports of an Omen here.*

They're charged with burglary, assault, vandalism, theft. A young female. Black hair, black eyes, pale skin. An omen stain on her back.

I swallow. They're talking about me. I've broken into many places. I've stolen many things. The lie I tell myself is that I have to. No one else in the world is looking out for me, after all, not anymore.

It's my turn to be looked over. The police eye me and wait.

I retract my arms from my airy shirt and pull it up over my head. And then I do what I always do—I hide my omen stain.

Hiding it is not something the others can do. I don't know why. All I know is that it's a simple thing, like holding my breath, where the black spill of my omen sinks back underneath my skin. But like holding my breath, I can't hide it for long, just long enough to get away with things like this.

The men and women turn me around and look over my skin, and I know they see nothing but the bumps of my spine, the bumps of my rib cage, the pinprick bumps over my white skin from the cold. They find no omen stain, though it's there.

It will always be there.

The police move on. I slip on my clothes. They look at the girl next to me, and she shrinks back against the wall, shakes her head, panics. A policewoman, her glove thick and squeaking, clamps her hand around the girl's arm and yanks. The girl yelps, struggles. She paws at the unfeeling glove and says please. *Please.*

So I step between them.

Wait, I say. *It's not her*, I beg. And I know. I should tell them, tell them the whole truth. (I'm the thief. I'm the Omen girl you're looking for.)

But I'm scared. I know I have no right to be. But I'm scared.

The woman shoves me aside. No one is listening. The girl thrashes and kicks and wails, and the more she does, the more something coils up from her too-worn shoe, up around her ankle, up her calf.

An omen stain, dark as a scab.

It thickens leathery as a hide. It crawls up her leg and hip until the whole of her skin is no longer skin, but rough like earth, and just as dark. Her teeth are lengthening. Her nails are sharpening. She growls and slobbers, and becomes something like a beast.

I've never seen anything like this before.

The stories were true.

We *can* turn into monsters.

The police have bolt pistols in their hands. They take aim against the no-longer-girl's head and fire. There is no blood. The monster collapses against the ground, doesn't move again. It's—*she's*—dead. I don't know. I can't breathe. I can't move. It's my fault she's dead.

Am I even allowed to mourn her?

Before the police leave, they turn to us where we stand, stupefied and petrified by the white, white wall. They say, *Stay away from Omens.* They say, *At best they're criminals. At worst, monsters.*

One of them looks at me and asks me if I understand, and I can say nothing. I can't even nod. If I move, I might break. If I open my mouth, I might hurl.

But I understand.

I don't want to understand, but I do.

Against a dead end in the night full of smoke, a woman named Esp finds me.

Three years have passed since that day against the wall. I'm huddled underneath a dripping red tarp, and a pipe beside me trembles with hot water and hisses and hisses. My reflection in the laundry-gray puddles is like the reflection of a stray—small, dark, dirty.

A shadow is cast over me. I look up and see Esp.

It's like looking up at a vulture, a black vulture. Her jacket is puffy and dark, with fur fat around the collar to guard her against the nighttime chill. Her legs are slender, long, slick with the reflected reds of neon lights. She's chewing gum and blowing a bubble. Her hair is electric green.

"You lost?" she asks.

"Are *you*?" I reply.

She pops her gum and stares. I stare back. This is my dead end; I got here first. And if I act afraid, act small and soft, she'll take it from me.

I notice her omen stain then, her stain like a loud afterthought, curved like a sickle from the corner of her lip over her cheek and ear, up into her hairline. I don't know how I missed it.

She snorts at my glare. "Put your gun away, kid. You got a name?"

"I'm not a kid."

"No? You look like one, talk like one, act like one."

I bare my teeth. "Zap off."

"A kid," she repeats. "But a kid I could use." My silence is stunned. I've never been of use to anybody.

She says, "I hear talk you're special."

My stain, and the way I can hide it.

"You tired yet," she asks, "of being lesser than?"

Gutter-walkers. Alley-dwellers. For us, mothers pull their children closer to point and to say look, look, that lump against that corner, that one there is evil.

"You got a wish, kid?"

I'm startled again. I'm an Omen. Omens don't deserve wishes. I recall my faded memory of the races, and of stars, and of the things I felt then. But I don't have a wish.

I have many.

I wish I were good. I wish I had a bed to call my own. I wish people didn't spit on my shadow when I passed by, and that I told the truth that day against the white, white wall.

I wish I could go back to that warmth underneath the stardust, to the days when I didn't need wishes.

Maybe the woman sees something in my expression, because she nods. She says, "I have a wish. People like us all do. Omens, they say. Monsters, they say. We're the unlucky byproduct of some genetic lottery. That's all we are. Ten people could commit the same crime, and only one of them would be stained. A city and a world where the unlucky are punished. What a joke. What an absolute joke."

It's unjust, she says, and I agree. With a force like thruster fire, I agree.

It needs to be rectified, she says, and I tilt up at her, wait for her to tell me the answer. How will this be rectified? How will we monsters be given justice?

Instead she looks at me and asks, "Do you understand?"

I don't. I told her I'm not a kid, but I am. Justice and wishes are beyond me, have always been beyond me. She turns from me then and steps away. My heart drops—I've failed her, somehow. She's leaving, just like my parents did.

So I lie, the way I've always done. "Yes."

I tell her, "I understand."

And she stops. She twists back at the mouth of the dead end. Her voice echoes off the edges of the alleyway when she says, "Good."

She tells me to come, and to follow her, and so I do.

She doesn't need to know I've lied. And maybe one day, when I'm grown, when I'm stronger, I will no longer need to lie.

ONE

Four Years Later

In the gentle haze of morning, in the open courtyard of low clay roofs, burnished verandas, and manicured bonsai trees, a boy in white falls from the sky.

His skin is staining black.

That's what does it. That's why nobody moves. Everyone knows, after all, what that staining over his skin could be.

I push through the numb crowd, but I am too far, too late.

The boy lands shoulder first against the stone of the courtyard. The snap of his bones echoes. His eyes roll white from the pain, and then his body slides down and away to sink into the dark mouth of the pit behind him.

It's the training pit—a concrete bowl gouged deep into the earth, curved enough to catch the wind. Some days, windy days, all it does is howl and howl, like a hungry thing.

Still no one moves. We're all here for our morning exercises, dressed in our school's training robes and single-toed socks and bamboo sandals, to warm up and to wait our turns to fly. But now, no one knows what to do.

Something bitter twists through me.

In the matter of a single fall, the people here have drawn a line between him and them. But all I know is that a boy like me is down there, and that boy is hurt.

I leave the crowd. I cross that empty stretch of courtyard alone.

Behind me, the boys and girls—from as young as seven to as old as seventeen—stay huddled, watching and waiting. They are afraid some monster is going to claw its way up and out of the pit.

"Did you see?" one of them whispers. "His skin bruised all black."

"The silhouette of the sun," someone else answers.

"The sun's not even up that high yet."

"And he fell. It's so close to the Joining now. No one should be falling."

"He's dead," someone wails, someone much younger. "I bet he's dead. Or the stain's overtaken him and he's a monster now. We should go get the master. We shouldn't be here."

Some of the people murmur, and nod, and pull away. Some others laugh and say things like, *Don't be silly—only stupid babies believe omen stains turn people into monsters.*

No one stops my going. No one stops me because they are curious, and because I have by now a reputation in this school. The infamous Sozo, the girl who grew up on the streets of Tall Titan. The unfriendly girl who never smiles. Bump into Sozo in the halls of the school and she'll bite your ear off, they say. Look at her wrong, they say, and she'll bite trenches into your skin.

I don't correct them. The rumors about me keep all of them at a distance, after all. It keeps all of them from looking too hard and seeing the truth of who I am.

I step to the edge of the drop and peer over it. In that dimness, the first thing I notice is the white of his robes, like a messy smear of sunshine.

The boy is sprawled on his back. He writhes and clutches at his arm, but he is alive and still just a boy, not a monster. When he sees me, he sobs. The arm he is clutching is bruised, but not only from the fall. I know that color. I've seen it many times in the mirror, on my back, when no one else is around.

To the gasps of those behind me, I slide down into the pit.

The training glider he was flying on is beside him, splintered in two. Its engine is shattered open, along with the gears seated inside. In a real glider—or anchor, as they're called—that engine is where the star would sit and shine.

"It hurts," he cries.

"I know," I say, and I wish I knew how to comfort him. But I've never been taught how.

I help him to his feet and position myself against his side. When I loop my arm around his waist, I realize he's small. Young. If I'm about fourteen, he can only be seven or so.

Fear pricks me, suddenly. The Joining is at the end of this week. Now that I've been seen helping the boy, people will be wary of me, suspicious of me. There are many superstitions about the omen stain. I've come so far hiding who I am. Could this jeopardize everything?

A silhouette appears at the mouth of the pit above us.

It's Lumi, a girl my age and height. She's robed like us, but with her face completely covered by a smooth porcelain mask. Even her eyes are hidden behind mesh. Her hair and mask are bound by a gossamer veil.

"Hang tight!" she calls. She also slides down the pit.

As a Veil, as a soul perfectly in tune with the nature of stars,

Lumi is considered holy. As a holy being, only those who have taken their temple vows may ever see her face. Even portraits and pictures of her are forbidden things.

Holy or not, I think she's a fool, and aggravating.

Despite how I scowl, or ignore her, Lumi's cheer toward me forever beams, like a glare of light that stings. I imagine she's always smiling underneath her coverings.

The girl slots herself against the boy's other side and coos soft nothings at him—*There, there. It's okay. You'll be okay.* Then she says to me with her usual cheer, "Always knew you were a good egg behind all that teeth."

I scowl. "Always knew you were a fool behind all that veil."

"What's so foolish about helping someone?"

She can see that the boy is stained, and still she can ask that question. Lumi really is a fool. But a fool privileged enough to get away with it.

Together, with the boy sniffling between us, we pull ourselves back out of the pit.

The courtyard hushes. The abrupt silence is thick, and thickening, like cement has been poured all around us. Someone cries out. Someone else bursts into tears. All the eyes in the courtyard can indisputably see now. They see the blackness spilling down and over the boy's left arm like a coffee stain, and there is no mistaking it. It's an omen. He's marked.

"Get away from him, Lumi!"

"He's an Omen! Has he always been an Omen?"

Some of the children are rushing forward, but even as they do, they linger out of our space. They don't come any closer. Instead, they look at each other, and bite their lips, and fumble in silence.

The mark of the corrupt. The mark of the sinful. But stains

aren't contagious. That's the truth. They're not a virus that can be spread, and everyone knows this. The schools teach it. Medical groups carry out study after study to prove it. I know it by living it. I've touched and bumped into plenty of people, many in this very school, and none of them have ever caught my stain. I've been training with them for half a year, and still they're unblemished.

But it doesn't matter what's known. Superstitions passed from generation to generation are a hard thing to bleach away. And superstitions hold sway here and now, in our school as we train for the Joining. One vital requirement for the Joining is that we must be pure. We must be stainless. Only those without blemish may fly.

No one is willing to risk touching the boy. Lumi and I are the sole exceptions.

Lumi rests her hand on top of the boy's head, a protective thing, and says—berates—"Silly, all of you. Crying and acting all scared. He's the one who's got broken bones, not you."

The others pause, but murmur all the same, "Not just broken bones."

"I'm not stained," the boy blurts. "This is . . . this is just blood."

I look at the boy. I watch his mark. Now that I am up close, I can see his stain is spilling further, creeping ever down the expanse of his arm.

"They say," I warn him, my voice low, "that lying makes the stain worse."

The boy pales. He twitches his eyes toward his arm and whimpers. He hangs his head, then trembles, then begins to wail.

"I don't know why this is happening. I really don't know why. It's never happened before. Nothing like this has ever happened before."

He splutters on and on. The courtyard fills with his sobs.

I believe him. There have been cases of people living all their lives unstained, and then waking up one morning with a mark on their cheek or a mark on their hand. The omen doesn't always appear after the first sin.

I want to put my hand on his shoulder. I want to tell him to be strong. He reminds me of myself, red-faced and bleary-eyed, the first time I realized I was stained.

Lumi rubs the boy's back and coos soft things again, gentle things, like any of that is going to help him. They're not. Nothing can help an Omen once they're stained. The stains are for life. There's no cure. There's no hope of going back.

"Everything will be all right," she promises. Lies. "Maybe it isn't really the omen mark," she says, even though it is.

It's not fair.

Why is it that she can lie and not be marked for it?

Heat rushes through my chest; I am bitter, jealous. On my back, I can feel my own omen stain trembling over my skin.

Murmuring ripples through the courtyard, and I turn to look. It is Maven—master of the school.

His robes are thick, heavy, brown and white and rustling with his steps. His head is shaved, like all the masters are. And like all masters, his face is stern. Strung over his shoulder is the long, thin cord of his whistle-sling—a sling of flexible metal—and in the pouch of the whistle-sling is his star.

Behind him is a train of people, teachers and aides, and a student whose face I don't recognize. It's a boy my age with a too-long neck and too-large ears, and his head is shorn clean. He must have come from the temple.

Maven speaks. "Explain."

I don't answer, because I know Lumi will. And while she explains the falling, the breaking, the spreading stain on the boy's arm, I move away to rejoin the crowd. Maven's expression tightens and tightens the more Lumi explains, like a gear being wound, wound tight enough to snap.

"Thank you, Lumi," Maven says. "You may return to the others."

He gestures at the teachers and aides then, who move to flock around the still-sniffling boy. They don't touch him, but they watch him. They eye the stain on his arm.

Maven turns to the other boy, who smiles. They speak in low tones. I can't hear it. I'm too far away. Then with a nod from Maven and a bow from the temple boy, they all turn to leave. They take with them the stained boy, caged among them like a prisoner with his jailers.

Departing with their robes rustling and rustling, in that hush, it occurs to me that no one asked the boy how he was. No one at all. Not even Lumi. I imagine he hurts quite a bit. He fell from a great height. The snapping of his bones echoed.

No one cares now. No one cares when you're an Omen. When you're an Omen, that's all you are.

In the lunch line, waiting with my empty tray, I hear that the boy who fell has been expelled and detained. He's to be questioned by the authorities.

The stain that bloomed over his arm was large, after all. He must've committed quite the crime to go with it.

"But he's so young."

"Doesn't matter. Always knew there was something wrong with him."

"Liar. Weren't you helping each other out in drills before?"

"As if. People like that are scum. I know better than to mingle with them."

Red heat swells in my chest. My hands creak over the edge of the tray I am holding, but I don't turn around. I wait in line. I stay silent. My back itches—I can feel my stain thickening underneath my robes, crawling up the bone of my shoulder blade and over my shoulder. If it grows any more than this, it'll crawl out of my collar and up my neck. I'll be exposed.

I breathe in and out. I have to control myself. My anger aggravates it. Aggravate it enough, and I won't be able to control it.

The people behind me continue. Their voices are hushed, but I hear them.

"Master Maven was talking about a cleansing."

"For who?"

"Everyone that was in the courtyard."

"But we didn't even touch him!"

"Better safe, though, right? We've got nothing to be scared of, anyway. Not like—" The person stops. I know they are looking over at me. I was one of the only two who touched the boy, after all.

The line moves up. It's my turn to receive my food. Lunch at the school is always two things: a type of congee plus a side dish. Pickled radishes, pancake rolls, marbled eggs. Today is pan-fried dumplings.

I balance my food on the tray and leave the lunch line. I exit the mess hall the way I always do, to eat alone, the way I always do. But today, I go further than my usual nook by the garden.

I down my congee—hot as it is—as I walk, and when I am done, I flip the empty bowl over the plate of dumplings. I leave the empty tray on the veranda and slip on my sandals while balancing the covered plate, then I move through the school, through its many halls of paper screens and around its many corners, to the kitchen. The cooks there do not ask where I'm going. They're busy gambling in their corner, and smoking. And it's lunch hour. A friendless girl can do as she likes.

I exit out the back, onto the streets of Tall Titan.

Tall Titan is urban, packed in with corners, dense in verticality. Its streets wink metal-toothed in the sun with railings and walk-ways, parked hovercars and bikes. I pass by shop after shop selling bubble tea and shaved ice and palm readings, though most of the stores are closed. Their rusty roll shutters are pulled down and shut because the sun is at its height. No one—not even tourists—wants to be out on the streets. Heat wavers all the lines.

I work through the maze of the older districts, with the canopy of wires like brambles above me. I pass by an oily display window where a duck has been roasted and step into a damp tunnel seamed with weeds. Heat-grayed neon lights, off during midday, line the curved walls.

By the mouth of the tunnel is a telephone booth that no one has used in years. Its plastic walls are fogged with age and molded over with moss and weeds. And there, I wait.

A slender woman comes down the street. Esp. Her hands are in the pockets of her overlarge silk bomber, and her hair is split white and pink, straight down the middle. She approaches. The height of her looms.

"Sozo," she greets.

I unveil the plate of dumplings and hold them up to her.

She looks at them. "You don't need to bring me food each time."

"I know," I say. "But I always get too full to finish," I lie.

Esp hums. She plucks up a single dumpling and eats it while I hold the plate. I want to smile at her, at this, but I don't. Esp wouldn't appreciate it. Me giving her food, me eating a little less— it's the only kind of softness she will allow from me.

"Heard something happened at the school," she says. Esp has ears in many places.

I nod. "A boy fell during morning exercises. He caught stains all over his arm."

"And?"

"They've expelled him. The police have taken him. Maybe he doesn't have parents."

"If he didn't, he wouldn't be able to pay the school."

"I don't have parents."

"You don't need parents," Esp says. And I agree. I don't need parents, not when I have Esp.

After that night in the dead end, she took me to her other Omens, children like me and adults like her that she had gathered and led over the years. It's easier in a group, in a gang, to get away with petty crimes.

But pickpocketing only gets you so far. It doesn't quite explain how Esp gets her capsule-coin.

I don't know how she's done it so far. I don't even know what she does, not really. Omens can't get jobs, not the good kinds, anyway. So maybe she deals, and that's how she gets the capsules we need to put me through this school. Maybe she knows people in powerful places, or knows things other people pay to know.

I asked, once. We were standing on the fire escape outside

a pachinko parlor, in the manic din of its slot machines. It was drizzling. Esp looked at me, pulled on her cigarette, and told me not to ask again.

I say, "The master's doing a cleansing because of what happened."

"Should I be worried?"

"No," I say, even as my back itches, even as I remember the stares. "Nothing to worry about."

"And your training?"

"Going fine."

"We need better than fine."

"I started much later than the others." I don't mean it like an accusation, but it comes out as one. "Some of them have been training for years already."

"Just like the temple-folk. There's no time for excuses, Sozo."

"I'm not making excuses."

"It's now or never," she plows on. "You can only enter the race once in your life. And adults rarely win. Next decade will be out of the question."

"I know."

"Do you?"

"I know." I grit my teeth. My shoulders tense. Esp doesn't trust me. She doesn't trust me with the truth of her job, and she doesn't trust that I can do this, that I understand what's at stake. Even now, after all these years, she still treats me like that kid in the dead end.

Esp hasn't touched the rest of the dumplings. She's unwrapped a piece of gum instead and popped it into her mouth. My omen scab tugs and tugs. I need to leave, to calm down, before my omen tugs out of control.

I leave the plate on a ledge in the booth and turn away. I think about leaving just like that, without a word, with the silence of my back like defiance. But when I step into the shade of the tunnel, Esp says, "They consider the temple a holy place."

I pause. I know that. After the Joining, if I pass, the temple is where I will go. For a month, I will be allowed to train in the temple with a real anchor, a real star, and then the Decade-Races will begin. I know all this.

"You know what they do to people like us in holy places?"

My stain quivers. My breath stutters. Esp is reminding me because I've made her unhappy, because she's displeased. She wants me to fear.

"Get caught with a stain outside the temple, and they'll expel you, lock you up. Get caught with a stain inside it?"

Touching their holy things. Breathing their holy air. I know. I do.

If I lose control inside the temple, if I am caught, there will be no excuse for me, no second chance, no way out. I see the girl with the blue eyes by that white wall, on the ground, unmoving. That would be me.

And the world would move on. No one would mourn.

One less Omen in this world, after all, would only make a better world.

TWO

The boy with the too-long neck and too-large ears has a name: Naqi.

He's an acolyte of the Temple of Celestial Ichor, the holy temple in the heart of the city of Tall Titan. The city gets its name from the temple, I think, because the temple looms tall like a titan, and because in the center of the temple is the eye of one.

I don't know if the eye really exists. Titans aren't real, after all.

Near the training pit, Naqi is preparing for his demonstration. He was sent here to demonstrate what flying a true anchor will be like. He's to show us a star-bonding.

According to his self-introduction, he likes birds and sunflower seeds and long walks by the artificial sea sector. According to the gossip around the school, he's one of the best fliers in the temple. A true contender, they say, for winning the race. He knows all the starsongs by heart. He flies so fast, so sure, the whistle of his flying can cut.

He smiles a lot, that's all I know. His black eyes curve into crescents with his smile, and his skin is sun-kissed. He's still smiling as he says, "I'll get to the good stuff quick."

He nudges the silver anchor by his feet, a real one, not like the training ones we use. Its shape reminds me of a surfboard, or a calligraphy brush's bristles, and seated by the head of the board is the metal globe of the engine-lock—a kind of woven cage where the star is held.

He points to the lock and says, "Engine, where the star goes, so that its blood—its ichor—can be pumped out, enabling flight."

In his hand is a whistle-sling. In its pouch is a star. The misshapen pearl of its body is dim, and like glass. It's asleep.

It blurs out of view because the boy is swinging his sling around and around. The sling whistles. The whistle thickens into a hum. The gathered crowd is oohing and ahhing and pressing closer to see, and so the boy smiles ever wider. He swings his sling in a figure eight, then passes it from hand to hand all spin and flair. He's showing off. He's laughing while he does.

I had no idea boys could be so annoying. *Khab* is what we would call him on the streets. A fool.

"Rotating force wakes the star and activates its fire. Like this. Stay back."

Naqi quickens his pace. With four firm swings, the star bursts into light and life, the sound like a flare being struck. Liquid fire sloshes white, then ebbs away. The skin of the star swirls with a metallic iridescence.

It is beautiful. Otherworldly. The people around me have broken into applause, and I want to. My heart aches to. But admitting to beauty is something like a weakness; I've never been allowed weaknesses.

"Once the star is on, whip it into the lock, like so."

The boy twists his torso and hip and slams the pouch of his sling into the lock. The metal teeth of the lock clang open then shut over the star. The cord of the sling, still connected to the star, is left exposed outside the lock.

"Don't be afraid to use the full force of your body. The star can handle it. And never touch the lock once a lit star is in there, unless you fancy yourself a hand barbecue." He smiles again. The crowd laughs.

"Step onto the anchor, like so." Naqi steps onto the glider, facing the side and slightly crouched, like one would with a longboard. Then slowly, slowly, ichor bleeds gold through the cord.

It shifts and moves with a life of its own, lacing itself around Naqi's leg. It tightens. With a sigh, with a blooming like the coming dawn, Naqi becomes like the sun. Light spills through him and swallows him whole. It pulses with his breath, in and out, blinding, then only almost blinding.

The ichor settles over his skin, then under his skin, and then the boy is just a boy again. He's no longer some divine being. He no longer shines.

Still, he's full of smiles.

The people roar, and cheer, and are lit up with awe. The noise of their words, of their questions, is like a wave crashing on and on and on. They sound like gulls scrambling to be heard.

"Will we look like that when we fly?"

Naqi laughs. "Pretty much."

"How fast can we go?"

"Pretty fast."

"How different is it from our training engines?"

"Pretty different." Naqi looks down at his anchor, at the star bright in its lock. "There's no real bonding happening with your training engines. No real connection. But with a star, every part of you is bared. Every part of you is seen. There's no hiding from a star."

The mood shifts. People quiet and shuffle from foot to foot. We've all learned about the baring of the bond, but hearing about it in the remoteness of a classroom is one thing. Here, before a boy who has bonded, *is* bonded, it's another. The idea of it is sobering.

Someone raises their hand.

"What's it like?"

Naqi thinks about it. "Like meeting an old friend."

"Do they talk to you?"

"The stars? Sometimes."

"Does it hurt?"

He shakes his head. "Not if you're of one accord with the nature of stars. You've been taught your Nine Ahs?"

The children around me nod. The Nine Ahs. The nine different principles of a star, all with the sound "ah" inside their names: Tahv, Hrah, Sha. No single word can describe an Ah. They are entire feelings or actions. Choosing joy in the coming future. That is an Ah. To be complete and whole is another.

Someone else, without raising their hand, asks, "But if you're not properly aligned, it hurts?"

"It hurts."

"How much?"

"Depends."

"Could you die from it?"

Some people laugh. But others murmur and shift. We've all heard the rumors—someone hooks themselves up to a star and is pumped full of ichor, and maybe they were particularly misaligned that day. Maybe they insulted the star, somehow.

They catch on fire. Their flesh gives way to golden flame from the inside out, and not even their bones are left in the ashes.

Naqi strokes his chin. He ponders, then looks up and says, "Sure. I've never seen it happen, though."

The students are silent, watching. They're waiting for Naqi to say more. So Naqi smiles a reassuring smile and says, "You'd have to be wildly against the nature of stars for that to happen. I doubt any of you are. You all seem like good people."

Good people. I go cold.

Someone says, and the sound is distant, "Weren't you here this morning?" They add, and the words are a blow, "There was an Omen here."

My chest hollows out. The people around me are saying things, all sorts of things, but I don't hear them. I can't hear them. Stupid, stupid. I've known this. I've known flying a star requires a bonding and a baring. I sit in the classes same as everyone else. I've learned the Nine Ahs. But the Ahs are nebulous things I don't understand. What does it mean to be complete or whole? What does it mean to choose joy in the future? How do I be humble, be compassionate, when I have never been taught those things?

An Omen like me—would I burst into flames?

The conversation around me has moved on. The boy, Naqi, is tugging his anchor up and off the ground, into the air, and it's one of my first times seeing a real anchor up close, a real star-flight— but my heart is thud-thudding. I see without seeing. I don't know how to breathe.

On the day of the Joining, the star will know I'm an Omen.

The day of the Joining could be the day I burn alive.

My omen is a wound in the shape of a snake.

It curves scab-dark around the blade of my shoulder and over my collarbone, edges splaying like fingers toward my neck, greedy to wrap around it and squeeze. I hold those fingers sheathed but wear my robes high around my neck, just in case.

Sometimes, on quiet days—when storm clouds sit above us to thicken the humidity, and we're made slow and drowsy in it—my stain slithers into a slip of a thing, a black letter-opener cut on my white-envelope skin. Other days, days where someone speaks loudly about Omens, my mark grows loud and brash, thick and scaly. Those days, I can check shoulder-first into corners and not feel the bleed and the bruise. I'm angry on those days, filled with hot air that rushes to my head and bloats it. My vision goes gray like the cruiser smog that sits over the city skyline.

Today, my stain will have to disappear entirely.

It's the day after Naqi's demonstration, and Master Maven has declared a schoolwide cleansing. It's to take place at the sauna, where we'll be buried in the trenches of the sand baths.

We will be stripped to nothing but our underclothes.

It'll be fine. I've gone through the cleansing before, months ago, when I first joined the school. It's the custom of all schools. The stardust purifies, and the sands are meant to symbolize the burying of bad energies, of misdeeds, and of rising anew.

I've done it before, and so I'll do it again. I've come too far to be caught now.

The redwood of the sauna is dotted with moisture. Steam mists the air. The hot sands have been mixed with stardust, glittering white like sugar against the volcanic black of the sands.

All the girls in their pale-yellow bathrobes are shuffling in. The boys have already left. Towels are wrapped around everyone's heads to keep the sand out of their hair. On the bamboo walkway, they step out of their robes, fold those robes, and set them aside. They step into the hot trenches. They lay on their backs and wait for the teachers and aides to shovel sands over them, to be buried from the neck down.

For most, the heat is a lulling comfort. The weight tucks them in, wraps them tight, like a baby in a swaddle. Some fall straight asleep. Others linger by the edges and whine, because stardust can prick, sometimes, like static shocks.

For me, the sugar-like stardust is like salt on a wound. For me, the shocks burn.

I'm an Omen. My stains are an affront to the stars, even their dust. And hiding my stain makes no difference, because the stars know it's there. I've only hidden the stain beneath my skin.

Still, I'll have to hide it. No one can see. And once I've hidden it, I'll have to endure the pain.

I take my time in the sauna. I toy with the towel in my hair and wait. When there are only a handful of students left in the sands, I approach the trenches. The remaining girls are clumped together to the side of the sauna, to chatter and gossip and giggle at one another. I pull in my breath and hide my stain.

I peel off my robes.

The far corner of the trenches is empty, and I go to it.

I step onto the sands with my bare feet, and it stings. The sand mixed with stardust feels like it is rubbing against raw skin, and I want to hiss, but I don't. My face is a smooth mask.

I sit down and lie back. I think about my breathing—in and out, in and out—as the aides make their way over, as they shovel sand over me then leave. I'm buried. I'm left with my pain. The flecks of stardust over and around me are like pinprick coals, and the pain of them comes to me in waves. Heat contracts over me and through me, and it's dizzying. I gulp. I shut my eyes. I let my stain spill free once more because I still can't manage to hide it for long, and because here, buried like this, I can afford to.

Ten minutes. Just ten minutes of this, and I won't have to hurt anymore.

"Hi."

My eyes snap open. It's Lumi. She's there in her bathrobe and mask, with the ends of her long, sheer veil tucked into her belt-sash. She leans over and wiggles her fingers in a wave.

"Can I sit with you?"

"No."

Lumi laughs. She steps into the trenches. Sweat is beading over my skin—from the heat, from the pain—so I make no expression at all. If I did, my discomfort might leak through.

"Well," she says, "too bad, I guess," and then she sits in the sand next to me and lies back.

Because she's a Veil, and because she must keep her veil and mask on at all times out in public, she's afforded the luxury of staying clothed, and the privilege of it twists at me. It mocks my pain.

Lumi is buried. Then we're left alone.

The group down the way is getting ready to leave. They cackle as they struggle against the weight of the sands, and one of them moves over to tug her friend free, and they stumble, and then cackle some more.

"My mom sent me a letter," Lumi says. "Can you believe it? In this day and age of data-packets and vid-calls? Sent it all the way from the farm-colony out on the Eurydice moon. I'm surprised it even made it here in time, or that she could afford it."

I close my eyes and say nothing. Lumi's voice softens.

"She's the only family I have. Never met my father. No grandparents. Life on the farms is tough, you know?"

I am silent.

"Hey, Sozo," she asks. "Why do you dislike me so much?"

And finally I say, "Because I can't stand your face."

She laughs, and it grates. I've never seen any part of her face, of course, and she knows it.

For a long while after that, she says nothing. I'm granted blessed silence. My body is twisted in pain, but I can't move. I can't writhe. They will know something is wrong if I do. I think, maybe, I pass out at one point. I'm not sure.

Lumi's voice shades back in.

"I didn't choose to be like this, you know."

I frown. I don't understand what Lumi is saying.

"To be called a Veil, to be treated like one."

To be *holy*. That is what she means.

Anger flares through me. With that anger, pain spikes. My omen stain is like a branding iron on my back, white-hot, searing, and I grit my teeth. Lumi dares to complain about her status, her holy status. She dares to complain to someone like me.

"Zap off, Lumi."

"What?"

"You heard me. I hope siren's teeth take you one day."

"That's not an awfully nice thing to say."

My pain spikes again. My vision whites out. I can say nothing.

I can only tremble and gasp. Lumi doesn't notice. She quiets. When she speaks again, her voice is soft.

"I'm not saying I've got it hard. I don't. There are expectations that come with being a Veil, yes, but I'm lucky. I know. I have it a lot better than others."

I shut my eyes; another wave of pain blooms through me. How long has passed? How much longer do I have to stay? When can I leave, and be free? My voice is a drained, faded thing when I say, "Why are you talking to me?"

I hate my voice. It sounds like I am begging.

"Because." Lumi shifts. Maybe she's turned her head to look at me. "I'm the one that's veiled, but you're the one that's hidden. Why do you push everyone away?"

"None of your business."

"I'm making it my business."

"To hell and void with your business."

"Sozo." Lumi is shifting again. Her voice is tight when she says, "You're pale."

I gasp. I thrash out of the sand and dust and roll onto my side, away from Lumi. I'm shaking. Every part of me is shaking. I want to hurl. I feel peeled raw all over, and I'm cold, yet burning, and I'm going to hurl.

Have I hidden my stain? I can't tell through the blare of my pain. I wrench my towel off my head to wrap around my shoulders, and then I am swaying. I can't stand. I'm going to pass out.

Someone's hands are on my arms. Someone hoists me up. I look, and it's Lumi. She's helping me out of the sands.

She's making me her business again, but I have no strength to spit, and no strength to curse. I let her help me out of the trenches and onto the bamboo walkway. There, on that smooth woven warmth, I collapse. I am panting, panting, like maybe I was drowning. The teachers and aides are here. They've hurried their way over at our commotion.

"What's wrong?" they ask.

"A contest." Lumi laughs, and lies—lies for me. "I was egging her on and took it too far. The heat got to her. We're sorry. I'll get her some water."

"Not like you to do something like that," they say. But I know what they mean: it's not normal that someone like Lumi would be bothering with someone like me. I push to my feet and hold in my quaking. Lumi's hand is on my back.

"See?" she says. "Right as rain. I'll walk her back to her dorm."

The grown-ups are nodding slowly, and I dip my head and take my leave. Behind me, I can hear Lumi following. Behind her, I can feel the adults watching.

Outside the sauna, the night air is a balm on my skin. Relief sighs over me. The pain of before, of the stardust boring holes into my skin, is ebbing away and away.

And then Lumi touches the towel on my shoulder where my stain is. I jerk away, backhand her touch, and snarl.

"Don't touch me."

"Sozo."

"Stay away from me."

"I'm just trying to help."

"Stop trying. I don't need it. I don't want it. If you ever touch me again, I'll make you bleed."

"Sozo. Calm down. I'm not your enemy."

I'm not listening anymore. I've twisted from Lumi and am stepping away, quick, curt. Did she see? Does she know how much the stardust hurt me? Does she know I'm an Omen? Maybe the adults have seen, and now they're on their way to tell the master. They're going to send people to my room, to hold me down, to expose me.

My stain is throbbing. If they were to examine me now, I wouldn't be able to hide it. They would see on my back my omen stain, trembling ever larger under the strain of my stress, and that would be it for me.

Esp asked me if she should be worried, and I said no. No. Nothing to worry about. But I've always been a liar. Ever since that time under the people like stars, I've always known how to lie.

THREE

No one has come for me. I'm still hidden. I'm still safe.

The days pass. They come and go mostly without trouble, except for Lumi. I don't know why.

Ever since the sand bath, Lumi's fixation on me has been stoked into something like a passion. She's been trying to get me alone, at the training fields after lessons or in the classroom after meditations. She makes an effort to sit beside me in the mess hall, or in the baths, or by the gardens as we're crouched in the earth.

She says hello, and asks me to stay, and I never do.

The days pass. We train and meditate, and the air trills with quiet anticipation. We sleep lightly. We eat lightly. Then, at long last, the end of the week arrives.

The Joining celebrations are a spectacle of tents and sails, vibrant as a feast. It's a market of delights, full of stalls selling stinky tofu or red bean pastries or treats like blown sugar and powdered mochi. Canvas sails like entire rivers—lipstick red and marigold yellow—soar above the crowds for shade. Banners and ribbons in the shape of stars snap in the wind. They are hoisted high up on poles, and like the tails of kites, their stardust tails stream.

I see parents with their children holding colorful masks in their hands, masks of smiling sirens and scowling titans. I see a path full of festival games—goldfish fishing and balloon popping and streetside mahjong. Another path is full of dancers. They twirl in their *ao dais*—tight-fitting silk dresses that flutter about the legs—to the tune of bamboo flutes and chimes and drums. Their loose sleeves have been sewn on specially, and their dancing in them is like looking at long drawn brushstrokes. It is mesmerizing.

Here, there, begging by the sides of the paths, are Omens.

I see a man with one milky eye, blind because his stain spilled over it. I see another with a crumpled hand, the way a hand crumples up after a stroke, because his stain clustered tight over it.

My scab hasn't deformed me yet, but I imagine it will one day.

I know Esp can't hear out of her right ear because her scab has grown over it, and if her stain continues to spread up into her hair and over her head, she might begin to lose her memories, or her mind.

We've all seen Omens like that, ones that hear things and see things that aren't there at all. You catch them sometimes, ambling from alleyway to alleyway, cackling at the face of the moon.

People say it's what we deserve for having done the things we've done.

I wish I could remember what it was I did that first time, my first immoral act, the one that made my mother and father believe I was no longer worth keeping.

I pass under a vast shadow, and look up.

We are outside the white walls of the Temple of Celestial

Ichor, at the base of it, where the Joining festivities are hosted every decade. The walls loom the way ancient things do. They cut arrogantly into the center of the festival.

I don't know if anyone else notices. I don't see why they would—the colors and smells and music of the festival are arresting. But I look up at the wall, and there, up that impossible height in that impossible white, is a break in the stones where the temple garden, walled inside, decided it did not want to be inside anymore. It peeks through with its roots and branches, staining the stones green. Its vines droop like ropes.

My stain itches. It's bizarre to me, seeing that gap marring the holy walls, like seeing a mimic of my own disfigured body.

Far beneath that hole in the wall is the House of Stars. The Joining will take place there.

The House of Stars is a sprawling tent that easily houses hundreds, and its white canvas is lined by gold. Its posts are lacquered blue pillars, tall enough to dwarf a grown man. Hung over the open mouth of the entrance is the ivory figurehead of a siren, beautiful, with her eyes closed and her mouth full of stars. Unfurled like her arms is her hair, a swirling denseness of nebulae that drips down and around the entranceway.

The tent is manned by four guardians in black and red. Their temple robes are layered with pauldrons and breastplates of steel and wood, and their hands are bound in leather. Their heads are shaved like all temple-folk—even the women's—and wound over their shoulders are their whistle-slings.

If an Omen were to walk up to them and try to enter the tent, they would unwind their whistle-slings and beat the Omen back. We are unholy things. We are forbidden in the tent.

But right now I'm not an Omen. I'm only one of the many

hundreds of children come to try their hands at the Joining. We come in our stark white robes, led by our masters and teachers holding their staffs. They shake the star-shaped chimes hooked to the heads of the staffs.

People cheer for us as we pass. They toss flowers and rice in our path. They watch us enter under the looming figurehead of the siren, into the darkness of the tent.

My eyes adjust. The dark is lit by tall braziers of ivory. We've entered into a curved hallway of canvas that leads only to our left and right. The tapestry before us covers the entire length—thick and midnight blue, and intricately woven, full of the impossible colors of nebulae, the golden rising and falling of stars, and the silver cuts of anchors whistling through it all. Here and there are the slender figures of sirens.

We turn left, while some of the other schools go right, though it doesn't really matter which route we take. The hallway is a circle. It wraps around the inner sanctum where the Joining will take place to connect at the waiting rooms in the far back. That is where we are going.

The din of the festival is muted through the tent. Inside, all of us are wide-eyed, giddy and smiling, or hushed and reverent. We pass by one of the two openings to the inner sanctum, and many of us stop to peer, clogging the hallway and slowing the crowds. No one complains. We all want a peek inside.

The inner sanctum is unadorned, but full of smoke and incense. To the left of the circle are stands for sitting, and a generous stretch of ground before the stands for when the seats run out. To the right of the circle is a ring of white pillars. Placed in its heart is an ivory altar in the shape of an eye. It glows. A shaft of light from the smoke hole above has settled on it perfectly.

There's something on the altar, but I can't quite see. The crowds are pushing on, and I'm pushed along with them.

We make it to the back of the tent, to the waiting rooms.

There are five waiting rooms—four for the four flying schools in the city of Tall Titan, and one for the acolytes of the temple. Ours is the one furthest south, and like all the other waiting rooms, it is sectioned off by thick canvas curtains, white like the rest of the tent.

We settle in to wait. Our school is going last, and so we will be waiting for a long while.

Lumi is here, dressed like the rest of us—white robes with bronze hems and sashes. She's bound a thicker veil over her hair today, with another sheer veil over her mask. In her hands is a letter, the letter she talked about at the baths.

The paper is crinkled and well-creased. She must've read it and reread it again and again.

Her head turns toward me, and I flick my eyes away.

She beelines for me anyway. So I twist away and make for the exit. There are many bodies in the way—near a hundred of us are crammed here—so I push and shove my way through. People glare and grunt, but I push on.

I have no time or space to be dealing with Lumi, not now, not on this day of days. I have to keep my omen in check. I have to keep it small and tucked away.

Ever since the sand baths, my stain has been harder to control. A simple twinge of annoyance and I can feel my stain scabbing down my side nearly to my hip. A sly glance my way and my stain thickens over my arm nearly to the wrist.

So I refuse to let Lumi speak to me, to upset me and anger me. I refuse to let her ruin everything we've worked for.

The Joining has begun. I am hidden in the crowd of the inner sanctum by the edge of the southern entrance. The crowd is thick, and it's hard to see. I am only fourteen years tall, while the others around me are grown adults, some with children perched on their shoulders.

But the altar is higher. On the altar, in a beam of light, is an anchor and its star.

The anchor is four times the size of a normal one, and so four times as heavy, and its body is gilded gold. The Nine Ahs have been cut into the gold, with strokes curling one into another like vines. There is no protective cage around its engine-lock. Its star is bared and asleep.

This Joining anchor, according to the myth, is what the first ever anchor looked like.

In the beginning, when the stars fell and turned into people, a great golden star gave itself up in the form of an anchor and carried the people out of the cosmic storm and onto the shores of this world. So this is why we Join—to remember our beginnings, to honor the sacrifice of the first star, and to recall the strength and power we had when we were free, so free.

A boy climbs the steps of the altar. His hems and sash are green like the rest of his school, who wait behind the altar in the shadows and the smoke.

This is the second school to go. The temple acolytes were first, and they've long since finished and left. This boy, being the youngest at his school, is first in the line to Join.

He stands before the anchor, and it is laughable how very small he looks in comparison, like a teaspoon in a bowl. He reaches out. He lays his hand upon the star and waits.

The star snaps into light. The boy howls.

The cord of the star is winding around his arm and pulling tight like it did with the boy who came to our school, with Naqi. Light is flooding into his skin and overtaking him, and I don't know if I am imagining it, but I smell the singe of burning flesh.

The boy does not let go. He crawls onto the anchor. With a grunt, and a great shout, he tugs. Ichor throbs over him and through him in waves, to the rhythm of a heartbeat I do not hear. And then the anchor lifts off.

Silently, silently, the anchor peels away from the altar to hover a meter in the air, then two, then three.

The boy has passed. He has Joined with the star and flown it.

The crowd bursts into cheers. My chest thrums with it. The ground shakes with it.

Out of the hundreds of children who try to Join every decade, only a few ever pass. Some years it is fifty, others a mere dozen. No one is sure how exactly stars choose their fliers—maybe they choose based on purity, or talent, or strength. Whatever it is, our school would be lucky to have even five chosen.

The boy touches back down and wrenches free of the star, then stumbles. He very nearly falls off the altar but crouches and catches himself. His smile for the crowd is timid. He holds up his hand in a wave—the skin of his palm is peeled raw.

I imagine myself up there on the altar, with my hand pressed against the star. Ichor floods into me, and then golden fire spews from my mouth, my eyes, my ears. Maybe I will choke to death before I burn alive.

Someone bumps into me, hard. I twist around. It's Esp.

Her hair is long and black. She is wearing a white leather face mask, one that covers her mouth, scar, nose. I didn't think she'd come, being an Omen. But Esp doesn't look like an Omen right now, the ones begging by the streets. She never has.

Right now, in her red ao dai, Esp only looks delicate, romantic. She points with her head toward the hall, and I move to follow.

Another child has climbed the altar and is trying her hand at the Joining. She settles her hand on the star, and the star snaps into light almost immediately. The crowd again bursts into cheers.

The hallway we walk is empty. Still, we keep our voices low.

"Your school is going last?"

I nod. "After this school is the third, and then us."

"I'll be watching in the crowds."

"I didn't think you would come," I say abruptly. "They're broadcasting the Joining everywhere."

Something like hope sparks in me, then.

Esp doesn't do tenderness. I know this. When she taught me to cut purses, and to slide the shiv down my sleeve to hide it, and when the shiv sliced my arm red, she only handed me a roll of bandage and told me to try again. As I bandaged my own arm, she was silent, only watching, unmoving and unconsoling.

When I managed to cut my first purse, and I showed Esp the gleaming leather of the wallet, she didn't smile. She said only, like that first time in the dead end, "Good."

Esp doesn't do tenderness. Still—I imagine her now, saying, *I came because I wanted to see you. I wanted to make sure you'd be all right.*

She says instead, "Some things you need to see with your own eyes."

I fall silent. The sting of my disappointment itches over my stain and then jolts it. I gasp and look away.

Esp looks at me. "What is it?"

My stain is crawling over my back and across my other shoulder blade, all pins and needles. The scabs are heavy. I never thought a pair of wings would feel like shackles.

"Nothing."

"Should I be worried?"

"No," I say, too fast, and so Esp stares. She doesn't believe me. Her stare bores into me.

We're moving past the curtain dividing the front of the hallway from the back, the back that leads to the waiting rooms. It's quiet here. Most of the curtained rooms are empty—everyone is in the inner sanctum, watching like I was, or waiting behind the altar for their turns.

"Once you pass," Esp says, because there's no room for ifs, "it'll be much more difficult for us to meet. The temple-folk like to keep their birds in their cages."

"I'll find ways to sneak out."

"Don't. You won't be doing anything that'll jeopardize our chances."

"But what if . . ." *I need help.*

I don't say it, because I know what Esp's answer will be. She'll look at me with the weight of her gaze like water, drowning me, pulling me under, and she'll say nothing. Her silence will mean: *You shouldn't need help.*

I never taught you to be weak.

Esp goes on.

"Everything will continue as planned. Pass the Joining. Win the race. Get us our wish. Nothing else matters. Do you understand?"

I understand. Of course I do. Getting the wish for Esp is all I've worked for over the past four years.

But then I remember the pain I felt in the baths. How much

more pain will I be in inside the temple, working day after day with a star? Will I be able to fly faster than everyone else? Will I even survive the Joining?

I don't mean to say it. I don't. My question slips out without my permission.

"What if it doesn't work?"

Esp says nothing. I pull in tight, and look over at her to gauge her silence. I can't read it. I imagine, then, her telling me it's not too late to back out.

You've worked hard enough, she'd say. *We'll come up with another plan*, she'd say.

She says instead, "I'm disappointed, Sozo."

Another sting jolts through my stain, and the stain spasms at it and claws its way down my back. It feels like the layers of my skin are being peeled with wax, like gravel is being pushed through my pores. The scabs bubble thick, and burn, and itch.

I fist my hands. I grit my teeth. Esp is still looking at me, so I look up at her and lie through the fog of pain, "Don't be. You've nothing to worry about."

Esp looks at me, and I lock my gaze on her. I need her to see the fierceness there. I need her to believe me, to believe that I can do this, that I will. For me, for her.

The flap of a waiting room opens. It is Lumi. I startle. The stain over my back ripples with it. Why is she here? Why isn't she with the others in the inner sanctum?

"Sozo." Her head tilts between me and Esp. Her tone is polite when she says, "I'm sorry, but other people aren't allowed back here."

Esp smiles with her eyes, then dips her head at Lumi. The line of her posture has curved soft and sweet; she's always been a convincing actor.

"A Veil," she greets. "It's an honor. I only came to wish Sozo good luck."

Lumi mirrors the dip, though it's slow. "You know her?"

"Yes." Esp nods. That's all she supplies. She turns back to me and grips my shoulder, and it hurts. I say nothing about the hurt. It's always hurt with Esp.

She tells me, "I know you'll do well. I'll be watching."

That's all the comfort I receive. Esp pulls away, and leaves. I watch the tail of her dress flutter around the hall and out of sight. I hear the dividing curtain pull open, then fall shut.

I am left outside the waiting room with Lumi.

"Who was she?"

"None of your business."

"Someone you knew from the streets?"

I don't bother to answer. I turn the other way to leave through the other exit, and Lumi follows after.

"Sozo," she calls. "I've been looking for you."

That's why she was in the waiting room, because she couldn't find me in the crowds. How long has she been looking?

"Leave me alone."

"I need to talk to you."

"What you need is to stop talking."

I push past the curtain and step back into the main hallway, and then Lumi says, "I know what you are."

I jolt to a stop.

Lumi says, "I saw your stain that night, at the sand baths. It was growing past your towel and up the back of your neck. The others would've seen, but I stayed behind you."

Blood is pounding, pounding, behind my eyes and through my ears. I can't think. Lumi saw. Lumi knows. Is she going to tell?

No. She hasn't. Not yet. She's been trying to tell me that she knows all this time, but why? What does she want from me?

Pain jars through me, abrupt. I cry out and stumble forward and sink to my knees. My omen stain is surging down my arms and thighs, and my vision blurs from the pain that comes in convulsions, a pain that burns like holding my breath for too long. My control is a thin string. I don't know when it will snap.

Lumi's arms are around me again like that time at the baths, and she's tugging us back behind the curtain, toward our waiting room. I thrash against her and shove her off.

"Sozo, please!"

My throat is tight. It is hard to breathe.

"You have to calm down, Sozo. It's spilling onto your hands and your neck. The others will see."

I shake out my head. Lumi's voice burbles, like we're submerged underwater.

I'm angry, so angry. I'm bloated on it. My anger flashes at Esp. The Joining could kill me, and yet she's come and gone like some doctor with too many patients. Her words toward me were clinical, cold. Maybe she doesn't know. If she knew, maybe she would be scared for me, scared that she might never see me again.

"Sozo!"

"Go on, then," I snarl. I slap her hands away. "Tell everyone what I am."

Lumi is shaking her head. "I'm not going to tell anyone."

"Liar."

"I don't lie."

I bark a laugh. Of course she doesn't lie. Perfect, pure Lumi beneath her perfect, pure veil. I hate her. I hate her for it.

"Leave the Joining."

"What?" My hands are cold. I'm cold all over, even as I burn. It's getting harder to see Lumi now. She's a messy smudge of white crouched before me, as I am crouched.

"Don't participate in the Joining," she says, *begs*. "You could die, Sozo. And if you go out looking like this, you really will. They'll kill you."

"That's got nothing to do with you."

"Sozo, please."

"Don't talk down to me."

"I'm not."

"You think we're charity cases, is that it?" I don't know my own voice. It is full of glass—broken glass. "All the poor little Omens, needing the high-and-mighty Veil to pull them out of their pits, to save them?"

Lumi is shaking her head again. She reaches for me and touches my hand, my hand that barely looks like a hand. My fingers are craggy and dark. My nails are long and sharp.

"Why are you doing this, Sozo? Why do you need to?" She pauses, then understands. "Is it the wish? There's a wish you're willing to risk your life for?"

I can't speak. My throat is all jagged edges, and my head is full of stones. I can feel my robes tearing. My scab is thickening and swelling enough to break through the fabrics and seams.

"Let me make your wish for you."

I look up at Lumi.

"Tell me what your wish is, and I'll make it for you."

She squeezes my not-hand and promises, vows, "I'll join the Decade-Races and beat everyone, everyone, and then I'll make your wish for you. The star I catch will be used for you."

I see red.

Who does Lumi think she is? Make my wish *for* me? Do it for me because I'm not good enough, because I'm an Omen, because I'll never be good enough? Esp already thinks that of me—she watches me in silence and stews in her disappointment.

But someone like *Lumi*?

Esp would be scared of losing someone like Lumi.

Pain cracks through me, winds me, blinds me. I double over and scream, maybe. I don't know. I don't know my body anymore. I don't know what it is I'm seeing and hearing and feeling. All I know is that my bones are distending against my skin, and it hurts. All I know is that I'm angry, so angry, and it hurts. The world around me is a blur.

I'm running, and then falling, and then my string of control snaps.

All is dark.

(Someone is shouting a name and shouting, *Please, no.*

Sozo, please. No.

I don't know who they are. I don't know who Sozo is.)

Waking is a heavy thing. I don't know where I am.

I register two things:

Scabs are sloughing off me like mud in rain, leaving behind the tatters of my robes. Esp is here in her red and white, and she is crouched over something a little way from me, crumpled by the curtain.

It's Lumi.

My body is numb. My mouth and eyes are dry. I stagger to my feet, and then Esp says, "She's dead."

She says, "You killed her."

I don't know what to say. I don't know what to think or feel. I'm still numb.

Esp rises. She turns to me.

"All these years of sacrifice on my part," she says. "Wasted, because of you, because you couldn't get one thing right. Destroyed in a single moment, all of it. Because of you."

Esp doesn't do tenderness, and she doesn't do rage—not the kind of rage that rails and roars. Hers is a keen edge, a surgical cut. Right now, with her lines held high and still, she is what I imagine a guillotine is like. Her gaze is being strapped beneath the blade. Her words are the fall.

"You're on your own now." Esp is leaving. "You clean up your own messes."

Everything crashes back to me. I'm buffeted.

I want to throw up because I've killed Lumi. Of all the sins I have committed, I don't know if murder has ever been one of them. (Lie. That's a lie. The girl with the blue eyes by that white, white wall was my fault too.)

I want to scream because I don't know what happened. I lost control. The world went dark. I think, maybe, I transformed into a monster. I think, maybe, my stain overtook me.

I want to fall to my knees and cling to the tail of Esp's dress, because she is leaving, and that want disgusts me.

I don't throw up. I don't scream. I don't fall to my knees and grovel.

My eyes sting—tears, I realize, but I don't allow them to fall.

There's no time for tears, for screaming, for falling. There's no space for weakness.

"Wait," I croak, and Esp stops. She waits.

I say nothing else.

I know what I have to do.

FOUR

Behind the ivory altar in the incense and smoke, I wait alongside the others from my school. My ears are ringing. I feel . . . untethered, like I am watching myself from above.

(Lumi is dead. Don't think about it. Don't think about it.)

I am next in line to Join.

The girl before me has placed her hand on the star, but the star doesn't stir. A breath passes, then two and three and more, and still the star remains dark. The girl has been rejected. She turns from the altar to the sound of scattered applause, and wipes at her tears. Her head is dipped in shame as she leaves.

It's my turn.

I step onto the altar. I mount the stairs. I stand before the anchor and its star, and then do nothing but watch it. For a long while, all I do is watch it. The gold of its body sheens in the light. Its star hums, even in sleep. Up here, up on this peak, I feel removed, set apart. I didn't ever think that holiness could be so very like loneliness.

This is not a dream. This is reality. This is happening.

I lick my lips. The air is electric.

The crowd below me is hushed, because they've all been waiting for me.

Of course they have.

If anyone is to be accepted by the star, it would be me. If anyone is to pass the Joining like no other, it would be me.

Because I am wearing Lumi's veil. Because I am wearing Lumi's mask.

Right now, all the world believes I am her.

It won't matter to anyone if Sozo disappears from the Joining. She's just a street girl, a friendless girl, someone with no ties to anyone at all that matters. But Lumi must participate. Lumi must be here.

And once I'm inside the temple, only temple-folk can see my face, and those people will have never seen Sozo's face, my face. And the only family Lumi has is a lone mother out in some empty farm-colony, too poor to do anything at all.

I'll be safe. I'm sure of it. I'm banking on it.

If I can survive.

I stretch out my hand and, with a steadying breath, settle my palm over the star.

Nothing happens. The glass skin of the star is dim. Its hum peters out. I grit my teeth. I tighten my grip over the star because no, it will not end like this. I've come too far. I've done too much. And if I don't have this, I'll have nothing. The crowd remains hushed, watchful. They wait.

To the side, someone shouts. Everyone turns. Guardians are running, and things outside the tent are crashing, falling, and I know from the scandalized screams exactly what it is.

Esp's Omens.

When I told Esp my plan, and when Esp listened, she responded by taking a cell-piece out of her pocket and calling someone, speaking hushed and quick. That someone would come, she said, to help her hide the body. And then more people would come, she said, to make sure my job gets done.

I'm not the only Omen she's gathered up over the years, just the one she's invested in the most. And now, in this moment, those Omens are trespassing loudly into the festival, into the tent, all for one purpose: to sow chaos.

When everyone's eyes are on them, none will be on me.

I turn back to the star. *Please. Please.*

Nothing happens still. I dip down. I press my forehead to the star and pray again: *Please, please.*

I abhor begging. The Omens that resort to sitting by the sides of the streets, to while away their days on their knees, with their palms outstretched—I abhor them. I will die before I become anything like them.

But right now, alone with my star, with Esp's Omens scrabbling outside the tent, I can do nothing but beg. No one knows exactly how a star chooses. No one knows exactly what a star wants.

Please. Please.

Lightning like taser-fire sears through me. *Oh.*

The star cracks into light. Its heat punctures through me, bruises me open, and my teeth ring, and I think, *Ah, this is what being shot feels like.* I'm going to die. But I still can't let go. I can't let go.

Power from the star courses. My body begins to hum. Light breathes from within to without my flesh, and jagged lines like porcelain cracks scrawl and glow against my veins.

The cord tightens around my arm. Abruptly, through my dying, I understand only one desire: to fly.

I strain onto the anchor. My stain is boiling and bubbling over my back, but it doesn't spread, not yet. I don't burst into flames. Not yet.

Then slowly, surely, the anchor begins to lift. I am flying. I have Joined.

I've passed.

Relief blows through me. I've passed. I did it. And I didn't have to die.

(My stomach rolls because Lumi had to, and it was my fault. All my fault.)

A voice blooms in my head.

Who are you? What have you done?

I hollow out. The star is speaking to me. And it knows.

We see you. We're with you. There is no hiding from us.

Golden flames unfurl like wings. I am engulfed.

In my panic, I pull up and up. Yet somehow, I don't burn to death. Somehow, I'm still alive. The flames lick over my skin, and it hurts like dying, but I don't die.

People are noticing. They've turned away from the noise outside the tent and are pointing at me. They gasp and cry out. Many shield their eyes against the burn of the star's brightness, and I imagine I must look like some bird of white fire, rising high and higher above the crowd.

The altar is several meters below me now. I wrench against the star and its cord, but it doesn't let me go. In my head, it continues to speak. The words overlap one over another, asking the same questions again and again: *Who are you? What have you done?*

Who are you?

What have you done?

I can't stop. The star won't let me free. It will eat me up from the inside out and then I'll fall to my death.

Dimly, I realize I've lifted out of the smoke hole. I have flown up and out of the tent. There's no stopping it. Jamming thick through my veins is the singular desire to fly.

Afternoon light blinds, then passes, and then the noise of the crowd washes over me. I see men and women and children gawking up at me. I see overturned stands and Omens on all fours, guardians surrounding them. Below me, the festival and all its colors sprawls. Before me, the white wall of the temple looms.

I crane my neck at the height of it, at the impossible height of it. Trees burst from the top of the wall because a garden is walled inside. There, an absurd distance above me and halfway up the wall, is the gap, the gap I saw before.

The hole in the wall where the garden decided it did not want to be inside anymore.

It taunts me. It's my only hope.

My chest is heaving from the weight and heat of the ichor within me, which sinks heavy and heavier the higher I pull; flying is a weight that cements over the bones. But I will have to endure. If I want to live, I must. The star continues to lift us up, up, and I don't look down. I cling to the anchor, just as my eyes cling to that break in the wall.

By the time I near the gap, my arms are numb and quaking. My palm has blistered and popped from the fire of the star. Every breath I pull into my lungs is like pulling in salt, scraping my airways raw. I taste blood.

This close, I can see that the gap is big enough for a kid like me, maybe two. It's now or never.

My body lifts to the same height as the hole and, with a scream, I wrench my body hard to the side. I yank the anchor off course and veer against the break in the wall, and metal crashes against stone. Flesh crashes against bark.

The star lets me go. Heat drains from me. The drag of a strange kind of gravity, the gravity of stars, sighs out of me. I am myself again.

I roll and sprawl onto the arm of some ancient branch and am cradled by moss and vine and stone. Dimly, I realize my veil and mask are no longer on me. I lost them somewhere along the way. Part of the anchor teeters precariously by the edge of the hole—the rest of it must've broken off and fallen. The star, knocked out of the engine, shudders out light, then shutters dark. It is asleep.

I'm no longer in pain. I'm no longer in danger of dying. And so, with a sigh, with a shudder like the star, I also give in to sleep.

Someone below me says, "You're not a bird."

I startle. I twist to see a boy in gray, halfway up the tree, looking up and smiling. He's a lanky, big-eared thing with buzz for hair. It's Naqi. That's right. I'm in the temple. He's an acolyte of the temple.

My vision blurs again.

"Not a bird," he repeats, awed, and his voice sounds far far away.

He sees something in my face that has him frowning and saying, "Sorry. Came up here to feed the birds, not a girl. You okay? You don't look so great."

It's the last thing I hear. The world swims, and then all is dark again.

FIVE

Lumi, on the ground. There is no one else around.

She sits up slowly, slowly, with the white of her robes glowing. She turns to me. I can see the hills and valleys of her eyes, nose, lips through the silk of her veil, her veil like a funeral shroud.

She opens her mouth and says, *Hey, Sozo.*

Why did you kill me?

I wake.

The ceiling is not a ceiling I recognize. My heart is pounding. I fold my arm over my eyes but am too stunned to cry.

I haven't cried in a long, long time. I don't know if I'd even remember how to.

Esp. The Omens at the tent. The Decade-Races.

Did I fail the Joining? How did I survive?

What happened to the Omens at the tent? I imagine some of

them must have been caught by the guardians. I imagine some of them must've been caught inside.

Esp. Did she get away? Did she see everything? What did she do with, with—

I stay stewing that way for a while—arm over my eyes with my body wound tight—but eventually, I pull my arm away.

I look around and take in the room.

The walls are minty teal. It's dark outside. The curtains are sheer white, and they ripple in the breeze—not the breeze. There's a fan that squeaks as it turns. There are other beds, white, with railings, sectioned by more curtains. No one else is in the beds. I'm in an infirmary.

My bones ache. My joints feel bruised. My teeth feel like I've been sucking on a lemon, and my hand is bandaged. It stings. I don't scratch it. And then I notice my robes have been changed. My veil and mask are gone.

I startle from the bed and touch my back through my new shirt and feel—my skin, my bone. I don't know if I can feel my scab. I wrench the blanket off me and stumble out of bed.

There's a mirror on the wall, and I go to it.

Briefly, I see myself—eyes wild and hair tousled—before I turn around. I tug my shirt up from the back, pull it over my shoulder, and stare. My shoulder blade is bare. My skin is smooth. My stain is gone.

It's gone.

All my life, I've fantasized about this moment.

And then, like the way blood bleeds into sheets, blackness begins to spill over my skin. My omen stain is returning. It stretches like it is waking from sleep and then re-forms around my shoulder blade, the way it always has, my constant companion.

I don't know how, or why, but my contact with the star must've jolted it dormant while I was out. Now that I am awake, it also wakes.

The door opens. I yank my shirt back down.

Several adults enter the room—all of them tall, some of them old. Three of them are wearing headdresses like fans, red like the setting sun. The fans are studded with golden spikes like sun rays.

These men and women, moving slow and regal, are High Suns—the high priests and priestesses of the temple. Out in public, like with Veils, their faces are kept obscured. Now, I can see their faces all lined by age. The crow's-feet by their eyes. The age spots that splatter over some of their cheeks.

Behind them is another adult, a guardian. Her hair is shaved. Her neck is long. Her lines are hard the way a tall tree is hard, and she holds herself with a stillness that reminds me of Esp.

"Ah." One of the High Suns speaks. "You're up. How are you feeling, Lumi?"

I jolt. Lumi. They still think I'm Lumi. I haven't been recognized.

(This is where I fall to my knees and tell them the truth. I tell them what I am, that I am a murderer, that I do not deserve to be here.)

I manage a nod. "Fine."

"The doctor's looked you over. Said everything seems to be in working order. Your palm should heal in two weeks or so."

I nod again.

"Do you remember what happened?"

I recall the Joining, and the star and its many voices. I recall the hole in the wall. I recall the boy, Naqi. He didn't recognize me from his demonstration; there was a whole crowd of us at the time, after all.

"Yes."

"And what happened, exactly?"

I frown and look down. "I don't know."

The star could have burned me up, but it didn't.

The High Sun sighs. He turns to the others. They murmur among themselves.

I stand there and wait. I await my fate. It is all that I can do.

The High Suns have decided that I, Lumi, need to be placed in solitary confinement.

It's not punishment, not really. They took my flying into the wall as a holy sign of prosperity, or as the star's prophetic declaration that I will win the races this decade. But I did disrupt the Joining, even if I did not mean to, and I did break the anchor. Many children will have to wait several days now before they can try to Join again.

So I am to be placed in solitude for three days. And for three days, I am to reflect upon my actions. My isolation will be how I atone.

I'm led by the guardian out of the infirmary and onto the temple grounds. It is nighttime. The moon is like a searchlight above us.

The temple cells are blocks of cement set in the earth, dug near the back of the gardens—all dense and dark in the night. A metal grate on a hinge, the sole entry doubling as part of the ceiling, slants up from the earth. Deep inside the cell is a woven bed, a blanket, a stool. A small counter juts from the side wall, and behind the counter is a squatting toilet and a faucet for water.

The guardian pulls open the grate for me. The hinges screech with rust.

She waits for me to move inside but says nothing. She's said nothing to me all this time, not a single word.

I don't ask why. I prefer the silence.

I climb down the ladder and into the cell, and the grate is closed over me. The woman locks it, then moves to the side and disappears from my view. I can hear her still. She's settled somewhere by the cell, in the grass. She must have been assigned to keep watch over me.

I'm tired, so tired, but I know I cannot sleep, even as I crawl onto the bed. I know that if I sleep, Lumi will come to me again. I don't know if I could bear to hear the things she will have to say to me.

Morning comes. It's cold.

When I look up past the grate, at the temple grounds outside, all I see is mist. It rolls through the garden and drapes and chills, and thickens white like clouds. I move to the ladder to sit on it, to press up against the grate to stare.

The woman must've left sometime without my noticing, because she's reappeared with a tray of stick crullers and steamed egg pudding and a tall cup of hot soy milk, and she slips that tray through the bottom slot of the grate. I stare at it. My stomach grumbles enough to be heard.

I push the tray back to her.

"I'm not hungry."

She tilts her head. Maybe she didn't hear me.

"Take it. I don't want it."

The woman frowns. Then her hands go every which way, quick, precise, like she's braiding or weaving, except there is nothing but air between her fingers. I don't understand.

"What?"

Her hands flutter again. She grunts *ah*, *ah*, and opens her mouth and points at it. Inside her mouth, I can see that her tongue is not there.

"Oh." That's why she didn't speak.

She smiles and presses the tray toward me again. I shake my head. I pull away from the ladder without touching the food or the tray and return to the bed. I lie on my side with my back to the grate. I don't want to see the food, or the woman. The scent of sweetness and oil wafts.

In the afternoon, the woman leaves and returns with another tray. Lunch is fried rice and tofu and crispy pork chops, and my stomach twists. It hurts. But I know if I eat, I will not be able to keep it down. I know if I eat, the food will turn to ash in my mouth.

I curl up tight and close my eyes. When the woman grunts and taps the grate, I pretend I don't hear her.

Night falls. Someone rattles the grate and says, "Definitely not a bird."

I turn around. Naqi is there with one of his many smiles, and he is holding another tray of food, this time a single large bowl of noodles. It's steaming. I frown.

"Why are you here?"

"Hello to you too." Naqi laughs.

"If you're here to get me to eat, don't bother."

"Even though Yashi's so worried?"

I pause. "Who?"

"Yashi," Naqi repeats and gestures his head at the guardian behind him. I notice, for the first time, how broad the woman's shoulders are. Her arms, even through her black robes, are well muscled.

He says, "If you ate something, it'd really put her mind at ease. Mine too."

My frown sharpens into a scowl. "Why do you care?"

"Why?"

"You heard me."

"What kind of a question is that?"

I say nothing. It occurs to me, then, that Lumi wouldn't talk the way I do. With her, a conversation meant putting the knife away, opening the door, smiling and laughing and asking—asking and accepting.

I've never been taught how to do any of those things.

Naqi continues. He crouches and balances the tray on his knee and says, hushed, like he is passing over a secret, "I still can't believe that you flew the wall. When I saw you, I wanted to bombard you with questions: You flew? From the ground? On that massive anchor? How? How did you do it?"

I wrinkle my nose. I would've tossed Naqi out the hole in the wall if he'd done that. The khab and his questions grate on me.

Naqi sees my expression and laughs again.

"You really should eat something."

"Don't tell me what to do."

"Hey. Even birds need to eat. And if you're feeling guilty, don't. It's not your fault. Everyone knows it. No one blames you."

I say nothing. I curl onto my side again, my back to the others.

So Naqi raps the tray against the grate again, again, again.

"C'mon, Lumi. I brought you your favorite, and if it's not your favorite, you're kind of wrong. But we can work on that. Juicy, succulent beef noodle soup, extra onions. You could bounce off these noodles."

I twist around. *Zap off*, I want to hurl, to curse, but then I remember again that I am supposed to be Lumi. Lumi wouldn't curse. Lumi would nod and stretch out her hands and thank Naqi for this delicious meal.

But I'm not Lumi. I never will be.

I can only stare, unimpressed. Naqi laughs.

"The dish really is very good."

"I don't care. I'm not hungry."

"You haven't eaten all day."

"And I'm not hungry."

"Liar."

I flinch. I twist away again.

Naqi falls silent. I don't see what he does, but I hear him set the tray down. I hear the rustling of their robes as the two of them move. Yashi might be speaking with her hands again, and I can hear Naqi say things like, *Yeah, I know. Do you think I can?*

He's able to understand her hand language.

The lock clicks free. The grate is pulled open.

"Hey," Naqi says. "I've got your letter."

I go cold. Lumi's letter, the one she was clutching before the Joining, the one she read again and again. Is he going to ask me what's in it, to test me?

"I'll give it to you if you eat something."

I breathe in and out. I smooth out my expression. When I look over my shoulder, it's to ask, "How did you get it?"

"Your friends found it," Naqi explains, "in the waiting room after everything happened. They're not allowed in the temple since they didn't pass, so they gave it to a guardian, who passed it along to me since I was coming by. What do you say?"

In the dark, his smile sheens white.

I shouldn't. The letter isn't mine to read. The letter was something dear to Lumi. And then Naqi says, "If you don't want it, guess I'll have to toss it away."

I push up and glare. Naqi has the nerve to *laugh*. He holds up his hands and says, "Don't shoot! I'm unarmed!"

"Khab," I say, then realize too late that that is also not something Lumi would say. Would she even know street slang?

"Ooh!" Naqi's smile is impish. He hops down the ladder. "Did you just say a bad word?"

"No."

"Sounded like one."

"Give me my letter."

"I will. Once you eat something."

"I'm not hungry."

"Then I guess your letter is going into the trash."

I push to my feet. I want to scream, to rail, to bite. I want to punch Naqi's teeth out of his smug smile. He stands before me in the dark of the cell, hand over his sash. There, I can see the creased paper of Lumi's letter. He's telling the truth.

I say nothing, not for a while. I stew in the heat of my anger. My back itches.

I push past Naqi and stomp up the ladder. I break apart the wooden chopsticks on the tray and use them to guide the noodles into my mouth as I tip the bowl, as I drink and slurp and halfway choke. It burns. I don't stop. I deserve to burn.

My cheeks are swollen with food when I turn back to Naqi.

His shoulders quake; he's trying not to laugh.

I hold out my hand, and he pulls the letter out of his sash and hands it over to me, like he said he would.

I take the letter as he says, "I'm stoked to be racing with a Veil, you know, since it looks like I'll finally have"—he waggles his brows—"real competition."

Of course Naqi passed the Joining, the annoying khab. I toss him another glare; my mouth is too full to curse him.

He raises his hands like I am holding him at gunpoint and finally laughs. He steps around me, hands still up, and then lowers them to make his way back up the ladder.

"I'll come visit you again tomorrow, okay?"

I chew and swallow. "Don't."

"But you'd miss me."

Yashi steps over then and nudges Naqi on the shoulder. She's frowning and weaving her hands at him. She's scolding him, I think, because Naqi dips his head and rubs the back of his neck. His laugh is sheepish.

"Yeah. You're right. Okay."

He steps away from the cell. The grate is closed, then locked.

Naqi waves as he leaves. Yashi again settles down on the grass. I look down at the letter in my hand.

I touch the edges of it—it's been folded enough times that the paper is wearing, almost tearing. Touching is all I do, in the end. I don't open it. I don't read the letter.

I place it closed on the counter, away from the bed, and then spend the rest of the night on the ladder, looking out.

The second morning comes around. I still haven't slept.

Yashi brings more food that I don't touch, that I don't bother looking at. And when I retreat to the bed with my back to her, she unlocks the grate and comes inside and touches my head. It is soft, like maybe she's afraid of breaking me.

I close my eyes and pretend to be asleep.

The afternoon is much the same. I don't touch the food. Outside, I hear the rhythmic cries of people training and the rhythmic clacks of wood striking against wood.

I roll onto my back and peer past the grate. Yashi is watching a little screen that she's propped up in the grass. She's scrolling through the feeds as she eats her own lunch, and the small square of a vid plays.

The images are too small and far away for me to make out—I see only smudges of gray and white and brown. I hear a man announcing that the Omens they caught at the House of Stars have profaned the tent and are to be executed at the end of the week.

I go cold, so cold. I roll back onto my side and hug my knees to my chest, and cannot stop trembling. I wonder if they're my fault too.

Hours pass. Yashi comes into the cell again. This time, she reaches around and slips Lumi's letter between my hands, and I want to scream, to weep, to tear at the letter and then at myself. The letter burns. Yashi's gentleness burns even more.

I do nothing in the end, and don't move. Yashi leaves the way she came, quietly, softly.

Night shades in. I don't know why. I really don't. Twisted curiosity, maybe.

I fold open the letter. I read.

Darling Lumi,
I miss you, and I'm so proud of you.

I can't keep it in. I let go of the letter and scrabble from the bed. I stumble to the toilet in the floor and hurl, and hurl, except I have hardly any food in my belly. The smooth yellow of my stomach acid rolls out of me and burns.

Yashi is here. I don't know how she got here so fast. She's folded her arms around me and is opening the faucet and wiping water over my mouth. I push at her, but she's strong. Her muscles are tensed. She doesn't let me go.

We sit like that on the floor for a while, a long while. I don't cry, but I fall asleep. Somehow, I don't dream.

I wake in the bed. The sky is all blush red and shy violet, the colors of late afternoon, early evening. I've slept most of the third day away.

"Hey."

It's Naqi, standing on the other side of the grate, his lines bloomed orange by the setting sun. He's back to visit, like he said he would.

"Heard you're not feeling well."

I consider saying nothing, but then Naqi is opening his mouth again, so I cut in with, "Yeah."

I say, "Stay away or I'll throw up all over you."

Naqi laughs.

"Never been puked on by a Veil before. I imagine it'd be like a cleansing, really."

I wrinkle my nose but say nothing else. I'm drained, a husk. Sleeping the day away hasn't made me less tired.

"They pulled together a makeshift Joining today. Finished up the rest of your school. Two more people passed, so including you, that's eight."

Still, I say nothing. That's seven sets of eyes I have to be wary of, seven that could expose my lie.

Naqi falls silent. He watches me. He crouches by the grate and then says, quiet, "Something happened, didn't it?"

My eyes flick up to him.

"The Joining. The star. It said something to you?"

"Why do you care?"

"You asked me that yesterday." Naqi looks up and ponders it. "And I think my answer is: because I'd like us to be friends."

An Omen and a temple acolyte. Friends. A murderer and someone who has never sinned. Friends. I want to laugh, but I'm too tired for it.

"You're sick for wanting that."

"Am I?"

"Yes." I realize now he wouldn't understand. I shouldn't have said what I said, but it's too late. "Now go away."

"Taking solitary confinement real serious, huh?"

"Better to be alone than with a khab."

I imagine Naqi will laugh again or take offense. He'll turn and stomp away like any sane boy. But instead he hooks his fingers through the holes of the grate. He presses in close and says, softly, "You don't have to shoulder whatever this is alone."

Heat brews in my chest. Right now, in this moment, Naqi reminds me of Lumi at the tent. She crouches from her high-and-mighty place and asks to save me, to help the charity case that I am.

In that beat, in that breath, I swell with a bitter idea. I say, "All right."

"All right?"

"Don't let me shoulder this alone. Since I can't go out, you'll come in."

"What?"

"Instead of you," I drawl, "sleeping in your cushy acolyte bed, you'll sleep here, on the ground of my cell."

Naqi says nothing. He looks at me, unmoving. I flash him my teeth. "Maybe if you lock yourself in here with me, I'll even be your friend."

The boy is frowning now. I can see it, the bumps of moonlight over his brow. He rises from his crouch and moves to the side, where Yashi is, and so I taunt, "What's the matter? This all your friendship is worth? First sign of an inconvenience and you're out?"

He doesn't return the taunts. He's talking instead with Yashi, quick, low, so I can't hear them. After, they come to stand before my cell.

I open my mouth to taunt him again, to mock and to sneer, but then Yashi is unlocking the grate.

Naqi pulls it open and hops down into my space. I don't understand. I sit up.

"You can't be serious."

The grate above us screeches closed and clicks locked, and that is Naqi's answer. I look up at Yashi and say again, "You can't be serious."

Yashi shrugs. She returns to her post to the side, out of sight.

Naqi, of course, smiles. "Nice to meet you, roomie."

"You," I scowl. "Your mind is full of static."

"Yup." He heaves a sigh, and dusts off the ground with his foot. "They say it's a condition that can only be cured with friendship. Hey, want to learn something cool?"

I bare my teeth. Speaking to Naqi is like trying to speak to the wind, and I'm left tossed. I don't know how he can pretend like any of this is normal.

He continues with, "Copycat me, okay?"

"What?"

He settles crisscross on the floor, then holds up a fist and tucks a thumb between his middle and fourth finger. Then he nods at me. "Go on."

"What is this."

"Just copy me."

"No. This is stupid."

"What, don't think you can?"

I glare. Like with all my glares, Naqi laughs and holds up his hands: *Don't shoot, I surrender!* His smile remains after his laugh, and it's a challenge.

So I hold up my right hand and tuck my thumb between my fingers.

He nods again. He pulls his thumb back out to rest against the side of his fist, and I copy him. He points his index finger and thumb down toward the ground, and I copy him. He swings his pinky up in the air, and I copy him.

His smile at the end of this is bright. It's something like proud. He holds up the first shape again. "*N.*"

He holds up the second. "*A.*"

He holds up the third and the fourth and says, "*Q, I.* Naqi. My name is Naqi."

I know his name, of course, but he doesn't know that I know it, and I repeat the hand letters back to him. His laugh is delighted.

I don't know why. The way the shapes settle in my hand eases me, lulls me. It gives me something to do. It distracts. I ponder the shapes of Naqi's name—a vein embedded in the center of a heart, a gentle fist, plucking up seeds, a promise.

I look up at him and wait, but I don't ask. Asking is also something like a weakness. Naqi understands anyway. He scoots closer to the bed I am on and teaches me another letter in the shape of an *L*. Then two straight fingers. Another embedded heart. A promise again.

He teaches me others: an open palm, a promise, crossed fingers, a single finger pointed at the sky. And like this, on and on and on, Naqi in silence teaches me words. We do not speak. He murmurs the letters he is writing for me, and I rewrite those letters in the shapes of my hand.

He stays the night like I dared him to. I don't know if that will get him in trouble.

He falls asleep right on the ground of the cell, the cold cell, with one arm tucked under his head like a pillow and his other arm draped over his belly.

I cycle through all the letters he taught me and murmur them to myself, like some lullaby. But I don't sleep. I rise from the bed. I pull my blanket off and away, still warm because I've been lying on it, and drape it over Naqi.

In the morning I will peel it off him. I don't want him to know.

SIX

I don't mean to fall asleep, but I do. In the morning, Naqi is gone. My blanket is tucked over me.

The grate is open and Yashi is there, waiting. In her hands is a bundle of things: temple robes and a veil and mask, towels and a toothbrush, sandals. Outside the cell, by the ladder, is a plate of baked wheat cake with egg and a glass of black soy milk. It's my breakfast.

I rise from the bed. I climb up the ladder and eat the cake and drink the milk.

Yashi turns away while I change into my new robes, so I do not have to worry about hiding my stain. My scab has been quiet these last few days. Tired, like me.

But from here on out, I can't afford to be tired. I can't afford to hurl and to tremble. I'm Lumi, now. I'm to fly in the Decade-Races. There's no time to be weak.

I drape the veil loosely over my hair and clip the mask to my belt-sash, to be slipped on around anyone from outside the temple.

I fold Lumi's letter carefully into my pocket. The letter crinkles as I move, as I walk into the sun.

The dorms are several buildings of woven willow and redwood, looking like delicate birdcages. The windows are rice paper, and the verandas are thatched. The smaller buildings include the mess hall and the infirmary and the storage and the larger dorms, stacked three or four floors high. Spacious decks and balconies sweep from the upper floors, casting wide shadows.

The grounds are empty. Even inside, it's empty. The bamboo halls are polished, and they echo.

"Where is everyone?" I ask.

Yashi looks over her shoulder at me and presses a finger to her lips for quiet. Then she points up. I look up at the ceiling. In the morning hush, I can hear the sound of chanting, maybe, or of singing, and of bells. Everyone must be at morning meditation.

I'm led up the stairs and down a hall, a hall full of bead-curtained doors. There's a girl loitering by the doorway of her room, fidgeting with her nails and chewing on the inside of her cheek, staring off at nothing.

She sees us, then smiles and straightens. She continues to fidget. "Oh! Is this her?"

Yashi nods. She turns to me and spells out letters to me, because she knows what Naqi was teaching me last night.

R. A. M. A.

"Rama?" I try.

The girl perks at her name and nods. "Hi. It's nice to meet you. I'm sorry you had to be in isolation for so long."

Rama is my height but fuller, with a health about her that glows. Her head is shaved like all acolytes', but the downturn of her blue eyes reminds me of the beautiful women I've seen in vintage films.

"It's cool that you can understand Yashi."

I pause. "You can't?"

Rama fidgets. "Most people can't."

"Oh." I thought it was something all temple-folk could understand.

"We're going to be roomies. The Suns and High Suns thought it'd be better for you to stay with the temple acolytes instead of the others, so you don't have to worry about the mask and veil." She fidgets again. "Unless you prefer to be with your friends. I heard seven others from your school have passed. Would you want that instead?"

My answer is immediate. "No." I pause, and try again with, "No. Whatever the Suns and High Suns want is fine."

Rama smiles a timid smile, and nods. "Lumi, right?"

No. Not right.

"Yeah," is all I manage.

"It's really neat meeting a Veil." She smiles again, then steps out of the doorway to let me inside her room. She says, "I hope you don't mind the cramp. I don't know what kind of accommodations you're used to."

"It's fine," I say.

Yashi touches my shoulder and passes me a bundle of clothes and necessities, then folds her fingers over her palm again and again—she is waving goodbye. I nod at her, and she takes her leave. I enter the room.

The space is small, crammed with eight bunks, a heater-stove, a pile of rugs and cushions by the window. Each set of bunks has a prim writing desk and a sturdy chest, and each bunk is a rigid hammock of threaded straw and cotton, strung up on thick bamboo. Rama brings me to the bunks closest to the window, tucked against the wall.

"This is ours," she says.

The upper hammock is hooked with wooden charms, strings of carved bees and bears, and cut-out pictures of chiseled actors I've seen in action or romance films. I didn't know things like this were allowed in the temple.

Rama fidgets with her nail and laughs sheepishly. When she brushes a hand through the charms, they rustle and clack.

"Sorry," she says. "I haven't had a bunkmate in a long time. I can move these if you want me to."

"It doesn't matter," I say. I test the bottom hammock. I slip Lumi's letter out of my pocket and tuck it underneath my pillow.

Rama is waiting for me to say something else, so I say, "You've been here a while?"

"In this bunk?"

"No." I frown. "In the temple."

"Oh. Yeah. I guess? Not as long as some of the others. Some people were dedicated as babies. I came when I was, oh, nine or so? So it's been four years."

I say nothing else. I don't know why Rama continues standing there. I don't know what she wants. She says eventually, "Want a quick tour of the grounds before your interview?"

"My what?"

"Interview. Oh. Sorry. I should've said earlier. All the people that passed the Joining are going to be interviewed by the stations later, after morning meditation. I'll take you where you need to go."

"Why are we getting interviewed?"

"Why? I mean, isn't it obvious?"

It is. It's the long-awaited Decade-Races, plus the privileged contestants of the Decade-Races. Of course the people of Tall Titan will want to meet them, if only to place their bets on who might win.

I nod again, can only nod, because my throat is tight. I can say nothing at all.

The Temple of Celestial Ichor is divided into four main sections:

The work tents and benches to the north. The cluster of buildings where we came from to the south. The gardens to the east. The temple to the west. Everything, save the face of the temple and its gates, is surrounded by the temple walls. We are bordered in, cloistered and safe.

Rama leads us to the work tents first, tucked right up against the temple wall. The space reminds me of the Joining festival, all soaring canvas of red and yellow, but instead of stalls and shops selling goods and treats, it's workbenches and furnaces and contraptions for weaving. Even now, in the early morning, priests and priestesses tinker away.

"Where are the others?"

"What do you mean?"

"The people from outside the temple."

"Oh. Probably still at morning meditation, but you'll see them later at the interview, and also when special training begins for those who passed. I won't be there, though."

I frown. Naqi said Lumi's friends didn't pass, but Lumi knew many people, and many more people knew her. If the other seven from my school approach me, speak to me, I don't know how I'm going to keep them at bay.

Rama is looking at me and waiting. Her eyes are very large.

I say, just to fill the space, "You won't be there?"

Those large eyes flick down with something like embarrassment. She shakes her head and fidgets. "No. I didn't pass. The star didn't light up for me at all."

Rama wears her weaknesses and fears so easily, so shamelessly, like some wide-brimmed sun hat. She would never survive out on the streets. Esp would've ground her to dust.

"Lots of people don't pass," I say.

"Yeah." She smiles at me again. "I know."

Rama takes us to the gardens next, though I don't think gardens is the right word.

The trees, looming high as the impossible walls, are jungle dense. They blot the sky green. Their ancient boughs are crooked with age but strong, carpeted with vines and moss and dots of white flowers. The great roots of these trees are like hills, curving high and large enough that nooks like caves form within them.

The tree that cradled me and Naqi is somewhere here, by the hole in the wall, but I don't know if Rama knows about it. I don't ask.

Above us, birds trill. Somewhere, water falls.

Within the denseness of the ancient trees are other smaller gardens.

I am taken to a vegetable pergola garden, a stone stroll garden, a garden of koi springs, and a lotus pond wide enough to require several connecting bridges. We cross over it to a flower garden full of colors and shapes I don't really know the names of.

It's serene. It's fragrant. I never knew Tall Titan could be either of those things.

"Were you scared?"

"What?"

"During the Joining, when the star started acting up. It's all everyone's been talking about for days."

I wonder what Lumi would say to this question.

"I guess," I say.

"I would've been terrified." Rama fidgets again. "The star flaring out like that? And flying that high? I would've fallen for sure. You're really brave."

I say nothing. I wasn't brave at all. I was terrified like Rama would have been.

She stops us, then, before a particular patch of flowers—delicate ruffled things looking like a cluster of suckling butterflies. Their colors are a gradient from dainty pink to gentle lavender.

"Sweet peas," she explains. She bends and touches one of the petals. "This is the patch I take care of."

The flowers suit her, look like her, and so I say, "They look like you."

Her eyes flick up at me, surprised. I must've said the wrong thing. But then she smiles. The apples of her cheeks swell. "My friends call me Pea sometimes, so maybe you're right."

"Oh," I say. "A nickname?"

"Yeah." She pauses. "You can call me that, too, if you want."

"Oh," I say again, and nothing else. The idea of calling anyone a nickname is a foreign thing to me, as foreign as the idea of having friends.

The interview will take place inside the Temple of Celestial Ichor, and the only solace I can take is that I will have my mask between me and the others, between me and the racers and interviewers and camera lenses. I can claim stress, maybe, or the mysterious nature of my Joining for why I am acting unlike myself, unlike Lumi.

I slide on my mask as Rama leads on. The temple looms.

Entering it is like entering the snout of a great slumbering beast, and I step lighter. I breathe shallow. This space is what myth made material looks like.

The doorway I enter through is the size of an aircraft tunnel, and the interior of the chancel is so vast that I forget to breathe. I can't fathom it. I didn't think any one thing could hold this much space. I didn't know space itself could echo.

A bell gongs. Incense wafts. Sounds mute to a hushed reverence.

The carved walls are white stones lined with gold, stacked tight with reliefs. The space itself is ringed by pillars and crowned by tiers and tiers of balconies and floors, more than I have time to count. The bell I heard, made small by the great distance, hangs from the ceiling of the temple.

The ground is polished like some still lake, a mirror of patterned marble. The many lights—candles on racks, torches on walls—bloom against the burnish like dancers swaying over a dance floor.

In the eye of the chancel floor, behind a great ring of high walls dotted with the golden masks of sirens, is a circle of shallow steps that lead down and down to a vast swirling well—the titan's eye.

It's real. It really does look like an eye.

Its iris is an impossible brew of sand and of smoke, and of the winking of stars. The ever-changing colors—pale blue to gold to white to pink—roll and wisp from the dark of the pupil, the dark like the end of all things, a dark with no end.

The pool sighs and whispers. It breathes out warmth, even though the temple air is chilled.

I forget myself and stare.

Set up near the titan's eye are cameras and lights. Interviewers and reporters with mics clipped to their collars are reviewing their cards or reapplying the red of their lips. The other racers are there, too, gathered on stands before the cameras. There are forty-five of us in total, according to Rama. The Joining star was generous this decade.

I see Naqi with his acolyte friends, chatting brightly and nudging one another. I see someone who looks over at me and waves. I recognize the person's face. It's one of Lumi's friends.

Naqi was wrong. One of Lumi's friends did pass.

Rama touches my arm, and I flinch.

"I think they're just waiting for you now. I'll be here, okay?"

I open my mouth to say no, I can't do this, take me back—but then a Sun is calling Lumi's name and coming over, ushering me to the stands. I'm late, he says. They're about to start, he says.

There's a space next to Lumi's friend, and I'm made to stand in it.

The girl's a short thing with freckles and too much hair, and far too touchy. I've seen her laughing with Lumi with her hand on her arm or holding hands as they walk down the halls. Now, she slings her arms around my waist and embraces me.

I'm tense, so tense. I don't know what to do. I touch her back, but I can do nothing else.

"Thank the stars, Lumi. You're okay. All of us were so, so worried."

I don't know what to say. Will she be able to recognize my voice? Lumi's voice was bright and high, like the words she strung together. This girl could realize the truth if I speak.

So, I say nothing at all. I stay where I am, stiff.

The girl pulls back. Her brows are crumpled, confused. Does she know? Does she?

"Lumi, what's wrong?"

The lights snap on. Someone behind the camera is shouting that we're rolling in one, and a woman in a tight pinstripe suit is moving to stand before the camera. Her smile is practiced perfect.

I'm saved. I pull away and turn toward the cameras, and so does Lumi's friend, though her eyes linger on me with something like concern.

On a monitor before us, a news segment is winding down. The anchor seated behind his desk is talking the way news anchors do—curt and clear and somber. And then I catch what he's saying: recent executions, Omen-incited vandalism, newly rising tensions between the Omens and the city.

Esp and her group must be lying low right now out in the simmer of the city; she's always preferred the shadows and a silent knife to a brawl in the heat of the sun.

She'll be okay. She has to be.

The news segment ends. A man behind a camera holds up three fingers, then two, then one. A red light clicks on. We've begun.

"We're live now," the woman opens, "in the chancel of the Temple of Celestial Ichor before the walls of the titan's eye, with the chosen forty-five of the decade."

The others around me straighten and smile, and I am glad in that moment for my veil and mask. I've never been taught how to smile.

"Once they've completed their month of extensive training inside the walls of the temple, honing their bonds with stars, these bright young souls will at long last begin their journey in the Decade-Races."

The woman goes on, then, to refresh the viewers with race facts: that there are three stages to the Decade-Races, that fliers are often called whistlers after the whistle of their flying, and that the titan's eye is sometimes called the wishing well, after all the wishes pulled from it.

"Let's start things off by introducing the one most favored to win the first stage of the Decade-Races—Roaz Mal. Sixteen years old. And one of Tall Titan's own. They tell us you grew up in the night market district?"

The lights around us dim, leaving only a spotlight on Roaz—a strong-jawed, bushy-browed boy. He's two rows below me and far to the right, and I don't recognize him. He must be from one of the other schools.

"I mean," he says, and smirks, "which part of Tall Titan isn't night markets?"

The woman's laugh is indulgent. She says, "I suppose that would explain why you're most favored to win this first stage."

Roaz nods. He squares his shoulders. "Oh, yeah. I know Tall Titan like the back of my hand. Racing through it will be no problem."

"That's the kind of confidence we love to see in our whistlers. We're all looking forward to the lines you'll draw for us."

Lines, stardust tails, ichor drag. These were the trails I saw when I was four, when the whistlers drew lines of light with their anchors.

"Up next"—the woman turns back to the cameras—"is the

second stage of the races. And in this portion, the one most favored to win would be one of the temple's own—Naqi Imka."

I look over. Naqi is down the other way, also some rows below me. The spotlight blooms over him now, and he smiles, because of course he does.

"Fourteen years old. Dedicated to the temple since he was eight. They say you've memorized all the starsongs in the temple archives. Is this true?"

Naqi laughs. "Would make me a huge nerd if it were, huh?"

"No shame in that. Do you have any inkling what song you might whistle for us when the day comes?"

Naqi shakes his head. "I'm just going to focus on passing the first stage first. Don't want to be getting ahead of myself."

"A very levelheaded answer. You're mature beyond your years, Naqi. Thank you."

Naqi bows, and his spotlight fades.

"And now, introducing the one that requires no introduction, the one most favored to win the final portion of the races, and thus the race as a whole—Lumi Sidik."

The spotlight cracks bright over me. I can't breathe.

"Veil. Fourteen years old. From the humble farm-colony on the Eurydice moon. According to the High Suns' interpretations of what happened days ago at the Joining ceremony, she is to be a bringer of prosperity. Lumi, we are all dying to know: what exactly happened at the ceremony?"

No one warned me of this. No one told me this would happen. I didn't think to come up with a lie, but I have to speak. Naqi is looking at me. I see, down the way, that Roaz is glowering at me, though I don't know why.

In the waiting silence, I clear my throat and fist my hands.

I lighten my voice to what I think is Lumi's pitch, and manage only, "I'm not sure myself."

The girl next to me shifts. She's watching me. Her brows are furrowed.

"We all witnessed what happened that day. You flew nearly the entirety of the wall. No one in recent memory has ever managed to fly such a height. How did you do it?"

I shake my head. My veil shifts and rustles with the movement.

"I don't think I did. The star carried me."

"Truly a testament of the breadth of your connection to the stars. We're all watching with bated breath for what other feats you have in store for us."

I nod and say nothing else. The spotlight over me dims. I am released.

The interview continues. The girl beside me reaches over and grasps my hand, my bandaged hand, and when she squeezes, it hurts. But I don't pull away. I don't think Lumi would, after all.

The woman is asking questions now. She is asking us what kinds of wishes we would make, if we were to win the races.

All around me, the racers perk. The air is giddy.

All sorts of wishes are broached, with most being wishes for capsule-coin, the stardust currency of Tall Titan and of the known world. A decade ago, a boy wished for a mountain of it, and it took them a good month to clear every capsule out of the main temple hall.

Some wish for more personal things, like long health for their families, or seeing a dead parent one last time. Two decades ago, a woman wished for a child—she had been barren all her life. They say her belly swelled on the spot.

When Naqi is asked what wish he'd make, he smiles and says he doesn't know.

When I am asked what wish I'd make, I also say I don't know, even though I do. I've known since the beginning. It's what Esp and I have been working toward all this time.

But it's not a wish I can say out loud. It's not a wish anyone would ever think to make.

After the interview, I cannot flee. Lumi's friend doesn't let go of my hand.

"Something's wrong," she says. "What is it?"

And I think about the things I could say: *I've caught something and am sick. The race is weighing on me, and I'm anxious.*

The girl's gaze is intent on me, and so I straighten and say, "Yes." Something is wrong.

I say, "Something happened at the Joining, but not something I want to share. And I've been unwell since then. Not sure when I'll feel better. I'd like to be left alone until then."

I don't stumble on my words. I hold my tone clipped and clean, neutral.

The girl looks at me with a wide-eyed expression, like someone's pulled back the funeral shroud of some corpse she once knew. She's aghast.

"Oh."

"I'm sorry," is all I can think to say.

The girl pulls her hand back and shakes her head.

"No," she says. "I understand. Or, rather, I don't understand. But if that's what you're asking of me, then I can't do anything but respect it, can I?"

I say nothing. I'm glad Lumi's friend doesn't seem to be someone who pries.

So, with a nod, I turn to leave. I won't have to be in close proximity to her from here on out. At the most, we'll have training sessions together, but even then, I'll have other people as a buffer. During mealtimes, we won't have to eat at the same table. We won't be bumping into each other at the dorms, as I'll be sleeping with the acolytes.

I'll be free of the danger she could pose.

She catches my wrist. I stop and turn.

The girl is smiling through her tears.

"Lumi," she says. Her voice wobbles. "I just want to say, before you go, that you've . . . if it weren't for you, I wouldn't be here today. I would still be that sad, lonely thing angry at the world. You helped me out of that. And so if I can help you in any way, I will. Don't forget that. Ever. I'm here, okay?"

I see Lumi at the bottom of the pit with the boy who fell, helping him out of it, soothing him with her words, with her hand on his back. I see Lumi in the tent on her knees with me. My hand is no longer a hand, and she touches it anyway.

She offers to help me anyway.

I want to hurl again.

I wrench my arm from the girl and twist away, and leave. She doesn't call after me. Even if she did, I know I shouldn't stop.

If I stopped, I think I would break open. The floods would come. My strength would drown.

I'd tear the veil off my face and shatter my mask and confess to the cameras, to the vast echo of the temple and everyone in it, that I am the one who should have died.

Lumi helps, and Lumi lifts.

All I do is hurt.

SEVEN

Connected to the main chancel of the temple is an inner sanctum of black tourmaline. Walking through it, echoing through it, is like entering the dark of space, an endless galaxy that stretches on and on.

The sanctum houses a kori tower—a tiered structure like a step pyramid—also of black tourmaline. It is topped with a spiraling roof in the shape of cosmic clouds, gaudy in gold. Sirens of gold adorn every tier, crowding the steps and corners.

There are one hundred and fifty sirens in total, and each of them holds in their hands an unlit star like dark glass.

I wait with the racers at the base of the tower, watching, restless.

Standing before us is a stick of a man, very old, with skin like wet clothes left on a line. Like all Suns, he is robed in the colors of the sun—red and yellow, with a belt-sash of white. He paces in front of the group, slowly, because he is very old.

His name is Brother Marat, and he is the one in charge of our preparations before the month is up.

"There are three kinds of stars." The old man holds up one finger.

"The first is the Joining star—characterized first by its size, typically ten times that of a normal star. It is capable of bonding with thousands of souls, and it houses within it many voices. Its lifespan is a thousand years."

"The second"—he holds up another finger—"is the wishing star, one that has power enough to grant a wish, any wish. It is known to be cunningly fast, far more playful and mischievous, and bright enough to scorch the eye. There is no record of a wishing star dying."

Finally, he holds up a third finger.

"Whistling stars, or simply—stars. Typically the size of a fist, with a lifespan of a century or so. These are what we use in our slings, what we bond with in our anchors, and what you see before you upon the kori tower."

Brother Marat gestures behind him, and we shift. We know what's coming.

After passing the honor of the Joining comes the Choosing.

In the Choosing, each whistler is given their turn to woo a star for themselves, a star specifically set aside for the Decade-Races. These stars are swayed not by the time one has spent in training—years or months or weeks makes no difference. And no amount of capsules spent in preparation for this moment will sway the opinion of one.

Instead, the star looks at a person's Ahs, the Ahs that I still don't quite understand.

Brother Marat gestures for us to follow, and he leads us slowly, slowly, up and around the steps of the tower.

He points as he goes and explains.

"This siren here," he says, "holds in her hands the star that bonded with Tiras, who won the Decade-Races twenty years ago. According to Tiras, he says, the star was a serious thing, with barely any sense of humor.

"This siren," he says, "holds the bonded star of Nim, who won forty years ago. He called the star stubborn, but also stubbornly loyal.

"This is the star of Avan. This is the star of Kit. This is the star of Togarath, who came back with not one but three whole wishes."

On and on and on, Brother Marat relates each story. I don't know how he's managed to remember the names and stars of so many people, even the ones who didn't win, only participated. Combined, the names number nearly a hundred. Maybe that's why he looks so very old—the ages of all the people he carries in his head end up writing themselves in the lines of his skin.

Some stars, fifty or so, are unbonded, untested, because they were newly harvested from cosmic storms just this year. These have the advantage of youthful vigor and speed, but the disadvantage of an unknown personality. The star could be unruly, or timid, or lazy. None of which will help you win the race.

We step down from the tower and gather back before Brother Marat.

He smiles a kindly smile at all of us and says, "Let us recite, then, the Nine Ahs, and so open the way for the Choosing."

He closes his eyes, unfurls his arms, and begins to story-sing.

"Hrah, adopting joy in the coming future. Sha, to be complete or whole. Sav, not giving in to anger even in the face of provocation.

"Sahd, a helping hand, a blow to the head. Tahv, choosing goodness over evil. Rahv, to be loyal and devoted and firm in truth. Anvah, humble to and compassionate of others' struggles and shortcomings. Enkrah, to manage one's actions, thoughts, and emotions.

"The reigning Ah of Ahavah—to seek someone's well-being without expecting anything in return."

The recitation ends. The sanctum resounds with it still.

"The Choosing," Brother Marat begins, "requires a surrendering, a humbling, and a giving up of what separates us from stars. Our souls must first be aligned through the Ahs, yes, but now our bodies must be, as well. Surrender to the star your sight. Humble your hearing to it. Give up the feel of your robes against your skin and the taste of the air upon your tongue."

People shift. Somewhere to my side, Roaz speaks up. His voice is clipped, harsh in the echo of the space.

"We need to go deaf and blind and whatever else for this?"

"Correct." Brother Marat's smile is still kindly. "But only for the duration of the Choosing, until you have properly bonded with your star."

"So we get everything back after?"

"Correct. With a few stray exceptions, of course."

"What?"

People are grumbling now. Some are already panicked.

Brother Marat holds up his hands, hands dark with age and full of veins, and he soothes, "In my many decades overseeing the Choosing, I have only ever witnessed such exceptions twice. The first was a most troubled young man—one horribly misaligned. Yet he was able to regain his senses after an extended stay in the proper medical facilities.

"The other was discovered to have been a criminal, a murderer. Only the stars know why he was allowed to pass the Joining in the first place."

Criminal. Murderer.

I fist my hands against my robes. Cold ruptures over my skin, and for the first time in a long while, I can feel my omen stain stir. I try not to tremble.

Roaz's brassy voice claps over the murmuring and gasps. "So what happened to him?"

"Unfortunately," the old man answers, "the star never returned his senses to him. And he was beyond aid. Unable to connect at all with the world around him, he passed shortly after."

A world devoid of sight, sound, taste. A world where your skin transfers nothing at all. A consciousness in a vacuum.

Death would be kinder.

"So as long as we're not filthy Omens, we'll be okay?"

"The man was not an Omen," Brother Marat says. "But I understand your meaning. And yes. You are correct."

Roaz sniffs. He crosses his arms. I see him flick his eyes over to me then, me underneath my veil and mask, and I'm reminded of his glare on me during the interview.

A smile curves over his face. It's a mean slash of a thing.

"I think our Veil should go first."

Brother Marat tilts his head. "Oh?"

"Oh, yeah," Roaz says. "She's supposed to be the best of us, after all. So she should do the honors, you know?"

The boy is sneering.

Brother Marat does not seem to catch the disdain. He only smiles on and nods. "Certainly nothing wrong with a Veil opening the Choosing for us. What say you, young Lumi?"

I can say nothing, because I have no breath in my lungs. I can't breathe. Everyone is watching me and expecting me to nod and to go and to bond. But criminal. Murderer. If that man passed the

Joining despite his sins, just like me, then I will be just like him here: blind, deaf, senseless, a grunting thing scrabbling in the dark.

I'm hyperventilating.

"Young Lumi?"

I shake my head. It is all I can do. And then I hear to the side, "I'd like to go first, Brother Marat."

I know that voice. Naqi.

I don't need to look over at him to know that he's smiling.

"I've had my eye on a particular star for the longest time. First come first serve, right?"

Roaz snorts. "Like you're going to get your first pick."

"I would if I went first."

"Because wooing a star is just that easy, huh?"

"Sure."

Roaz barks a laugh, the sound like a crack. "Get a load of this clown."

"What?" Naqi smiles again, this one like a challenge. "Don't think you can do it?"

The older boy returns the smile, but it carries the stench of malice. "All right, temple boy. I'll bite. Granted you're willing to eat your words, after."

"I don't see why not."

"How very exciting." Brother Marat's old face is tugged by amusement. He steps aside and gestures for both boys to approach the tower, and I can breathe again. I have been given time, time to think, time to plan.

I can't fly without a star of my own, but how can I fly if I am blind and deaf and senseless? Maybe it won't happen. Maybe that time long ago was only a fluke. Maybe I can be the exception to the exception.

Naqi and Roaz are climbing the tower now. Whenever one of them nears a siren, Brother Marat reiterates the kind of star they are approaching: that one is full of joy, that one is protective. That one is bold and courageous, and that one has been known to delight in poetry.

Roaz is looping around the tower to a siren near the back, and the group shifts to follow and to see. There's a siren there seated with her lower form tucked to the side, one hand on her chest, her other hand outstretched with the star.

"The star of Nim," Brother Marat says. "Headstrong, willful, but loyal."

"This is the one." Roaz's grin is full of teeth. He cracks his knuckles and looks out at us on the ground, then over at Naqi.

Naqi is going straight to the top. I can't believe it. None of us can.

"You can't be serious," Roaz scoffs, while the racers around me are thrumming, gasping with giddy disbelief, because we all know—stars are strongest at the alpha of their life, and at the omega. The stars placed nearest to the top of the tower will be the ones nearing the very end of their lifespan, at which time they will burst open in a firework of stardust.

Nayha's star is there, eighty years old, full of hope. Togarath's star is there, ninety years old, vivacious and playful and brilliant. Gaia's star is there, a hundred years old, set to die at the end of this year. Not much is known about this star, only that its power is vast.

"You'll go blind just touching them, temple boy."

"If I do, then I do."

Roaz curls his lip back. "You're not impressing anyone."

"Good." Naqi smiles. "I'm not trying to."

He finally stops before a siren. He's chosen the star of Togarath.

Brother Marat is applauding.

"Splendid. Splendid! Good to see the youth of today are still ever full of life and fire. Now, boys, when you are ready: close your eyes, open the door of your mind. When you feel a calling, a push, do not reject it. Do not turn it away. Allow the presence to come within and welcome it close. Remain humble to it.

"And most of all," he continues, smiling, "do not panic."

Brother Marat pulls back. The Choosing begins.

Roaz and Naqi close their eyes. They bow their heads to their stars.

The old man is chanting again, chanting the Nine Ahs, and the stars little by little begin to shake. They vibrate. Their skins bump against the gold of the hands cradling them and chime and chime, bright like the ringing of champagne glasses.

Before both Naqi and Roaz, their stars begin to glow.

Roaz is frowning, and shifting, and muttering under his breath. He clenches and unclenches his fists. Naqi is frowning, too, but in concentration. He stands very, very still.

Brother Marat drones, "The more we are like stars, the more we may fly like them, as they do—faster than the eye can comprehend, higher than the mind can grasp. So let us give of what separates us from stars, our physicality—how we see, how we hear, how we feel."

And then, with a force like a great wave crashing, slamming, swallowing whole, light bursts out from the two stars—a solar flare, a whip of flame. I have to clap my hands over my eyes even with my mask and veil.

The light recedes.

When it no longer hurts to look, we look. I see Roaz with

one hand on his knee and the other on his star. He is heaving for breath and shaking out his head. His eyes are the white-blue of blindness, but slowly, surely, that color shades back to black. He can see again.

I see Naqi with one hand on his hip and the other on his star. His own blindness is still bleeding away, but he is beaming. He looks so very proud of himself.

He tosses his star up in the air, catches it, and waves it at us. The people around me are giddy again. They laugh, and clap, and shout. The sanctum rings and rings with their mirth.

"Well done, boys. Well done!" Brother Marat is nodding and nodding, most pleased. "Named stars on the first try. Most auspicious. Your journeys in the Decade-Races have now officially begun. Please. Come and join the rest of your peers."

They dismount the tower and return to the group, and people clap their backs and ruffle their heads. Words and questions pour one over another—*That was incredible! How did it feel? Did it hurt? I can't believe you got Togarath's star.*

"Young Lumi."

No. No. There has to be a way out of this.

"Would you do the honors by starting for the girls?"

Everyone turns to me again. Roaz turns to me. His brow is beaded with sweat, but he smirks and says, "Should be a piece of cake for someone that flew the wall."

"Roaz," Naqi says. "Anyone ever tell you you talk too much? And that's coming from someone who talks too much."

"Oh, people tell me lots of things."

"Boys, boys." Brother Marat pats at the air for calm, for peace. He looks at me again and smiles. "No pressure, of course, my dear. Perhaps another girl would like to start for us?"

"Do we—" My voice cracks, and I clear it. "Everyone has to go through the Choosing?"

"Correct."

"We can't . . . there's no—other way of bonding with a star?"

"There are the weaker stars we use day-to-day throughout the temple—the ones found in our slings, or the ones Naqi would have used when he visited the schools. Those require far less stringent bonding."

I gulp. Maybe that's my way out. I can bond with one of those stars and keep from going senseless.

"But there would be no winning the race at all with a star like those. They are far too meek."

Roaz leans into my space then, and sniffs at me. He bares his teeth in a grin. "I think I smell fear."

I want to snarl. I want to hiss words back at him—*That's the smell of your own stench.* But Lumi would not say those words, so I don't speak. I fist my hands again in my robes and say nothing.

Roaz watches me, then snorts and leans away.

His dislike of me is blatant. He pinches his eyes at me like I'm a soiled thing to be trashed.

I realize then, with a pang, that this is what I did with Lumi. I saw her only for the veil she wore. I judged her for it.

Other girls like Lumi's friend have raised their hands and are volunteering to go, so Brother Marat lets them. Two of them mount the steps like Naqi and Roaz did and find stars that have won in the past—stars of Erla and of Avan.

They bow their heads and close their eyes, and Brother Marat begins his chants anew. The stars chime. Light like a storm flares.

When it is possible again to see, Lumi's friend is holding in her hand the star of Erla, while the other girl stands rejected. Her star remains in the siren's grip. She flushes, embarrassed, and tugs on her ears—her hearing must still be returning to her.

The group waits while she makes her way further down the tower to another star, this time belonging to a whistler who did not win but came close.

When she bows her head and gives of her senses once more, she is accepted. The star is hers.

Two other girls mount the tower, along with two boys. And like this, in fours, the Choosing continues on and on. Most people try for the named stars first—the stars of Ro or of Elis or of Kit. Most people are rejected. Some go straight for the newest stars but are also rejected. Young stars are fickle things.

Then slowly, surely, everyone has chosen. Everyone has chosen except for me.

I shouldn't have waited this long; now all eyes will be watching. The veil I wear to hide my face invites eyes instead, and I hate it. The veil is like permission given to turn me into a public thing, to be viewed whenever anyone would like.

I don't know what to do. I don't know how to unshackle from my panic.

Will an Omen like me come out of this unscathed? Or will the star judge me and hand me what I deserve?

Brother Marat turns to me and nods at me, and I go. There is nothing else I can do.

I mount the steps and walk the tiers.

The star of Elis is courageous and bold, so I don't think it would accept me. Fear has been my constant companion since the Joining.

The star of Ro is gentle and patient, so I know it will not accept me. There is no bone in my body that is gentle. And if there were, Esp has long since pruned me of it.

So I observe the others, over a hundred others, and am lost, unsure. I don't know which star to woo. I don't know which star would be safe.

Something brushes over my understanding then, the way a stray hair brushes over skin. It itches. It distracts.

I look up and see the highest star—the star of Gaia. A hundred years old, known only for its vastness of power, and how much greater that power must be now that it is at the apex of its life. It's calling for me.

I don't understand. But even though I don't understand, I go to it. I climb up and up and up, and I can hear the people hushing. The Veil, they say, is going to do the impossible. She's going to claim the star greater than even Togarath's.

I make it to the top. There are no more steps to take. The siren before me is large, larger than all the other sirens, with her lower half bound up in clouds. She's kneeling, holding the star between the tips of her fingers and the pucker of her lips, her face tilted heavenward.

The brushing is a buzz now between my brows, inside my ears, and I shake my head. I'm dizzy. This presence reminds me of the Joining star. The buzzing reminds me of its many voices. It is trying to enter. But I don't know if I'm willing to allow it.

Brother Marat is chanting. The stars are beginning to quiver, to chime, and I'm out of time. I have no choice.

With my breath trembling from me, with my heart like a bird railing against its cage, I close my eyes. I bow my head. I open the door of my mind.

The voice that resounds knocks my breath from me.

Who are you?

What have you done?

Hell and void. It's the same words, the exact ones from before. It sees me for the Omen I am, for the things I've done. And though this time there is only a singular voice, still it bloats through me with the force of many, and it hurts. I bare my teeth and clench down, because it feels like the voice could sweep me away, far away, until I am lost.

Answer me.

(You know. You already know. You don't need me to tell you.)

I long to hear it in confession.

I shake my head. Siren's teeth.

Surrender, Brother Marat had said. *Humble yourself. Give it all up.*

How can I possibly, possibly do any of those things when there's a chance I'll never get anything back? When there's a chance I'll be exposed?

Power is building, surging, rolling to a swell. I know what's coming. The star is about to make its choice: I am to be accepted, or rejected.

I can't hear.

It's taken my hearing. Sounds burble and muffle and become like held breath.

My eyes snap open to vision that blurs, then sharpens, then blurs again. Colors are blending and lines are smudging, and I want to hurl.

I can't do this. I can't do this.

I jerk and wrench away.

The presence that was engulfing my understanding pulls from me, stings the way a slap stings. I push from the siren and stumble and topple, down and down the steps of the tower. Bruises slam into me. My skin tears. My veil tugs against my sash but somehow remains secure.

People are crying out. I hear them. Stars, I can hear them still. But there's a ringing that will not go away, and the floor beneath me is like the rubber of a trampoline. I cannot find my grounding.

Brother Marat lifts me to my feet, and I shove him off.

Naqi touches my shoulder and says something, and I can't bother to listen to what he is saying. I knock him back, knock everyone back. I tear through the gathered crowd and flee.

I don't know where I am fleeing to, but I can't stay.

Beneath my mask and the thin silk of my veil, it is hard to breathe.

EIGHT

I have never seen Esp's real hair.

I don't know why, but as I'm running through the echo of the temple, as pillars and windows and corridors blur past me, I remember how I spent hours holding up her wigs on my fists as she bleached them, dyed them, cut them. When the bubble gum in her mouth turned stale and stony, she replaced it with a cigarette.

We worked in silence. It stifled like the smoke.

But sometimes, sometimes, she would look at me with a gaze that drowned and talk about *them*. The Omenless. The people who have stepped on us and spit on us. Sometimes as she talked, she gripped me by my shoulder and squeezed without realizing, and I never pulled away. I never cried out, not even when it hurt.

I don't know why I'm remembering this now—except maybe I do. Me and Esp in the silence. Light muted through dust-filmed windows. Air that stings and her hand that stings.

These are the softest memories I have of her.

Rama finds me in our dorm on the rigid bamboo frame of my hammock, where I am pondering my hands. The room is quiet, still, empty, because the acolytes are at the work tents. Here, it is safe for me to be veil-less and maskless, so I am.

"Lumi?"

I say nothing.

Rama comes over to me, sits next to me, and touches the back of my hand.

"You can try again."

I laugh. It's a mean sound. Rama understands nothing.

"You can." But Rama is fidgeting again, the way she always does. "Isn't that what everyone does? If they're rejected, they can try again?"

I can try as many times as I want. I can try every single star that's left on that tower. But nothing will change. The possibility that I might be like that criminal from before chokes and smothers.

My hands are trembling. I can't do this.

"You can," Rama says, and I startle. I spoke aloud without meaning to. She continues.

"It's just all these changes happening: new home, new friends, new bed. But once you get used to everything, everything will turn out all right. You'll feel better about trying again. You'll see."

Rama makes lies sound like such pretty things. She smiles like she believes them.

A question, an ugly question, bubbles up my throat.

"Why do you bother with me?"

"What?"

"Why," I repeat, "do you care about this? Why are you here?"

Rama fidgets, like I knew she would. But she doesn't pull away. Her eyes lower to both our hands, and she says, "You're my new bunkmate, so I want us to be friends."

"Easier that way?"

"No." She frowns. "Well, yes. But. I don't want to be friends because of that."

"Then why?"

"Because I want to." Her blue eyes flick back up at me. "I don't really know why."

I say nothing else. There's nothing else to say, really.

"You can talk to me, you know?" Rama squeezes my hand. Her frown is a soft thing. "I know how stressful it is, to suddenly be living in a new place with so many strangers, away from your family. So whatever is on your mind. Anything. I'll listen."

Whatever is on my mind. Anything at all. My omen is on my mind. Lumi's death is on my mind. The crime of being who I am and the sin of being where I am not allowed to be is on my mind, weighing, drowning.

"You can call me Pea," Rama says. "Only friends call me Pea."

I don't know what to say, so I say nothing. All I know is that someone like me doesn't deserve something like friends.

I stay in my dorm for the rest of the day.

When night falls, I make my way to the mess hall. The space hushes when I enter. I talk to no one, stop for no one.

I don't see Naqi in the watching crowd, but I see Lumi's friend by the table of our school. She doesn't approach, though she's frowning. I see Rama at the end of the dinner line, and so I take up my tray and wait with her. She fidgets. She opens her mouth to speak, and then somewhere behind me, a boy cackles.

Roaz calls, "Look!" He mocks, "The Veil who's too good for training. And also too good for stars, apparently!"

Nobody laughs. It might be a sacrilegious thing, after all, to laugh at a Veil. Not that Roaz cares. He cackles at his own joke; I don't turn around to watch. Seeing his face contorted by derision would make my fist fly.

Beneath my robe, my omen stain tugs against my skin.

Rama next to me opens and closes her mouth like a fish out of water, but no words come out. She doesn't defend me. She ducks her head and turns back toward the line.

I don't eat in the hall that night. I eat behind it, alone, in the dark on a stone by the well. No one comes for me.

I go to none of the Decade-Race training. Not for days. I don't dare to.

Word of my rejection has spread throughout the temple, from the young to the old, and I am watched wherever I go, judged.

So I loiter alone in the gardens, by the koi springs, on the many bridges of the lotus ponds. The fat fish clump wherever I go, because they think I have food, except I have nothing. Clouds overhead roll on and on, and I hate them for it.

Training has already begun for the others. I hear from a distance the pitches of whistling from the training pit, the rhythm of silence that comes from the drop, and I hear the voices of other Suns like Brother Marat—priests that coach for the races—calling out instructions, overseeing the anchor flights.

I know I need to be training. I only have a month—less than a month. I'm letting Esp down, letting all we've worked for go to waste. Still, fear coils tight around my neck. Sometimes I have to tuck into a ball, head on my knees, because I cannot breathe.

That night, after eating by the well—I don't know why—I return to the cells.

The way is dark. My mask and veil don't help, so I tug them off and clip them to my sash. The trees above and around me are old, foreign things, and walking through them is like walking through the dense cabling and overbearing hulk of a cramped hangar.

Past the denseness is a wide-open hill, and over that hill, the cells in their trenches. I walk the length of those trenches and peer through the grate of each cell. Some drip and leak, with puddles in the corners. Others are nested with birds, or with small skittering things that hide when I come close.

My old cell is the same as when I left it. I tug on the grate. It's unlocked.

I don't jump inside. It'd be a stupid thing, to go back inside. I close the grate again and climb up the slant instead. I sit on the concrete hood and lean back on my hands.

I look up at the stars and find three, four, more letters in the shapes of hearts and fists and promises.

The grate rattles. I start. There's nothing for me to throw, so I glare. My shoulders pull tight. It's just Naqi. He's already got his hands raised.

"There you are," he says, and smiles.

"Khab," I say. My shoulders loosen. I haven't seen Naqi in days. I haven't seen much of anyone in days. "Did Marat send you?"

"What?" Naqi frowns. "No. Though some of the other Suns have asked him to talk to you, or to get you to come back. But all he said was"—Naqi clears his throat and adopts a wispy voice—"'The stars will fall where they will.'"

It is my turn to frown. I don't know what any of that means. "Why are you here, then?"

"Oh. I was looking for you."

I squint. "Why?"

"'Cause I couldn't find you anywhere?"

"That doesn't answer my question."

"Wow, you got me there. Okay, let me try again." And he puffs out his chest and beams. He says, "Because I'm your *friend*."

"Ugh." I look away.

He laughs. He clacks up and up the grate to sit beside me, and I don't know why, but I don't stop him. He settles next to me on the hood of the cell, and like this, side by side, we settle into silence. We gaze up at the stars and their invisible lines forming invisible words.

"You know," Naqi says, "you're nothing like how I thought Veils would be."

Something like indignation pops through me. Is he going to taunt me and mock me like Roaz did? Is he going to rub salt in my wound and say things like, *You've failed. You've failed everyone's expectations.*

Beneath my robes, my scab itches.

I hold myself still. I keep my tone light.

"What's that supposed to mean?"

"I mean," he says, "I thought Veils would be these, I don't know, soft, faraway things. People that you can't quite ever know. People that don't quite feel like we do.

"Instead, you're all punch and bite." He laughs, delighted. "Instead, you're all emotion. It kind of takes my breath away, sometimes."

I look at him, and he looks up at the night sky. I don't know what to say.

So I say, "Shows how dumb you are, I guess."

"Wow." But Naqi is laughing, like I knew he would. He doesn't bring it up again.

We don't talk, not for a while. I tuck my hands under my arms because it's cold at this hour, out in the trenches, on top of a cement cell and its metal grate. The stars wink cool above us.

Naqi says, then, "I have an idea of what'll help."

I look over at him.

"This block you're having, with the Choosing. We'll play pretend."

I frown, baffled, and am lost.

"What?"

"Play pretend."

"The void is that?"

"You know," he says. "Like make believe. I used to make believe all the time as a kid. Pretend I was in a movie or something. I wanted to be an actor when I was younger, before coming to the temple."

I stare at him, because he's not making any sense, and he shakes his head and doesn't bother to explain.

Instead he hops from the cell and back onto the ground and tells me to follow him.

We're at the training pit. The anchors are lined up on racks in a shed to the side of the pit, along with the whistle-slings and their meek stars. Naqi pulls out an anchor and sling, and I do the same.

He winds up his star as he explains.

"It's a game you play in your head, where anything can be whatever you want, and you don't have to see something or feel something for that something to be real."

"Sounds like a game you'd get thrown into the ward for."

"It's fun," he insists. "Here. I can start. I'll still be called Naqi, but I won't be an acolyte anymore."

He narrows his eyes. He holds out his hands at the star-studded sky and deepens his voice and says, "I'm a dashing pirate whistler, versed in the ways of cosmic storms."

He sounds ridiculous. "This is a baby's game."

"Baby?" Naqi's voice is throaty. "I see no baby here."

"I'm not playing this game."

"Game?" Naqi's star cracks into life and light, and he twists and slams it into the engine-lock of his anchor. "A life of piracy is no mere game!"

He hops onto his anchor and strikes a pose, and it is ridiculous, so ridiculous. An itch grows inside my chest. I want to laugh, I realize.

Instead I say, "I'm not doing this with you."

"What, don't think you can?"

My eyes narrow. "Khab."

"Better a khab than someone who can't even play."

I know what he's doing. He's smiling at me, and I think he's figured out by now that I take his smiling as a challenge.

With a scowl, I tighten my grip over my whistle-sling and swing it. I wind it around and around until the star, with a crack, bursts into white flame. With a twist of my back, I swing the pouch into the lock of my anchor, but the caging does not part. The star pings against the metal.

"Swing it harder," Naqi says. He pats his hip. "Shoulder and hip and back. No hesitation."

I scowl, but I try again. I spin the sling twice to build up momentum, and, with a harsh twist and a grunt, I slam the star against the lock. The metal cage bangs open, then shut. Stardust puffs. The star is inside.

Naqi laughs. "There you go. Now, who are you going to play?"

I nudge the anchor with my foot. "You're actually serious about this."

"Playing pretend is serious business. Hey. If I'm a pirate, maybe you should be an officer."

"What, you want to be caught?"

"Oh ho!" Naqi's smile is impish. "Bold of you to assume that you can catch me."

The cord of Naqi's star is soaking gold with ichor, and that line of gold twitches around his leg, then laces tight. Power floods into Naqi's skin the way it did that first time I saw him.

He lifts from the ground as easy as a sigh.

Like meeting an old friend, he said. But to me, that friend is all sharp edges and voices I don't know. That friend, if it were less meek, would steal my senses from me.

I step away from my anchor.

"Okay," Naqi says, because he sees me moving away. "You don't have to be an officer. You could be, I don't know, a vengeful siren out to get me, or a member of my pirate crew. A captain?"

"Khab," I say. "I don't want to play."

"Even if it'll help?"

"How the void will any of this help?"

"It will." Naqi hovers his anchor closer to me. "I mean. It helped with me. I don't see why it wouldn't with you."

I frown at him, because I don't understand. So Naqi explains.

"Making believe," he says, "slips you into a skin. Playing pretend turns you into someone else. When I first got to the temple, I was . . . pretty scared." He laughs, and it's something like embarrassed.

"All these new rules and lessons and Suns watching over us. But instead of staying in bed all day because I was scared, or staying cooped up in the vegetable gardens because I didn't want to talk to anyone, I decided to act like someone who wasn't scared, even though I felt scared. I decided to play pretend at being brave.

"I got out of bed and out into the sun. I said hellos, and how are yous, and listened. I told the star at my feet that I was scared of it, but that I was going to try anyway."

"Stop." I don't know why, but my heart is pounding. "Stop it. I'm not you. And I'm not scared," I lie.

"Aren't you?"

"No."

"Then what is it?"

"You wouldn't, you wouldn't understand."

"Then help me understand."

I shake my head. If Naqi understood all that I am and all that I have done—no, no. He can never know. I'm an Omen, and Omens are unholy, unclean. Omens were never meant to fly. Playing pretend won't change the fact that I'll never be good enough.

Oh.

I'm crying.

I startle, and swipe at my cheeks, at my eyes, but my tears roll and roll, and they blur my vision. They clump over my lashes. Naqi is here. He's stepped off his anchor and is touching my arm, my shoulder, but I can't find strength enough in me to push him away.

For a long while, he says nothing. He stays in my space and sits in my sorrow, and in the quiet of the cradle we've formed, I shudder and shudder. I don't even know why I am crying.

(I do. I do know. All my life I've already been playing pretend— an unmarked girl, innocent of crimes. Worthy. Unafraid.)

"You don't have to tell me," Naqi is saying. His voice is soft. "You don't have to tell me anything. But you can tell the star. It'll listen. And whatever secrets you tell a star are safe with it."

I look up at him. It's a question.

Naqi nods. "Safe. Not like a star has a mouth, right?"

He smiles again, and I realize in that moment that I no longer mind his smiling. I don't think I've minded for a long while now.

He holds out his hand, and I take it.

He leads me to my anchor, and I step onto it.

When ichor bleeds out into the cord, and that cord laces around my leg, I close my eyes. I don't know what it is I'm supposed to tell it. I don't know what it is the star wants to hear. All I know is that I am tired.

I'm tired of being afraid. I'm tired of running.

I wish I could go back to that place in the tent with Lumi, and I wish I could change things. I wish I weren't so scared, so angry, all the time. All the time. Lumi might still be alive, then.

"Open your eyes! Look, look!"

I open my eyes. I see. I'm off the ground. Ichor has passed through me, and I didn't feel its passing. I look at my hands. There's a glimmer and a sheen to my skin when I tilt it this way, that way, like the iridescence of stars.

How is this possible?

Naqi is laughing and hooting. He hops back onto his own anchor and joins me in the air.

"Come on," he says. "Let's fly. Let's fly!"

"I've never—with a star."

"Right. It's okay." Naqi reins in his giddiness. "We'll go slowly," he says. "Gently. Like rocking a baby to sleep."

"I've never done that before."

"It's okay." He laughs. "We'll just make believe that you have."

I want to call him khab again, but just like that, he's tugging higher. He glides his anchor over to the edge of the great pit and, with the darkness thick enough to be a material thing, he leaps. He falls. I forget to breathe.

I don't move, and I watch the pit and watch the pit. I listen for the thud of his body or the crack of his anchor against stone. Nothing happens. A thin whistle builds and thickens and vibrates loud and louder.

Naqi bursts out of the pit, laughing.

He drags a line of white-gold behind him as he tears through the air, as he soars up and up along the curve of some invisible dome. At its peak, he flips over and hangs, unmoving, before gravity catches up with him. He falls, hooting. He disappears back into the pit. He bursts out like he did the first time, laughing still.

Caught on some unseen current, Naqi soars round and round, from pit to sky and back again, twirling and twisting and free, so free.

"Fly with me!"

And I want to say: *I can't. I shouldn't. I have never flown for flying's sake. I've never flown because someone wanted to fly with me.*

(But Naqi was warm by my side, telling me that he make believed bravery. And that I can too.

So I do.)

I lean my weight toward the pit. The anchor is tugged along. I teeter by the edge of the blackness, and leap.

I fall. Wind howls past me, cold, loud. My hair billows. I don't know how deep the pit is, and I can't tell one darkness from the other, so I keep falling, and falling. I don't pull up. Above me, Naqi shouts.

I yank up. Gravity sinks into my flesh and my bones and vibrates against my teeth, my bared teeth. Ichor coats through me and scrawls over my veins. The heat is heady. For a breath and two and three, all I understand is a blooming of lights behind my eyes.

Then I fly.

Naqi is cheering. He shouts words as I hurtle vertically past him, but I don't comprehend them. The air is rippling too loud and wild against the speed and violence of my flight, and I'm going too fast then falling too quick to catch his blurring words. In the end, Naqi trades his words for the sounds of his anchor.

He catches my current, and together, we fly.

My line is white-gold like his. It makes paths over Naqi's line as we criss and cross. Our anchors hum and harmonize, and I never knew. I never knew anchors could make music.

Naqi is flying close enough now, matching my speed, for me to hear him when he shouts, "You're incredible!"

I don't reply. It's because I'm . . . laughing, I realize.

This time, when he asks to play pretend, I don't call him stupid.

We play pretend in the air. Naqi is an upstanding captain of some great mining cruiser, and I'm the pirate who's stolen his haul of stars. Naqi is a desperate fugitive dodging through the dangerous burn of wishing storms, and I'm the law enforcement, come to see justice done. We shoot at each other with invisible ichor. We tumble and free-fall whenever we are shot.

I forget that I'm an Omen, that he's an acolyte. I forget that I am supposed to hate myself. I forget to hate.

NINE

At five in the morning, when the older Suns ring their handbells out in the hall, I rise with the others. It's my first time since coming to the temple.

I wait for Rama.

She's a deep sleeper and a sluggish waker, so I reach up and nudge her shoulder, again and again, until she grumbles and rolls onto her side. She draws her blanket up over her head, but sits up and climbs down from her hammock.

"Don't look at me." She rubs her eyes through the blanket.

"What?"

"I'm gross."

I don't understand. There's nothing gross about waking up. So I tug her blanket off and away, and she covers her face and whines. An itch bubbles in my chest again, that foreign feeling from before—a laugh.

I wait in silence instead, arms crossed, as Rama wipes her face. She looks at herself in a mirror she keeps tucked beneath her pillow, then, when she is content, she leads us outside.

The hall reminds me of the packed markets, but there's no shouting, and nothing smells of dung. Acolytes in gray and guardians in black fold out of their rooms, one after another, like a muted dance. The music is the rustling of their clothes.

Everyone congregates on the sprawling balconies of the upper floors. Morning mist swaddles us thick and blankets the canopy in white. In the distance, the temple pierces through the thick like some mountain.

Around us, the Suns in red and yellow light sticks of incense. They weave between us with the incense until the scent sinks into our clothes, our skin. It sticks to my hair, because I still have mine.

Then the temple bells toll, and it's like a field of flowers closing, because everyone kneels row by row. They kiss their foreheads to the floor. They chant on the same pitch, the same rhythm, the same words. It's a prayer I don't know the words to.

To the side, I see Naqi, bent like the others. His eyes are closed, and his mouth is not moving. The khab is asleep.

An older Sun clears his throat at me, so I kneel. I press my forehead against the floor. I close my eyes, but do not pray.

Naqi sleeps on even after the morning prayers are over.

He rolls to his feet, eyes closed and swollen with sleep, and auto-paths away from the dorms and down the stairs and out to the mess hall. I don't know how he doesn't fall or knock into things. It doesn't register to him that I'm there, or that anyone is. I scowl.

Rama by my side explains, "He's been doing that for years."

"Someone should knock him awake."

"People have, and it's never worth it. Naqi doesn't know his own strength when he's scared awake."

I snort. Rama watches me and fidgets.

"Hey, Lumi?"

I look over.

"About what's been happening, with everything, and at the mess hall. With that boy. Are we—okay?"

I frown. "What do you mean?"

Rama doesn't elaborate. She casts her eyes down and is silent, silent in something like shame. I know she's talking about my days as a recluse, and about how Roaz mocked me, though I don't know why that has anything to do with Rama.

But to break the strain of the silence, I say, "Hey."

I say, "Can I still call you Pea?"

Rama—Pea—looks back up and brightens. Her smile swells her cheeks. "Of—of course!"

"All right."

"I'm really glad, Lumi, that things are okay."

I nod.

"Are you hungry?"

My stomach grumbles, and I scowl. "Very."

Pea laughs. She tells me I catch all sorts of angry wrinkles when I scowl, like a pug, and I scowl some more just to make her laugh again. So this is what having a friend is like.

In the mess hall, Pea helps set the tables, while I'm brought to the kitchen in the back to wash up in the sink. Naqi's already auto-pathed himself there. We're ten minutes into washing fruits before he finally wakes. He blinks at me and says, "Oh."

I stare. "Khab."

He smiles, sheepish, then yawns. "Sorry. I didn't bump into you or anything, did I?"

"Would've bumped you a new nose if you did."

114

He laughs. He leaves the fruits in the water and raises his hands. "So I'm not a morning person." He waggles his brows. "And don't tell me you aren't impressed."

"What?"

"Takes skill," he says, looking puffed with pride, "to walk around perfectly without my eyes."

I flick water at him. He wrinkles his nose and laughs.

I agree to go with Naqi to the archives, for starsong lessons.

We're inside the Temple of Celestial Ichor, making our way up and up one of its many winding staircases. Here the quiet is an echo that bounces against the vastness. I speak softer because of it, like I am in some dream I don't want to wake from.

"You're lucky, you know." Naqi looks over his shoulder. "If you were a regular acolyte, skipping out on things would get you some form of punishment."

"Like what?"

"Depends. There are these things called the katohs, where you kneel and kiss your head to the floor, and they make you do like, a hundred, easy. Or there's this thing where they make you kneel while holding a bucket of water over your head, right outside the mess hall."

I scoff. "Those aren't punishments at all."

"They are when you live in the temple, with the same people day in and day out. Shame like that gets spread around."

I am reminded of the eyes I felt throughout these days, and of that night in the mess hall, in that silence, when Roaz sneered. My cheeks burn with the memory, but I shrug and say, "Not like I'm going to be here forever."

"I . . ." Naqi pauses. He looks at me with a strange quiet, and a smile that lags. "Yeah. I guess that's true."

I don't understand what's happened, so I push the conversation along. "Will you?"

"Will I what?"

"Stay here, in the temple."

"Like, forever?"

I nod.

"Stars. Forever is an awfully long time. I haven't thought about it much, to be honest. Plus I've got two more years left to my dedication anyway."

Acolytes dedicated to the temple must give to it eight years of their life. After that, they may either continue on to become Suns or return to the world they came from.

"But now that we're friends," Naqi continues, "I don't think I could bear to be parted from you. So the obvious choice here is to find you when my time is served."

I narrow my eyes. He smiles, and it's the right smile again. He raises his hands in surrender. "Don't shoot!"

"One of these days, I will."

"And when that day comes"—he looks so, so amused—"the stars will have fallen where they will."

"Whatever that means."

"If you went to classes, you'd know."

"Don't need classes to know your head is full of static."

Naqi laughs. "Static or not, you'd really like starsong lessons, I think."

I stare at him, unconvinced, and he says, "You will. Trust me."

"As if," I say.

"That's okay." He smiles over his shoulder. "We'll just make believe that you do."

Sister Ena has the appearance of strictness—squared shoulders carrying the lofty tilt of her head, pinched lips, tall nose. The angle of her brow is harsh and haughty above the prominent lids of her old eyes.

She's in charge of the archives, and she pinches her lips at me when I arrive, because I skipped her classes, and that's such a wasteful thing to do, she says. These lessons are a privilege, she says.

The archives are, like the rest of the temple, vast without compare. Yet somehow, the space feels like a secret space, tucked with shelves and made intimate with scrolls and books and parchments whispering against one another.

Here, everything is made of wood, dark and rich, and afternoon warmth from the skylights floods and soaks the aged burnish.

Sister Ena begins my lesson by explaining to me that I am very behind, and that I will have to work twice as hard to catch up with the others. And like with Naqi's smiles, I take that as a challenge.

We start by reviewing the basics.

Starsongs are like spells. The ichor line manifests whatever is flown.

There are nineteen consonants and six vowels, and the line of a starsong is divided into three sections or forms—beginning, middle, and end.

The first letter of a word always uses the ending form, while the last letter always uses the beginning form, because words are flown backward. Bird becomes drib and stone becomes enots.

Beginning forms look like blots and smears and sparks. The middle are loops and glides. Ending forms are large and graceful and full of curls.

There's an inkstone on the table carved in the shape of a turtle, and she plucks off its shell to pour water into the grooves of its body. She passes me an inkstone and teaches me to rub out ink in the water.

She hands me a calligraphy brush so that I can draw the lines of those forms.

A beginning *R* is a single dot. That same *R* as a middle form is two loops with a gap between the loops. An ending *R* is a swirl with a bottom loop that curls back up with a smear.

"Easy," I tell her, because I already know all this.

And she says, "Oh, very good, see how much more you could've been learning if you had come? How lovely it is, to be learning new things."

Sister Ena is talkative when she forgets to be strict.

Starsongs, she says, *are the language of the Nine Ahs, of stars themselves, and so are written from top to bottom, vertically, like stars falling to the earth.*

By connecting the letters, our line creates meaning.

A dot, circle, dot is *V*. Two simple loops is *A*. A pointed swirl with a dot in the center would be *N*.

Strung together, the line creates *nav*—light, brightness, to shine.

The line that says *rahka* means fire. *Mha* means water. *Mehsa* means to help. *Tuv* means to bury.

I look down and down the table. The top of Naqi's head peeks out from a wall of rolled-up bamboo books. Between a gap in those rolls, I can see his brush sweep back and forth and all over the page in broad, sure strokes.

I ask Sister Ena, "When can I start doing what he's doing?"

"Ah, so eager. It's admirable, dear. But only when I am sure you can read all the lines right proper, darling. He's doing translations, is what he's doing."

I wrinkle my nose. Sister Ena uses lots of names when she's talkative, names I have never once been called. I say instead, "I can read. This is *kuh*, this is *duh*, this is *ee*, and this is *oo*."

Sister Ena trills, and claps, and squeezes my shoulder. "I'm so proud," she says, and I don't know what to do with that, with her pride, so I duck my head and scowl at the page. I copy the lines again and again, until my awkward lines are smooth and sure. I copy again and again until the brush in my hand no longer feels like a foreign thing.

"How was your lesson?"

"Fine, I guess."

"Yeah? How'd you like Sister Ena?"

I think on it. "She talks a lot."

Naqi laughs. "Yeah. She gets a bit lonely in the archives all day, I think."

"And she calls me names all the time."

"Names? What do you mean?"

"Like"—I wrinkle my nose—"I don't want to repeat them."

"Oh. Oh, you mean like: darling, dear, sweets?"

"Yeah."

"You don't like them?"

I look at Naqi. "Do you?"

"I mean, I guess it can get annoying sometimes. But the way she talks reminds me of mothers, you know?"

I don't know. I don't know mothers. I only know the smell of bleach and stale bubble gum and cigarette smoke. I only know the weight of eyes that drown, and scars. When Sister Ena squeezes my shoulder, it does not hurt. How is she supposed to be like a mother if it does not hurt?

TEN

The week comes to a close. I still haven't chosen a star.

My scab has been a sleepy thing, drained, though thinking about the Choosing jolts it and sends it quivering over my shoulder blade.

When it's like this, I remember that night at the pit.

I recall lifting off the ground and into the air and feeling no pain. I recall cutting through and through the air with Naqi, with his laugh whistling by me, and just like that, my omen stain settles into something like sleep.

I spend most of my days in the archives now, mostly alone, with my turtle inkstone and brush and sheaves and sheaves of calligraphy paper. Sister Ena coos at my company and offers me butter cookies that I turn down, because I don't want crumbs on my pages.

I memorize the shapes of the lines and their sounds, and their meanings. I memorize them even though there's no racing in the second stage if I can't pass the first.

There's *albash*, ugly. *Nabal*, foolish. *Kahah*, weak. Sister Ena sees the list of words I am compiling and shakes her head, and insists that I cease learning only mean words, sad words.

I pause, because I didn't even realize I was doing it.

So I learn the words for beautiful, kind, strong. I learn *yir*, bird. *Hra*, flower.

If I am to win the second stage, I will need to write a line that impresses and exhilarates. The line for fireworks, maybe. The line for capsule-coin. Can a whistling star write that? What would the word for capsules be? Or would it need to be the word for wealth?

I wonder if there is a word for Omens.

I've been wondering that for a while. The thought, like a weed, roots into me. I ask Sister Ena, and she tells me that there is no such word, not in the starsong language.

"Why do you ask?" she says.

And I think about it, and say, "If starsongs are like spells, couldn't we write the stain away?"

Sister Ena coos. "If only it worked that way," she says. There are songs of healing, yes, but stains are not broken bones. Stains are not punctured flesh. Omens bubble forth from deep within, from the Ahs written in our souls, and so washing away one's stain would require seeing which Ah it has corrupted.

"Even then"—she flaps a hand—"there is no word for Omen, so all this talk is moot."

Moot, she says. Still, the thought of it clings to me, stains into me, like cigarette smoke in hair.

When Sister Ena is busy with something or someone else, I look in secret through bamboo scroll after scroll; I don't want to deal with her questioning my search.

I find the words for disease, for sickness, for dirtiness, for scar.

I find the words for sin, for crime, for wrongdoing, for murder. The lines for these words are ugly things, crooked and full of breaks, like I'm looking at a reflection.

I think about what it is to be an Omen.

I think about making up my own word.

Ten people could commit the same crime, yet only one will be marked, stained, exposed. So I dig for that line—exposed. I find it.

Exposed, *arah*—a smear-circle-smear, four loops, a gap, a perfect swirl.

Sin, *avah*—a smear-circle-smear, four loops, inner loops, another perfect swirl.

Perhaps this is what the word for Omen is, someone whose sin is exposed.

The more time I spend in the archives, and the more words and lines I memorize, the more I wonder with something like awe at Naqi, at the breadth of the claims made about him.

Was he really able to memorize everything?

"Well, certainly not *everything*," Sister Ena titters. "But the boy gives it a good go, bless his heart."

"How much does he know, then?"

"Well, quite a bit. He's drawn lines that I've never even seen."

I don't know what to say to that, or what to think. Who could've thought a khab could know so much?

The next day, Brother Marat tells all the racers, "We're going to take our anchors and stars outside the temple. Practice by the pools. And then perhaps"—he smiles his kindly smile—"some free time to explore the markets, yes?"

Everyone is rosy cheeked and brimming. I shift on my feet because it's been too long since I've felt and smelled the city, but I don't know if I am included in this field trip. I still have no star, after all.

Maybe Brother Marat reads my mind, because he pulls me aside. He settles his old hand on the top of my head, and I tense; I don't know what to do with his gentleness.

"Naqi's told me of how you flew at the pit."

I frown, though he can't see through my mask.

"He says you're an excellent whistler. Better than even him."

I don't know what to say. "So what does that mean?"

"It means, young Lumi, that I want you to join us by the pool. Take a meeker star. You may still practice, after all, though you've yet to gain an official star."

I look over at Naqi, and he senses me looking, maybe, because he looks back.

He smiles the way he always does.

The bathing pools of marble and stone sprawl by the edge of the districts between the slums and the gambling houses. The water is full of flowers.

Patches of sunbaked rugs are laid out over the tiled courtyard, for food and for wares, and for people to dry on and lounge on. Here and there on the pool steps, or by the shade of an awning or tree, are beggars and children looking blown and wild like weeds. They flock to us when they see us, because the Suns that came with our group are carrying baskets of food.

There's sticky rice wrapped in bamboo leaves, the ones tied

up with string, and steamed buns, and the little rectangular milk boxes that never seem to expire or go bad. The beggars and the children crowd close and paw and paw.

I would be begging like them, if I hadn't met Esp. My face would be dirt crusted and sun peeled, my skin pulled taut over bones. They are what my reality will look like after the race, if I don't win it.

Esp has no use for people who have failed her.

Brother Marat is gathering the racers close, and we stand with our anchors by our sides and listen as the old man begins to teach.

"This past week, starsong words have been flown and practiced at the pit, and admirable progress has been made. So today, at these pools, we shall weave the words we've learned into complete sentences.

"Starsongs," he reiterates, "are spells. And when the words of these spells are strung together, strung properly, reality is woven. Draw the line for *tummˈmha*, for example, and watch as rain is brought into existence."

Tumm, fall. *Mha*, water.

Someone raises their hand. "But where would the water come from?"

"The same place all wishes come from."

"From the star?"

Brother Marat nods.

Roaz says, "Thought whistling stars couldn't grant wishes."

"And you would be right, young Roaz. What we are doing here instead is making a statement. A proclamation."

"Sounds like the same thing to me."

"Perhaps," Brother Marat concedes. "But with a starsong, one is limited by their line and their ability to fly. While with a wishing star, one is limited only by one's imagination and desire. Now." The old man claps. "Shall we begin?"

The racers are eager to start. The crowds that have gathered around us are the same.

Roaz, being Roaz, mounts his anchor before all the others. He laces up to his star, light billowing through him, and is the first one out onto the water. A pang strikes my omen stain. I'm jealous, I realize. Roaz—though he's a brute of a boy—looks sure and strong and free on the water. Already, he is carving out sounds.

A circle and three dots, then six loops, four with extra dots, and a looped swirl with a smear in the center—*rahka*, fire. The ichor line remains in the air, ever gold-white.

It's a difficult flight pattern, but Roaz has done it. The broadness of his frame and the strength of his legs can manage all the extra loops and blots. His smile is broad and smug, even though he hasn't completed his sentence yet.

He puffs out three stardust rings, followed by a blot. He transitions into simple twin loops, then, at the tail of the curve, releases a spark of ichor—a crack of starfire like sparklers.

I don't know what word he's trying to fly, but I can see that the crack has jarred his bones and rattled his teeth, and he winces. He forgets his next sound, and loses his shape, then he loses his footing on his anchor. He falls.

So this is why Brother Marat chose the pools.

Roaz slams into the water. The spray of the splash is high and wide, and the crowds are gasping and cheering, some confused, others delighted. Roaz's anchor bobs to the surface, and then Roaz himself breaks through, gulping in air. He's scowling, but fine.

So it begins.

Other whistlers begin to fly. The pools are vast, able to fit five or six starsongs above them comfortably so that no one's line writes into another's. Someone is whistling the sentence *yir'agnia*, birdsong, and birdsong fills the air. Someone else whistles *hra'rahira*, the aroma of flowers, and floral scents waft.

I notice, for the first time, that when people are joined with a star, when they fly, something like zero gravity settles over them. Their hair floats. Their anchor sometimes bobs against the soles of their feet, or seals tight against them like metal to magnets.

A golden line soars high, higher than all others. It's Naqi. His line is long and unbroken, elegant and practiced. While the others stay tucked close to the water, he ascends without fear. His loops are bold. His glides are like flashes of light in your eye, quick and blinding and gone in a blink. My heart is pounding, pounding.

I want to fly like him.

The racers on the water are stopping to look, to gawk. Even Roaz is looking. Every eye in the gathered crowd is wide and watching. Every breath is bated.

Naqi has written words, complex words, ones I barely know. There's *nav*, light. There's *muumta*, full. And I think, maybe, I can read an *ain*-something, which might mean explode? Break?

The boy drifts down and away from his finished sentence, looks up at it, and then his line of light expands. The many, many glints of gold swell in color, in intensity, and then they *burst*.

It's a firework of stardust. It's a light show of stars. Awe rains down and down over us, coloring us gold, and when the dust settles over my skin, it itches, just like it did ten years ago.

I don't fly. My heart pounds to. My fingers itch to. But I don't fly. Brother Marat asks me if I would at least like to glide over the water, and I shake my head no.

Naqi is crowded by his friends. He is the center of all the chattering and laughing. People are turned toward him the way flowers turn toward light, and their eyes are bright. Their smiles are wide. Someone's arm is slung over his shoulders.

I've noticed that nobody dislikes him. Even Roaz doesn't dislike him, not really. He sees in him a good fight, I think.

Naqi's eyes flick over to me. I jolt, I don't know why, and twist away. Heat floods over my neck and cheeks, and my scab itches. I roll out my shoulder.

An hour or so passes. Brother Marat gathers us together again.

He passes each of us two silver capsules and five bronze capsules, each one about an inch in length, aluminum casings stained bronze or silver with the numbers one or ten embossed on their sides. Within their closed seams is stardust, different weights according to the numbers on the capsules.

One bronze capsule will be enough to get us a marble soda. Two bronze capsules, a bao. Three, a cup of goopy rice flour noodles. A silver capsule would be enough to get us a good hour inside an arcade, or a seat inside an air-conditioned restaurant.

I've never been given this much money before.

"The rest of the day is yours, young whistlers." Brother Marat's wrinkles fold over themselves with his smile. "Meet back here by six, yes?"

"Yes," the group resounds, and then they're off, scattering like birds taking wing.

"Lumi."

I look over. Naqi's got his anchor and star slung over his back, and I move to do the same. He's alone, strangely. Why isn't he with his friends?

"What?"

"You lived out here, right?"

I did, yes. All my life. But Lumi moved here only two or so years ago, to train in the school.

I nod. "For a bit."

Naqi's smile blooms. "Show me around?"

"What?"

"Us acolytes are cooped up in the temple most times," he explains. "Lived here six years, and still don't know what half the streets are called. Do you know where they sell coffin bread? Or ice cream burritos?"

I wrinkle my nose, though he can't see. "They sell those everywhere."

His smile beams. "Take me to the best ones?"

"The best ones take forever," I say, but I'm already thinking of the roads we'll take, and the district tiers I'll take him to. "If you complain, I'm not taking you."

"Complain? With you around?"

I call him khab. He smiles. I take him where he wants to go, and play pretend that I'm not excited, giddy even, to show him the city I know so well.

The lineup for the coffin bread takes twenty-six minutes, because the shop I take Naqi to is the best one on this tier. The lineup for the ice cream burrito takes forty-two minutes, because the shop is the best one in the city.

We eat the bread in the burrito line. The toast is large enough, thick enough, to fit an entire hamburger. Inside, underneath its sliced top—the top like the lid of a coffin—are shrimp and peas and onions, lathered in a mixture of milk sauce and creamy cheese. Naqi, cheeks puffed on bread he cannot swallow fast enough, will not stop humming.

The ice cream burrito is three scoops of taro ice cream on a bed of peanut brittle and a sprinkling of cilantro, all wrapped in a soft, thin crepe. Naqi takes his first bite, then moans, and I wrinkle my nose and shove him. He says nothing about it. He says nothing because his mouth is too busy being stuffed. Peanut shavings coat his lips. Ice cream dribbles down his chin.

"You animal," I call him. And he grins, all taro-smeared teeth, and howls.

I take him to the gambling district, to the pachinko parlors, just to see his face light up. He laughs and laughs at the cacophony of colors and of noise, his white teeth flashing like the lights, and covers his ears and shouts words I cannot hear, so I shout back that I can't hear him. My shout bounces against the inside of my mask. Naqi laughs again.

Afterward, at the junction of the tofu street and the silk vendors, we bump into other acolytes from the temple. Pea and Yashi are there too. Everyone must've been given leave to explore the city.

"Lumi!" Pea comes over to me and loops her arm around mine. Her smile is so very full and content. It strikes me again how beautiful she is. In the angles of her lines is the kind of elegance you'd take pictures of, the ones you blow up big and hang from the walls.

"I'm having so much fun," she declares. She doesn't fidget. "I saved up for nearly a year for this. Can you believe it?"

"You get allowance?" I look at Naqi as well.

They nod, and Pea says, "Just a bit, from the work we do at the tents and benches, weaving baskets and making pots and things. I was going to get some bubble tea, but there're so many, I don't know which store to choose."

"Lucky for you," Naqi says and grins, "we've got the best guide with us."

"Do we? Do you know the city well, Lumi?"

"I guess."

Pea laughs and cheers. Yashi, behind her, smiles and raises a hand and flutters it through letter after letter. The signing is far faster than I can comprehend, but I think I catch the word *yaki*. Then she pinches her fingers together and points them against her mouth. I can't read that one; I've only been taught letters so far.

"Ah." Naqi is translating. "Yashi wants to try—dorayaki?"

"What's that?" Pea frowns.

"Pancake burgers," I explain, "with red bean paste filling."

Pea giggles and shakes her head. "That sounds gross."

"It's good. Sweet." I stole some once, when I was eight or so. "You'd like them."

A crowd of children—scrappy-looking things with mismatched clothes—bump past Yashi in their hurry to get by, and I know exactly what has happened. I've pulled this same trick many, many times myself.

I reach out to stop the first child, but then Yashi's hand flashes out. She grips the child's wrist—a boy, only six or so. It's no trouble at all for her to drag him close.

She signs an open palm from him back to her, and I don't need to be taught to understand what she is saying: *Return what you stole from me.*

The boy screws up his face because he doesn't understand. He begins to struggle.

"Let me go," he cries. "I didn't do anything wrong," he lies.

On the back of his neck, unobscured by his sleeveless shirt, is the bold black of an omen stain.

Pea sucks in a breath and jerks away. She tugs me back with her by my arm and fists her hands into my sleeve.

Yashi hears the gasp and understands the mood, and so she hauls the boy away from us, further down the street and into the shade. There, she holds her hand out at the boy again and waits, stare stern, until the boy hangs his head and relents. He digs about his pockets.

I feel eyes on me.

I jerk a look over my shoulder at the bustle of the crowd, at the slanted shadows, but see no one looking back.

That's right. That boy is an Omen. Maybe he belongs to Esp.

Pea clings tighter to me and pulls my attention back to her.

"Stars," she breathes. "An Omen, and now he's—she's—I can't believe Yashi is touching him."

Naqi turns to us. He hasn't reacted, not like Pea—wide-eyed Pea looking like some frightened animal—who continues to babble. "They're unclean, and . . . and Yashi is just touching one. It makes me think the rumors are true."

Naqi's eyes narrow. Something in me draws tense—I've never seen Naqi verge on something like anger before.

Pea doesn't notice, maybe. She turns to me and continues, urging and urgent, "They say Yashi used to have a stain on her tongue, and that's why she cut it off. Went to black market doctors for it and everything."

"Rama."

Pea flinches. Naqi's voice cuts crisp, curt. "Don't talk about things you don't know."

"Yeah, well." She fidgets. "I don't see why you're always defending her."

"I wouldn't have to," Naqi replies, "if people stopped attacking her."

"I'm not attacking her. I wouldn't do that. I'm just saying—"

"Bubble tea, right?" Naqi smiles, but it's faded, polite. It occurs to me I can tell the different kinds of smiles he wears, now.

"We should go and get some before we need to head back. It's already almost five."

Pea fidgets again, but nods. She doesn't argue.

Evening draws near. We return to the pools.

Pea is a happy, fluttering thing, chirping at all the things she's seen and tasted, and the pretty things she's bought. She found for herself a new lip stain, even though she can't wear it inside the temple. She found a new string of colored beads and fake gems that she can hang above her hammock.

Naqi's smiles are normal again. He makes easy conversation with Pea, despite what happened before. Maybe forgiveness is something that comes easy to him, or forgetfulness.

The boy didn't buy much for himself, just the food in his belly, and some seeds he thinks the birds might like. I've never had money like this to spend before, and guilt pinches my stain each time I spend it. So I don't buy much either. I look at things. That's all I do. I can still hear the remainder of my capsules clinking and clinking against each other in my pocket as I walk.

We're some of the first few to arrive at the pools. Brother Marat is nowhere to be seen. Roaz is with some of his friends by the edge of the pools. The courtyard is empty. The air is still sweet. Sunset red highlights every ripple of the water and tinges every surface with a blush, a lethargic rose-gold smog. Pea takes off her sandals and dips her feet into the water. She kicks at flowers that drift too close.

Naqi unslings his anchor and whistle-sling, and for the first time, I'm able to look at his Togarath star up close. It looks much the same as any other whistling star, form like a misshapen pearl, but larger than most others, the size of two fists.

If Naqi wins the race this decade, it will no longer be called Togarath's star. It will be called Naqi's star.

"Our holy Veil!" Roaz booms. Already he is making his way over. "Lucky us. We were just talking about you."

Pea shrinks. Naqi rolls his eyes. I tilt up my chin, though it's obscured by my mask, and stand firm as the boy swaggers up to me. Oh, how I wish Lumi could swear.

Roaz smirks, all teeth, and says, "You see, we've got a bit of a bet going on. Taigo there thinks you're just pretending you can't get a star, can't fly, so on and so forth. But I know better." He touches his chest. "A pure Veil like you wouldn't ever *lie*, so it's only right to assume you really can't do anything at all."

He cackles. My stain bubbles. I want to bodycheck him into the pool. If I let my stain take over a little, I would have strength enough to.

I sense Naqi tensing beside me, so I say instead, "How much did you bet?"

Roaz looks at me. "Huh?"

"I said: How much did you bet?"

Roaz snorts. "Nothing, obviously. Didn't know Veils were allowed to be dumb."

If I weren't here, if Lumi were still alive, she would be the one speaking to Roaz right now. She would be the one Roaz called all these things, the one he mocked. I don't know why, I don't quite understand it—but heat simmers against my rib cage. I'm indignant. I'm offended.

"Let's make a bet then," I say. "If I can fly a better line than you, you need to katoh to me ten times."

"Ka-what?"

"Katoh," Naqi cuts in. He shifts on his feet. The air about him is *giddy* now. "You'll have to bow to her in front of everyone."

"Bow!" Roaz barks a laugh. "Good to know you really do get a trip outta being worshipped."

"If *you* can fly better," I continue, "then I'll have to bow to you."

"Ten times?"

"Ten times."

"Make that twenty." Roaz's smile cuts. "Then you have yourself a deal."

"Fine." I don't care. If I have to look at him any more than this, my stain will scab over my shoulder, maybe even up my neck. I turn away. I unsling my anchor and whistle-sling and begin whirling my star.

Pea's gotten to her feet and is making herself small behind Naqi. Her eyes are wide, fearful, and she's frowning. Naqi's gaze holds steady on me, and when I look back at him, I'm struck with the sudden meaning of that gaze: he thinks I can do this.

"Gonna beat me with a common star?"

With the knowledge of Naqi's hope in me like wind in sails, I say, "Yes."

Roaz barks again. His friends have wandered over by now, and they cage us in, nudging one another, speaking to one another and laughing, but I don't hear any of it. My star cracks awake, and I slam it into my engine-lock.

I mount my anchor. I lace up.

Ichor pours into me and brims into my every line, and I swell with the victory of it, that I can do this without pain now.

Roaz follows suit. The color of his star when swung awake is a gold richer than mine, and when he laces up, he shudders at the power that courses through him. He lifts into the air with me, and together, we hover out over the water.

I'm securing my veil to my sash when someone parts the people on the shore—Brother Marat. The others will likely be returning soon as well.

Naqi is speaking to him, explaining the situation, and Brother Marat looks as kindly as usual. He nods at Naqi, and then at us.

Naqi turns to us out on the water and calls out, "Brother Marat will be the judge."

"Fine by me," Roaz replies. He rolls out his shoulders, then rolls his head at me. "You going to insist on going first like the Veil you are?"

"Why wait." I don't bother turning to him. "We'll go at the same time."

I can hear the sickle curve of his smile as he says, "You scared?"

I don't bother answering him. I shift forward and begin to glide.

The water beneath my anchor ripples as I pass, and I stay parallel to its surface for a while, in a long line. Then, with a harsh tug, I cut directly up. I pop out three blots of ichor and a stardust ring: *A*. I follow with six quick loops, one with two inner loops, one with two dots, one with a gap. A generous swirl, a ring and three dots. Eight loops. A looped swirl with a dot.

Naqi is laughing. I can hear it even up here, the brightness of it, because he can tell now. He can tell that I'm writing his line.

I'm flying what he flew this afternoon.

I still don't know all the words and the meanings of what he wrote, but I remember the exact blots and swirls and sequences. I don't need to see it more than once. The light of his line is like a brand behind my eyes, and when I close my lids, I can still see it burning clearly, brightly.

And the more I draw, the more I realize, with an expanding awe, how gifted Naqi is. Already, my knees are straining. My head spins and spins the further I glide from the water. Yet he was able to fly this complex shape so quickly, with careless joy, with fearless abandon. Like a bird that soars, the sky is his playground. Gravity is his friend.

Out of the corner of my eye, I see Roaz tearing by.

The sound of his line is a roar. He's writing *rahka* again, fire, but this time he's connecting that fire to a shape—*shakhal*, lion.

I don't know what he's planning, but I can tell he's deliberately writing his lines over mine, peaking the swirl of his *S* to cut through my words, disrupting their meaning.

Two can play at that game.

I abandon Naqi's line and pull into a large loop, up and over, to arrive behind Roaz's line. I corkscrew and swoop and cut right through his ichor drag so that his lion is severed.

Then I connect my line to *taqa*—a great sound, a blast. I'm going to write into existence the roar of a lion, a roar like thunder enough to fill the skies. So I soar high and higher so that Roaz cannot reach me. I fly the three dots and one ring, the simple loops, the loops with a curl, the sweeping pointed swirl, and I have only the puffed ring left to finish, then my line will be complete. I will have finished my first starsong.

Roaz enters my vision. He's caught up to me. He's overtaking me. I don't understand.

I tug against the cord around my leg, for more ichor, for more power, but I can tell—already I'm straining against the limits of this star. Its body quakes in its lock and squeals like a kettle on a stove, because it has nothing more to give, because it was never meant for starsinging.

Naqi said I'm a better flier than even him, but none of that will matter if my star is weak. I'll never be able to win the race like this.

When I look at Roaz, I see that his star—the star of Nim—continues to pulse ichor after ichor of power into him, thrusting him along, hurtling him faster and further from me.

He looks so free.

Envy sinks into me; it pinpricks over my stain.

Roaz cuts directly in front of my path; he's playing dirty. He blasts out a cloud of ichor, and the blow of the burst rattles through me, buffets me like wind. My stance wobbles. I lose my balance. I topple off my anchor.

I careen. My cord is still connected to my leg, but the wind is too loud, and the world is a blur, and I can't think. The air is going by too fast for me to gulp it in, for me to breathe, and then I slam into the water. I go under.

My mask and veil are in the way. I'm going to drown.

I thrash to the surface.

I claw my mask and veil away from my face and gasp for breath, but I do not tear them off. Even in the frenzy of staying afloat, I remember that Roaz and his friends are from outside the temple. A Veil can never expose herself to the vow-less.

But then Roaz is hovering by me and above me, and he is smirking, and something inside me uncorks, something like fire, like red. I don't care about being a Veil anymore, not now, not with him looking down on me.

My anchor has bobbed to the surface, and I grab onto it. I dip back underneath the water and kick my feet up, to realign them to the glider. The cord tightens against my leg again, and the star stutters back to light. I flip upright and float off the water.

"Was hoping the fall would rip your veil clean off." Roaz leans toward me and into my space. "Guess I'll have to make do with those katohs instead."

"You cheated," I spit.

"A loser *would* say that."

"You knocked me off my anchor."

"You fell. I didn't do anything."

"Liar." My scab is thickening beneath my robe, down my back, down to my elbow. Pain jolts through me from the cord. My connection to the star is beginning to burn. Still I stay where I am. I hold my head high.

Roaz bares his teeth in a smile. "Not my fault if you flew too close to me. Also not my fault if you couldn't get out of the way fast enough. And now you're going to throw a tantrum because you're not as good as me? Siren's teeth.

"You sure," he jeers, "you're even a Veil?"

I snarl.

I slam my fist into his nose.

People are clamoring. Everyone has long since returned, and the shore where they are is all commotion. Roaz rears back, stunned, and then his eyes flash. His teeth are like fangs. He swings for me. I jerk out of the way, fly high with my anchor.

"You're a liar," I fling. *And I'm going to expose you for one.*

With blood streaming out his nostrils and staining his teeth, Roaz comes after me. He shouts things at me, names, hateful things, things I don't hear because I'm writing another line. I'm spinning and twirling my way around him, twisting out of the way when he comes too close.

Arah, I write. Expose.

Avah, I write. Sin.

I'm going to expose his lie. I'm going to make him pay for making me feel small.

The line is complete. I finish the final swirl and bob down from the line, but I shouldn't have stopped. Roaz is right behind. The full weight of him crashes into me.

It's a violence of sounds. Metal cracks and snaps. Our bodies plow not against water but against the stones of the courtyard, and we roll. We tumble. Nails flash and teeth gleam.

Roaz reaches for my hair through my veil, and I slam my knee up into his stomach. He doubles over. I kick him off me, away from me, and scrabble onto my hands and feet to kick him again, but then people are holding me back by my arms, yanking me away.

Roaz's friends crowd around him to help him up, and Brother Marat is here. Same with Pea. Same with Naqi.

The old Sun's expression is stony, but he is not looking at me or at Roaz. He is furrowing his brows at something over the water—the line that I last drew.

Pea is by my shoulder, and Naqi is gripping my arm and frowning and hushing, "Lumi. Lu. What happened?"

One of the boys cries out.

He stumbles away from Roaz: Roaz, still on the ground; Roaz, who is staring at his hand and trembling, trembling.

There's an omen stain on his hand.

Blackness leaks out of the seat of his palm and bubbles over like tar. It slicks its way over the heel of his hand, down his wrist. A stain blooms over his temple. He winces at it, whimpers at it. It's hurting him.

"Roaz! He's . . . he's stained!"

Everyone is watching him. His friends have all pulled back. Brother Marat stands where he is, ever silent, ever stoic, and then he turns to me.

He says, softly, "What have you done?"

Pain splits through me. Brother Marat turns back to Roaz, and I double over onto my knees. It feels like my bones are trying to sprout their way out of the soil of my flesh and skin. Naqi is there, holding me close. Pea is there, fretting and frantic.

My omen stain begins to tear through my robes.

No. No, *no*.

Brother Marat is helping Roaz to his feet, and all eyes are on them, pinned on them, except for Pea's.

Except for Naqi's.

They see it. They see *me*. There's no denying what they see. My omen scab juts from my left shoulder and through the fabric, craggy like the face of a cliff, and Pea tenses. She tenses the way people do, right before a scream.

I wrench away from them. I cover my shoulder.

It hurts. My head pounds, and it hurts. My heart thunders, and it hurts. I can't stay here. I can't bear it, the weight of what I've done, the weight of who I am exposed.

I can't bear to see Pea and Naqi's faces.

So I don't. I turn away.

I run.

ELEVEN

I am running, still running, my feet thud-thud-thudding.

To my right, the metal teeth of the city screech by me and by me, all railings and walkways and signs and smoke. To my left, the ocean sector sweeps. The vastness of its water is something like loneliness.

I keep running.

I slip and stumble, and to catch myself I slam into a streetlamp. It's the only thing holding me up. I tear off my veil and mask. My omen stain still protrudes like stone from my shoulder, and my gasps are metallic things, blood-iron on the tongue. I do not know if it is possible for lungs to bleed from running too hard, for too long. It doesn't matter.

It hurts.

It does not matter.

The sun has set. The sky above is a somber blue, and the stars are shading in. Waning light clings to the horizon, and here, there, the streetlights are blinking on.

I don't know what to do. I don't even know what's happened.

I drew a starsong, *arah'avah*, around Roaz. I drew the omen stain onto his skin. I didn't even think that was possible.

My own stain bubbled out of control because of my emotions, or maybe because of the starsong I drew. Pea saw my stain. Naqi saw my stain.

I didn't look at their faces. I didn't dare.

I'm trembling.

What do I do now? Where do I go? Who can I turn to?

Esp will want nothing to do with me. I've failed her. I'm no use anymore, no good, no good at all. The temple—maybe they'll send people after me. Not only am I an Omen, one that entered a holy space, but I've *caused* an omen. They'll look for me, and take me, and like those other Omens who entered the House of Stars during the Joining, I'll be executed.

Footsteps, running footsteps, thud loud and louder behind me. My heart drops. Panic opens up in me, swallows me whole, and my stain bristles. They're here. I have to run. I have to hide. I don't want to die.

I push from the lamppost and turn to see, to see who has come for me.

Wheezing, groaning, hands on his knees, is Naqi.

He's the one who's come for me. Alone, in the dark, in the jagged bowels of the city. I don't understand.

"Lumi," he pants.

I say nothing. Is he going to attack me? Does he have a whistle-sling on him? No. He has nothing on him, no anchor and no star. I don't know how he's managed to keep up with me all this time, all this time of me trying to lose myself.

I move away from him.

"Lumi. Please. Stop."

I turn and step down the street. I keep going.

"Lu." And this time, Naqi comes close enough to take hold of my hand. He tugs.

I wrench against him. He tightens his grip. I throw a blind punch, and he jerks back far enough that he is not stunned, though my knuckles clip him over his lip and chin. He grapples my arms even as I punch and punch, and when my blows don't connect, I kick. I rail. My heartbeat roars in my ears. I'm shouting, I realize.

"Khab," I spit. "Let go. Let me go. Zap off. Zap off!"

Naqi winds his arms around me instead, to keep me from thrashing. He traps my arms in his hold. Somehow, from his body to mine, I can feel the rhythm of his heart, a rhythm like desperation.

I don't understand what he's trying to do. I don't understand what he wants. I could use my omen stain to push him off, to run away, far far away, but he's holding me still and anchoring me down, and within the weight of his embrace, my violence is sapped from me.

I am spent. My omen stain trembles away and away and sinks back beneath my robes. I sag against Naqi, and he holds me up, and I hate him for it.

"Come back," he says.

I laugh.

"I'm serious. Come back."

"And then what, huh?" I fist my hands in his robes. "Go quietly to my death?"

"You're not going to die."

"Zap off."

"You're not."

"This is real life, khab. This isn't another game of your stupid make-believe. I'm an Omen. I gave Roaz the stain. No amount of playing pretend will change that."

Naqi falls silent. He knows what I've said is true.

We stay that way for a long while, a long while. But he doesn't let me go. Beside us, the ocean laps and laps. The cityscape on the far shoreline glitters and is studded full of lights.

I say, finally, and my voice is small, "Why are you here?"

"I don't know," is Naqi's honest, naked reply. "I just . . . had a feeling you might not come back if I didn't go after you."

"I can't go back."

"You can. You didn't mean what happened."

I didn't mean to kill Lumi. I didn't mean to be born an Omen. But Lumi is still dead. And I am still an Omen. "My meaning doesn't change anything."

"It does. Lumi, it does. But it's—not about that. It's not about any of that."

"I don't care. I don't care anymore. Let me go."

"If I do, where will you go?"

"That doesn't matter."

"It does." *To me*, he does not say. But I understand it like light breaking through smog. It matters to Naqi.

I can't stand it.

"I'm an Omen," I tell him again. Why doesn't he understand?

In that moment, with a pull like overlooking the edge of a great drop, I think about telling him everything—that I've always been an Omen, that I'm not a Veil. My name is Sozo. I killed Lumi. I've been working for a woman named Esp, working for a wish, and I don't know if I've ever done anything good my entire life.

"I'm stained. And the temple is a holy space. And I've tainted Roaz." Why doesn't he understand?

"I know all that."

"So why are you still here?"

"Because." Naqi pulls back, and his face is—all wrong. His smile is missing. His eyes are dark. He looks like he's about to cry.

It does something to me, seeing him like this, the seams of him fraying like this.

I'm afraid of him, I realize. But I don't know why.

Naqi scrubs the back of his hand over his eyes, then reaches for my hand again, like he's fearful I will run. I let him take it. I don't run.

"I'll tell you why," he says. "But I want to sit down."

I don't know how to say no, not to this Naqi. So I nod. I take him from the street to the curb, but then he says no, he doesn't want to sit here, in the cold by the sea black in the night.

So I take him through the alleys. I wind us up the district tiers.

I take us to a series of narrow fire escapes, rusted over and missing sections, and lead us up to a walkway high above the junction of a pedestrian bridge and a shopping street. Here, nothing is in darkness. It's a feast of lights, of wares being sold, of food being made. People on people negotiate the flow of the crowds. Tall Titan rarely sleeps.

The walkway itself is narrow and decked with signage. The few people who stroll over it glance at our temple robes but otherwise pay us no mind.

There's a vending machine in the corner. I go to it while Naqi finds a large gap in the railings and sits between them on the walkway, legs dangling in the air.

I twist two capsules into the machine and return to Naqi with two marble sodas. I hand him one and sit beside him.

He works a while at the soda, because I don't think he's ever opened one before. So I push the marble down in my drink to pop it open, and hand him mine. He takes it. He trades me his.

He's still not smiling. Despite the warmth of the city radiating from below, the air about him is cool, distant. He ponders the soda in his hands, but he does not drink.

Then softly, softly, he begins.

"Mum and Dad," he says, "are both researchers. Botanists. We moved around a lot for their jobs, until I turned four. Then we settled into this small depot-town in the middle of some countryside. Don't know if it's around anymore. The depot, I mean."

I nod and listen.

"There was a boy there. Elis. Much older; ten when I first met him. He had long hair, and he was lanky and tall and slouched all the time, and I thought he was the coolest thing ever." Naqi laughs. "And he probably thought I was just some annoying scrapper he had to look after. But there weren't a whole lot of other kids around then. There weren't a whole lot of other things in general—just warehouses, greenhouses, labs. Fields as far as the eye could see."

I imagine little Naqi, standing on the bank of some artificial river. A solitary boy against something far larger than he is.

"So we stuck to each other. We told each other everything. He didn't like his family very much, so he'd never want to be home. He'd stay with us, sometimes. We'd bunk together. For three years, that's how things were. He taught me how to hack into warehouse systems, and how to climb diffuser towers, and we'd sneak into the comms room all the time, to ride the waves, to see what other sort of news was out there."

I stare at Naqi, because I never fathomed he could do anything like that—hacking, sneaking, misbehaving. But I don't speak. I don't ask him questions. I don't want him to stop talking.

Naqi rolls the marble about in his soda bottle, then takes a sip.

He continues, voice soft, and I lean closer to hear even though I don't need to. His voice carries clear to me. The din of the crowd below us sounds to me like a distant thing.

"A few weeks after I turned seven," he says, "we fought about something. Stupid, looking back now. I don't even remember what we fought about. A place he promised he would take me, maybe. He had a hoverbike that he'd managed to cobble together from scraps, and I wanted to ride on it whenever I could.

"A few weeks after that, we fought again. A week after that, same thing. And it went on happening again and again, for months. The smallest things. Dumbest things. I would do something to annoy him, or he'd lie to me about something, and I'd catch him. He'd promise to be somewhere and then not be there, or promise to get me something only to forget days later. Other children started moving into the town around this time, and I was—angry, with him. I didn't know why things were changing. I didn't know why he was changing. So I stopped hanging out with him. I hung out with other kids instead."

Naqi's expression is shadowed. Somehow, it looks like he's losing weight right before my eyes, thinning away into nothing, and fear tightens in my chest. But I don't move. I still don't speak.

"Then one day," he continues, "Elis asked to meet me, and I think he wanted to apologize. So of course I went, and he was there, and we talked. But I'm a stupid seven-year-old, and I said something, I don't know, and he got angry. And I got angry back. And we started yelling. And then . . ." Naqi frowns. His grip over his bottle goes white-tense.

"He started—saying things, things that were happening with him, with his family. He was confessing. All sorts of things. Vile things. Things you shouldn't be telling a kid, but he was, because he didn't know what else to do. He was saying things like how he was trying his best, but he couldn't handle it anymore, how he didn't want to handle it anymore.

"He was asking for help." Naqi looks down. "But all I could think about was how angry I was. I kept thinking: How could you? I'm just a kid. How could you unload all these things on me?"

Naqi stops. His gaze is heavy on his hands. His shoulders are hunched like he has no strength, and it makes me want to lay my hand on them, to lend him mine.

"So I decided to hurt him," he says.

"For the wrong he did me, I decided to hurt him back," he says.

"He told me he didn't know if he could handle it anymore, so I told him don't. Don't bother. I told him he could end things, and that he should, and that it'd be what he deserved after laying all his dirty laundry at my feet. And then I left."

Naqi says nothing else.

The sound of the crowd filters back in, and I am—lost.

I am, like that time at the Joining, untethered.

I know what he's saying. I know how this story ends. But I don't understand.

"Why are you telling me this?" My whisper shakes.

"I'm telling you this," Naqi whispers back, "because of what you asked me."

I shake my head. I still don't understand.

Naqi turns to me. His eyes hold on mine. He doesn't look away.

"You told me," he says, "that you're an Omen."

"And I asked you," I say, "why you're still here."

"I'm still here," he answers, "because I'm one too. You just can't see it."

Ten people could commit the same crime, and only one of them would be stained.

"They found him a couple days later," Naqi continues. "And I knew it was my fault. He was standing right by the edge, and I pushed him over. I knew what I was doing. I wanted to hurt him. I wanted to get back at him. I sat in my room for a good week, after, waiting for my stain to appear. And it never did."

Naqi's laugh is a broken thing. "It never did."

I don't know gentleness. I don't know words that soothe. All I know is that it hurts, listening to Naqi laugh out broken glass. It hurts, watching Naqi so small like this.

It's not your fault, is forever on the tip of my tongue. But I don't say it. I know it would not help. It never did with me.

We don't head back to the temple, not right away. I take Naqi to other districts, to the plazas of the soaring malls all crystal and glass, to crowded shopping arcades, to crooked back alleys bordered with little restaurants you have to duck into, and then—when we tire of the noise and of the lights—I wind us back to the shores of the sea sector.

The wide street is empty. The streetlamps shine for no one at all. In the lonely dark, moths congregate against the lights, fluttering, straining.

Naqi waits by the foot of a post while I stop at a public

washroom. It's empty, like the street. The cement stalls are cold. The smell of the place is damp. While inside a stall, I hear someone else enter to wash their hands. I don't hear them leave.

When I come out of the stall, I see that it's Esp.

She's waiting for me, arms crossed, leaning back against the sinks. She's platinum blond. Her hair is bobbed, with straight bangs that cover her eyebrows and most of her scar. A patterned surgical mask hangs from her neck. She wears it to cover the omen scar that stretches from the corner of her mouth across her cheek.

Her eyes are baby blue; she is wearing colored lenses. She looks high end in her black dress with black gloves and pert black heels.

"Sozo."

My breath blows from me, like I've been punched in the gut. It feels like a lifetime since I've heard my own name.

"Yes."

"Been following you for a while."

But she couldn't approach because of Naqi.

"Sorry," I say.

"Didn't know acolytes were allowed to be out this late."

"They're not."

Esp looks at me and waits, waits for an explanation. And so I pull in a breath and give her one. I tell her everything. I tell her what happened at the pool with Roaz and the stain I drew. I tell her how I've been exposed, and how I ran, and ran.

(I don't know why, but I don't tell her about Naqi.)

I don't realize I'm looking down at the stained tiles until those tiles blur in my vision. Tears have swollen behind my lids, and angry, I blink them away. My nails sting against my palms.

Esp has her arms around me suddenly, suddenly. I freeze. I

forget to breathe. Esp is embracing me. She has never, ever touched me like this before. I don't understand.

"You've been through so much," she says, soft. She touches the back of my head. "You've been working so hard for our sake."

I don't understand. I don't know how to reconcile Esp with softness. But she's still holding me, and she is caressing my head like I am not someone who's failed her, and so, whimpering, I cling to her. I let my tears fall.

"It's my fault," I whisper. "Roaz. My stain. Everything. Everything is my fault."

Esp doesn't deny it. Her silence is her affirmation. Then she says, "The boy with you. He's taking you back?"

Naqi is still waiting for me outside, underneath the light and the moths.

"Yes."

"And he thinks things can be mended with the temple?"

"I . . . think so."

"Sozo."

"Yes," I say. "He does."

"And he still trusts you?"

My throat is tight. Naqi smiles for me and races through the city for me. He looks at me and tells me why he's stayed. When I say, "Yes," it's a thin thing, a small thing, a word that hooks against the tightness of my throat.

I'm ashamed.

Esp nods. "Good."

She says, "You've come this far, Sozo, passed the Joining, entered the temple. Just a few more weeks, and you'll be flying in the race. Then you'll show them. You'll show them all. We Omens will never again be something they'll mock and spit at."

That's right. Our wish.

I go cold.

If I win the race, if I make our wish, Naqi—

"Esp."

She pulls back and looks down at me. Her hands are on my shoulders.

I don't know what to say. All these years, the wish has never been something I questioned. It's always been something I embraced and believed in. I yearned after it like an alcoholic would a drink. But now, knowing what I know about Naqi, I don't know how I could go through with it.

"What is it?"

"The wish," I begin. "Can't there be . . . couldn't there be another way?"

Esp's gaze is on me abruptly, like standing on the other end of a cocked gun. The hairs on my neck stand on end.

"What are you saying?"

"Our goal," I say, "is to be treated the way other people are treated, to erase the prejudice. So that means—"

Esp's voice is all edges. "Have you lost your mind?"

I flinch.

Her hands on my shoulders clench down, and it hurts. She says, "Has temple mush and brainless star babble turned you soft? Have you forgotten in this week the years we've all had to endure? How they treated us? How they all continue to treat us?"

I swallow. "No."

"They stripped you naked when you were just a girl, and looked you all over, because you weren't a girl to them, just an *Omen*. They barred you from work and stores so that you couldn't ever earn a living or buy food. They barred you from beds so that even their dogs slept better than you. Have you forgotten the looks? People pointing at us and calling us evil, warped, worthless, unclean?"

My hands are fists. I grit my teeth. "I haven't forgotten."

"Our goal is to be treated the way other people are treated? What a joke. What a sad joke. It's never been about that. And you know it."

I don't know what to say. My head swims. I can only nod.

"We're going to make them pay." Esp doesn't see me anymore, not really. Her eyes are on me, but they're glassy. "Our goal is to ensure they get treated the way we were treated. Give them a taste of their own medicine. And then we'll make them suffer. All of them."

Her words ring. The silence around us is loud.

I've been here too long. Naqi is still waiting for me.

"I'll find you again." Esp pulls back. "If you're ever let back out of the temple."

I steady my breathing. I nod again.

Esp says nothing else. She's watching me, weighing me. I don't know what she sees. In the end, she says, "Remember."

She says: "You're an Omen, and you've killed, and there's no coming back from that. You're not like the others, and you never will be."

I know. At least, I thought I did.

(What about Naqi? What about someone like Naqi?)

"Remember," Esp says, and she touches my head. "The race and the wish comes first. Nothing else matters. You do what you must to ensure this whole thing blows over. When they check you for stains, you hide it, the way you've always done. You deny and lie, the way you've always done. Then we'll move forward with the plan. We're so close, Sozo. We're so close."

She says, "Do me proud."

And then it happens—something I never quite realized I had been waiting and wanting to hear all this time, all this time. My eyes pull wide. Something in me opens, and it blots out my shame like bleach.

"If ever I had a daughter," she says, "she would be like you."

Brother Marat is waiting for Naqi and me by the temple gates. He isn't smiling. Naqi, for once, is silent. I also don't explain. We stand in the cold and the dark, heads down, while Brother Marat watches us and watches us. In the end, he sighs. He steps out of the way and lets us inside.

"Roaz is fine," is what he says. My head snaps up. The old Sun nods.

"The omen stains receded an hour or so after the starsong. He's shaken, but not unwell."

Naqi's eyes flick to the torn fabric over my shoulder, but he says nothing. He doesn't betray me. He must be thinking that my stain is gone too.

"How?" I ask Marat.

"Providence of fate and of the sirens. If you had been using a true whistling star—one full of power—I imagine the spell of his stain would've stayed for good. But lucky for him, and for you, that wasn't the case. Roaz will be fine."

Thank the stars. I don't like Roaz; he's a boor. But thank the stars. Even a boor like him doesn't deserve to be stained like me.

I frown. "And what about—"

"You, young Lumi? We'll think of a proper punishment for

you in due time. And I hope you know"—Marat pans his gaze down at me—"that this can't happen again."

I nod. My mind jumps, then, to Pea. She saw my stain too.

"Did . . . did Pea say anything?"

"Pea? Ah. Young Rama?"

"Yes."

Brother Marat shakes his head. "She seemed shaken, poor thing, but has said nothing to me. Should she have?"

"No," I say, too quickly, but Brother Marat only nods. He doesn't question it.

The gates of the temple are closed, and we're led back through the chancel to the temple grounds, and all along that dark, echoing stretch, I think and brew.

Esp has acknowledged me. Esp *needs* me. And she's right—I'm an Omen, one who has killed, and nothing will ever wash away that stain.

But Naqi has also acknowledged me. His running after me means that he sees me.

He sees me, and he stayed anyway.

I stop. Naqi notices that I've stopped, and he turns. He cocks his head. "Lu?"

I look down at my feet. Esp. Naqi. Her wish. His past.

I know what I have to do.

I look back up at Naqi but say nothing. I move away from him and from Brother Marat, away from the titan's eye, to the doors that lead to that inner sanctum of black tourmaline.

I push open those doors and slip inside, even as Naqi calls after me, even as Brother Marat turns with a frown and watches.

Inside, across the vast galaxy-dark of the sanctum, stands the kori tower.

My star calls.

In the deep of the night, in the silence that shrouds, fire from a sun blooms.

The temple quakes. The ancient trees tremble. Gaia has been claimed.

The star asked for my hearing, and I gave it.

(Naqi who sinned like me gave it, so I do too.)

The star asked for my sight, and I gave it. I don't need it to see what I have to do.

It asked what my wish will be if I win, and I answer: I'm going to make the wish Esp is too angry to make, too hurt to make. I'm going to make instead the wish that she needs, that I need, one that will not hurt Naqi.

The star says that I have a history of lying, and I say yes, I do. But this time will be different. This time, I will help. I will lift.

No longer will I choose to hurt.

TWELVE

News has spread in the night that I've returned with Naqi, and that I've claimed the star of Gaia, and people whisper that maybe it wasn't even my fault in the first place that Roaz caught the stain.

Surely a star like Gaia would not have accepted someone who did such a thing.

Brother Marat believes the stain appeared on Roaz because of the line I drew, and he is right. Naqi believes the stain appeared on me because of what happened, and he is partly right.

Both think the stains are gone for good now, and that is true—for Roaz.

In the morning, in the dorm, I wait for Pea the way I always do. When she wakes, she looks at me, then flicks her eyes away, then comes down her ladder quietly, quietly.

She must have questions about what happened.

"Pea?"

She startles.

"Oh, stars. Sorry. You don't have to wait for me all the time, Lumi."

I shake my head; I don't mind.

She's still looking away. She runs her hand over and over the back of her head, the scruff of it, and then she says, "Is . . . so is everything all right now?"

I nod.

I say, "Thank you," and the words are an odd shape in my mouth, "for not telling anyone."

She ducks her head. She fidgets. ". . . Naqi didn't tell?"

I shake my head.

Pea fidgets some more. But when she looks back up at me, she has pulled on a smile. "Okay. You're welcome. And you don't have to worry. I won't tell anyone. I mean"—her eyes flick to my shoulder—"it's gone now, right? Like Roaz's?"

"Yes," I say, and the shape of this word, this lie, is nothing like odd in my mouth.

I am washing fruits in the sink at the back of the kitchen when Naqi finally wakes beside me. He yawns and says good morning, and then Roaz pushes through to the kitchen and snarls, "You. *Veil.*"

It's far too early for this. And Naqi groans and says, "It's way too early for this."

"How is any of this right?" Roaz bulldozes on. "You cursed someone with the stain, and you're still allowed in the race? In the temple? How are you even still allowed to *live*?"

"Roaz," Naqi cuts in. "That's enough."

"Enough what? She wrote the omen onto my skin. You saw it. You all saw it."

"She didn't mean to. And the stains are gone now."

"She didn't mean to," Roaz mocks. "So let's acquit the poor

pure Veil of all blame because she didn't mean to. Poor Veil. Poor thing. She's pure, all right. Pure evil."

"Stop," Naqi clips. His brows and mouth have set into hard lines. "You've done nothing but pick fights with her since the moment you laid eyes on her. Stop."

"Yeah. I'll stop. I'll stop once the holy Veil gets hers. And you can bet that I'll make sure she does."

Roaz twists to leave. He stops at the exit and glares over his shoulder. He spits at me and says, "Should've been *you* that was stained. Scum."

He leaves.

I turn back to the sink.

My hands are trembling, so I dip them underneath the water to hide them.

Naqi wipes his hands on his robes and says, "Stay here."

I look over at him. "What?"

"Stay here," he repeats, and he doesn't look at me.

He turns from the sink and stalks out of the kitchen.

I pause, and then follow after, frowning, because I'm not letting Naqi tell me what to do.

Out in the mess hall, people are wiping down and setting the tables. They move light and slow in the morning. Naqi steps up to Roaz, who has picked up a heavy stack of plates. I pause.

Naqi says something. Roaz replies. Then back and forth until veins are bulging from Roaz's temple and neck, and Naqi is—I don't know. It's hard to see. The hard line of his back is mostly to me.

Naqi shoves him. Roaz drops the stack of plates, and the clay shatters like a scream, and then the two are throwing punches. They topple to the ground. They have each other by their collars and are scraping each other through broken pottery until their robes stain red at the elbows, at the backs.

Pea is crying. People are shouting. In the heat and the din and the taste of iron, Roaz fumbles his hand over a shard of plate. He's not thinking. He takes hold of it despite its cutting him and aims it at Naqi's temple, and I'm there, I've moved. I'm grabbing Roaz's arm. I wrench it down at the wrong angle. He yowls over the snap.

Roaz's friend comes in and kicks me in my mask, where my mouth would be, and the mask cracks. A shard of it falls and splits open my lip.

Someone else yanks me away—Naqi, it's Naqi—and just like that, the two of us are back to back, brawling. We swing out at anyone coming at us. I punch someone in the ear. Naqi twists someone's arm and slams them against the side of a table.

His face, when I see it, is red. I've never known that color on him.

I only know Naqi by the white of his smile, by the yellow of the sun around him. I never knew he could be this shade, where the white of his teeth is bared for me, where the yellow of his bruises is caught for me.

We're barred from breakfast and lunch and dinner, Naqi and me. We're given a bucket of water instead, to hold over our heads as we kneel in the dust of the courtyard outside the mess hall. People go about their chores. They brush their brooms around our space. They stare when they think we don't see.

I don't hang my head. I tongue the edge of my lip, the cut, and taste salt. I stare ahead and say, "I didn't ask you to do that."

"Yeah," Naqi says.

"You're crazy," I say.

"Yeah," he says.

"It's all your fault this happened, you khab."

"I mean"—and he can only twitch out half a smile, because his face is set with bruises—"I wasn't the one who broke Roaz's arm."

"You started it."

He pulls in a breath. "Yeah," he says. "And by the stars, did it feel good."

I shake my head. "I don't get you."

"What?"

"You heard me. Your head is full of static, you messed-up, make-believing khab."

He laughs. He would raise his hands if they weren't already raised. The water from his bucket spills. His arms tremble like mine, and he winces.

He complains about his bruises. He whines about the cuts stinging on his cheeks, over his back, and the aches that cut into his ribs from fists and heels. He doesn't complain about the bucket over his head.

He doesn't whine about kneeling in the dust with me, where everyone can see.

A few days pass. Everyone in the temple knows by now what has happened.

I'm made to suffer through a few more punishments—katohs before the titan's eye and incense prayers to the wall of sirens—and I'm made to tend to Roaz as he heals. Naqi is made to whistle starsongs over him, daily, to aid in his healing.

It will be tight, but with the help of starsongs, Roaz should be healed by the end of the month. If he isn't, Naqi and I may then be kept from the races as well, as punishment.

So Naqi flies twice as much over Roaz as he's required to, and I cross my arms and glare at Roaz as he eats, like maybe that will frighten his body into healing faster.

Roaz himself gloats at it all.

Serves us right, he says. *Now the two of you know your place*, he says.

But strangely, strangely, he no longer taunts with the same bite. He no longer mocks with malice. He quips at me, and smirks at me, but that is all. He trades barbs with Naqi, but something must have happened—either during that talk before the brawl or after when I was not looking—because sometimes after their barbs, they laugh.

I cannot believe it, but Roaz and Naqi are *friends* now.

As for me, I don't call Naqi khab as much anymore, but I will. I'm only waiting for his cuts and bruises to heal. There's a deep gash down the side of his back that's still scabbed over. He tears it all the time, when he twists and soars on his anchor in the air, when the sun glints white over his laugh.

Flying at the pit with the others is exhilarating.

Flying itself is exhilarating, breathtaking, like leaping and diving through the sky while gravity has loosed its strings on you and cannot hurt you. It's the end of the second week.

Gaia's presence is immense. I can fly twice, thrice, the speed I could before. The only one who can keep up with me and my lines is Naqi, and we fly on and on, longer than we should, long enough that Brother Marat needs to scold us to give others a turn.

The pitches we whistle out harmonize and twine, and it's music.

I don't think I could ever tire of hearing it.

Aside from Gaia's power, I can't pinpoint much else about her personality. Naqi's star is playful, and he says it helps him think up wild lines, fanciful lines, lines that make him laugh.

Others talk about their stars in a similar way, like they are people, friends that they can converse with.

But Gaia hardly converses with me.

The only time we spoke was at the kori tower, when she asked me what I wanted, when she wondered whether or not I would lie again.

I learn that Naqi has a habit of collecting things.

Soft things. Broken things. Things the others no longer want or need.

"You're more bird than boy," I say.

"Going by that logic, you'd be more hedgehog than girl." He grins.

I try not to bristle, because then I'd be proving him right. I ask instead, "What's the point of hoarding junk?"

Naqi thinks about it.

"I think," he says, "it makes me think of home, somehow, and I miss home. Or having one, at least. You should try it. Collecting things, I mean."

Omens don't own things. Owning things means you could have them taken away.

"Whatever for?"

"For fun. For the sake of it. And you know . . ." His voice lilts, so I squint because I know he's caught an idea. He grins and says, "If I'm a bird, I'm going to need a nest."

I argue with him, of course, that the Suns are going to confiscate his things, that he'll get in trouble with the other acolytes for making a mess, but in my head I'm already thinking of the places we could hoard his collection: my old cell, maybe. One of the unused work tents, maybe.

We'll need lots of space, space enough to hold something like a home.

In the end, of all the locations, we return to where Naqi and I first met.

By that hole in the wall, we soften the cradle of branches and vines with his worn blankets, moth-eaten cushions, faded fraying rugs. We light the space with his broken lamps and stumpy candles with barely any wick left, with warped vases that we fill with warped stars the temple no longer needs. We decorate the space with toys and figurines that don't get played with anymore, and hang colored glass from the branches so that reds and blues and yellows blur our nest into watercolors.

Tented in that space—warm, wrapped soft in dusty, broken, forgotten things—it's easier to give, to ask, to bare.

I ponder what he said to me, that I should try collecting things. But I think if I do, if I ever try to own things for myself, I could only have things that no one could ever take from me.

It would hurt too much, otherwise.

And in the quiet and lull of our nest, we waste time musing over things that don't matter at all, silly things, stupid things, like who we would want to be if we weren't Naqi and Lumi, what our jobs would be, what our names would be.

(And I wonder, in those moments, what my real name would sound like coming from Naqi's mouth.)

We draw shapes in the stars above us and make believe life on other planets, moons, colonies. We draw shapes in our hands, and then Naqi teaches me more hand signs, ones that mean yes, no. Eat, hug. Sorry. Thank you.

"What's the sign for *khab*," I ask, and Naqi laughs, because there is no such sign. So we create our own.

Khab, we decide, is tapping the side of our temple then pinching our fingers from the brow, like maybe there was a speck of something stuck on the eyebrow. The sign for *zap*, we decide, is snapping two fingers in both our hands, and rotating our hands like we are reeling in a fish. *Siren's teeth* is clawing our fingers and dragging our nails down the back of our hands.

Naqi scratches the nail of his thumb over his forehead, then wiggles his fingers, and already he is snickering. Static for brains.

I'm reminded, then, of Yashi, of her missing tongue, of what Pea said that time in the markets. So here, in the sanctuary of our nest, I ask Naqi for the truth.

"Yashi doesn't keep it a secret," is what Naqi says. "If you ask her, she'll tell you."

"So it's true."

Naqi nods.

I frown. I've heard of black market doctors that deal in omen amputations. They're wildly expensive, and the operation is risky, never guaranteed to work. Who's to say the stain won't simply appear somewhere else on the body?

"There's a hospital," Naqi continues, "that treats people like Yashi. A secret place. Don't know how she managed to find it."

"And the temple knows?"

"About her? Yeah."

"And she's still allowed to be here?"

"She's not an Omen anymore."

I fall silent.

Not an Omen anymore, Naqi says, so easily, so very easily. If I had done what Yashi did when I was younger—gouged out my flesh at my shoulder blade—I wonder if things would be different. I wonder if it'd be true, then, when I said I wasn't an Omen anymore.

"Hey."

I look up. My thoughts must've leaked into my face, because Naqi's voice is soft. He smiles at me, but it's different. This smile has no teeth, and no cheek, and it makes my eyes sting.

"*Ya'tuv mi-eh,*" he says.

It's the strung-together sounds of a starsong, and I know *ya* means you. *Tuv* means bury. *Mi-eh* means me. I don't understand. He is telling me to bury him.

Naqi raps his knuckles against his heart, then brings those knuckles up to his forehead. He says again, "Ya'tuv mi-eh."

And I remember one night, winter, with the glare of red neon lights over ice, a man opening his jacket and folding a woman into it. He zipped it up with her inside, and they kissed each other, and laughed.

The scene was soft, soft, like something I've never been taught.

That is how Naqi says it, and smiles, and how he reaches for me—softly. I block his hand, because I don't . . . I don't think this is something I'm allowed.

"Don't."

"I just . . ." He stops. His cheeks look red, but I don't know why. He asks instead, "Do you know what it means?"

"No. But don't. I don't want it."

"Want to learn more signs, instead?"

I nod. I'm grateful for the change in topic.

Naqi teaches me the signs for want, for need, for more. He teaches me *angry*—clawing his fingers against his stomach and pulling up and out. He teaches me *afraid*—clenching his hands before him and then opening them in shock.

He tells me that there are two ways to say *love*:

Crossing your fists over your chest and squeezing in a hug.

Combining three letters into three fingers, thumb and pointer and pinky, to spell *I* and *love* and *you*.

At the beginning of the third week, the walls full of siren masks that encircle the titan's eye are pulled away. Brother Marat gathers us by the steps of the portal. He gathers us for our final lesson.

"Should you be among the ones to pass the first stage of the races, and also the second, you will then be given the honor of whistling in the third and final stage, one that takes place within the titan's eye.

"Be forewarned," he says. "Not only is flying its depths already quite the dangerous endeavor, it will also be unlike anything you've experienced thus far in the races."

He stresses, "Or in this life."

The portal, Brother Marat explains, leads to a cosmic storm, one of many that dot the dark of space. Its flesh is rolling static and clouds, knit together by lightning. Its currents are said to be the very breath of sirens themselves.

In those storms, stardust is mined. In those storms, new stars are harvested.

"But once every decade, the storm takes on a different quality, one full of possibilities, of visions, of stars thrumming with wishes. If the first stage tests your physical strength, and the second your knowledge, this final stage in the titan's eye will test your very spirit, your very soul.

"Pair up," he instructs. "Use your lit stars as conduits. As the Choosing had you give up your senses, you are now to train in the trading of them—see as others see, hear as others hear, feel as others feel. Transfer your senses and put on another's, and in this way, shed the shackles of your own distorted truths. Only then will you be equipped to whistle through the cosmic bowels of the eye."

I don't understand. Neither do the others; everyone is shifting and murmuring. Brother Marat raises his hands for calm and says, "Simply remember your Nine Ahs. Cling to their undistorted truths, and they will guard and guide."

He explains, "The eye will test you. The eye will force you to see yourself, truly see yourself. If you are unprepared to be **seen**, then the storm will spit you out. If you are unwilling to be **seen**, then the storm will reject you."

Fear like tension winds through my body.

I am left with only two choices, then:

To hide all the depths of me and all that I've done and to be spat back out, to lose everything I've worked for, sinned for, suffered for.

To lay bare and be seen for all that I am, all that I've done. I wonder. If I choose this path—expose myself—and am not spat out by the storm, will I instead be swallowed whole?

Between our training and our meditations for the sense transference, Naqi and I idle away our time at the nest.

Sometimes we talk about Naqi's parents, but he doesn't **like** talking about them too much because, he says, "It makes me miss them," and then he admits, with a fearful quiet: "That, and I barely remember them anymore."

We're curled on our sides with our foreheads almost touching, and I touch them together in that quiet. Fear on Naqi is not a good color. Naqi smiles.

We find things to talk about, like the work tents and the things they make, and the people and the food. We find things to complain about.

"Roaz," Naqi complains, "has a thing for Rama, apparently."

"Oh." I think about it. "Pea is very pretty."

"Sure, but he doesn't have to talk about it all the time."

I look at Naqi, and look at him, and ask, "Have you thought about anyone?"

Naqi pauses.

He looks back at me, eyes blank, and then he laughs. It's an uncomfortable sound. He rubs his face, his eyes. Between his fingers, I see his skin is red. "I mean, maybe."

Something like a snake—coiling, open-mawed—twitches in my chest. "Who?"

"I'm not telling you that."

I frown.

He changes the subject. "What about you? Thought about anyone?"

I shake my head. I don't think about anyone. I ask again, "What's she like?"

"Who?"

"The person you think about."

"Oh." He looks down, and away, and rubs the back of his head.

"I don't know," he says. "She's—cool, I guess."

I frown again. Naqi whistles like the wind, flying here, there, until you're left breathless. The Suns talk about him in the halls when they think no one hears. They say things like: *He could lead us one day.* They say things like: *He should be the one to win.*

In the eyes of the temple, and in the eyes of the others, Naqi is what it means to be cool. There is no one else at his height.

"I don't know anyone like that."

Naqi laughs. "Maybe she's just a make-believe girl."

I scowl. "Fine. Don't tell me. She's likely full of static like you, anyway."

Naqi only grabs his middle and shakes and laughs.

I've been pairing with Naqi for our meditations. We sit crisscross across from each other with our lit stars between us, and we treat it like a race, like a contest.

Naqi wins.

I don't realize he's crested the peak into a trance until I hear him shivering. His teeth chatter. I open my eyes and press close to him, and I touch his hand so he knows I am there.

He comes out of the trance heaving, sweating, like an almost-drowned man floundering out of the water.

I ask him what it was like, and he tells me it was like popping your ears, where balance yawns open, except it opens in the center of your forehead, where a sense you've never known spreads over you.

"I could feel your lifeblood," he says—whispers. He is too tired for anything louder. "It burned through me like something holy, you know? And I could feel that your feet were cold, and that you didn't eat enough for breakfast, and warms and colds and colors ebbed like waves from everything."

"You sound insane," I hush, but I don't stop him. My eyes are wide. I lean closer to hear more.

He says, "I think words and pictures stamped over my mind, behind my eyes, but they weren't my words. Those pictures weren't pictures I'd seen with my own eyes."

"I don't understand."

His mouth twitches with a smile. "Maybe I was reading minds," he says. "Maybe I was reading yours."

I stop. I pull in tight. But Naqi only shakes his head. He says, "The pictures were a blur, a single color. You were just a pale white; you were meditating at the time."

I don't know what to think. All I know is that Naqi's hands are trembling, and his lips are dry, so I let him lean on me when we walk back to the dorms after.

He's too drained to smile, but I know he means to when he bumps his shoulder against mine.

It's the final week before the races, and it's morning. We're meditating in the gardens.

And then, just like that, my ears pop open.

They pop open between my brows. A sense dawns over me like light through parting clouds, or like slipping and falling, falling, falling.

I feel the beats of Naqi's heart. His blood jams through my veins, up and down, like sky-traffic. I see colors even though my eyes are closed, blooming from people-shapes, from tree-shapes, from star-shapes. And just like how Naqi described it, words and pictures that are not mine stamp behind my eyes. Someone on the field is thinking about food. Someone by the tree line is picturing what it would be like to kiss a girl.

The picture I see from Naqi is of him knocking his knuckles against his heart and then bringing his fist to his forehead. He says: *Ya'tuv mi-eh.*

Bury me.

I understand what it means.

Somehow, up on the height of this spiritual peak, all of Naqi's meanings are made known to me. I see what he sees. I understand what he understands.

Your fears and doubts, bury them with me.

Your hopes and dreams, burrow them with me.

Shoot me down with your secrets, because I will take them to my grave.

May death come for me first, so I never have to know a day without you.

I tear out of my trance. Sweat breaks over me. I'm breathing heavy and shallow, too quick and not quick enough. Naqi is pressed against my side because I have no strength to sit up.

"You did it," he says, soft. "Take it easy. You came down from it kind of weird."

"I saw, I saw."

"Yeah. A whole bunch of weird things, right?"

I look up at him, at Naqi, Naqi who tells me to bury him.

"I read you."

"Yeah?" He looks amused. "And what'd you read?"

I say nothing, but I'm still staring, and I'm panting. I try words that do not sound. They do not sound because I am comprehending now that Naqi kneels in the dust for me, that he bleeds for me, and fights for me. Naqi ponders futures with me and builds with me a nest, a softness, that I can accept. Ya'tuv mi-eh.

Naqi doesn't understand my staring. I can tell. His smile lingers, hangs, because he thinks maybe I am trying to be funny. And I let him think it.

His ya'tuv mi-eh is for Lumi, the Veil. Lumi, the good and the pure. She would be worth being buried, worth the weight of secrets and the burden of fears. His ya'tuv mi-eh is not for Sozo, the Omen. Sozo, the evil and the corrupt. Only a fool would die for someone who is not worthy to be saved.

Naqi was right.

The girl he likes is only make-believe.

THIRTEEN

The day of the Decade-Races. A day of jubilee.

The city has transformed into a carnival of awe, of music, a firework bursting again and again in celebration. Like a song that loops unending, the parade of colors and delight sweeps through and through the city.

We whistlers are dressed in white and starry night blue. Gossamer silk is draped over our robes and tied off with golden charms in the shape of stars, with golden tassels like star-tails. My veil is wrapped tight about my head and neck like a wimple, and then pulled sheer over my mask. Everything is tied off and secured for the race to come.

Everyone is here behind the temple gates, all forty-five of us.

Roaz healed four days ago and rejoined us at the pits, full of strength, teeth and eyes flashing. Naqi is here, standing by the edge of the group in his own spot. He's looking down at the star of Togarath in his hands, and is pondering it, quiet.

Only the first twenty-four of us, the first ones to pass the finish line, will be moving on to the second stage. It means that almost half of us standing here today will be going home after this.

Home.

There's nothing like that for me to go back to.

I'm trembling. I've been trembling since I woke.

I see Pea through the crowd, and she hops and waves. There's still time before the opening ceremony, so she pushes through to me. She takes my hands and squeezes them, and smiles so, so bright.

"You can do this, Lumi."

I say nothing. My words would chatter against my teeth if I did.

"You can! I believe in you. You're going to do so amazing. You've got the best star, after all. Remember me when you win, okay? Remember me when you make your wish, okay?"

I nod. It's a stiff thing.

Pea laughs. She throws her arms around my shoulders and squeezes me tight, her cheek against my mask, and then she pulls away.

Fear pings sharp through me.

If I don't win, I will never see Pea again. If I don't win, we will never do this again, never walk to breakfast together, to the dorms and the gardens. I'll never again hear her hushed chatter in our hammocks, because she'll be in the temple, and I'll be in the streets. She's one of the first friends I've ever had.

"Pea," I say.

Pea stops a little way away and turns back to me.

"I . . ." and I pause, because I don't know how to convey my fear. So I say instead, "I'll see you after."

She smiles and nods, and, oblivious to the fears puncturing holes in my chest, she departs.

Atop a great scaffold, in the wide open of the plaza before the temple gates, the opening ceremony begins.

The scaffold is an imitation of the kori tower in the temple, tiered and with steps, but bursting with colors like a cake. Instead of the statues of sirens, dancers weave and twirl. Their bodies are trimmed in gold that clinks and clinks, and on their heads are headdresses like entire gilded thrones. The tower is vast enough, tall enough, that thousands can behold it from even the edge of the plaza.

At the very top of the pyramid, the High Suns stand in their glory.

Mounted around each of their shoulders is a ruff of monumental size, the size of a canvas painting. The popped collars are of rigid wiring, of gossamer, of lace, and of heavy jewels—diamonds, pearls, rubies—and they sprout up and behind the Suns in an array of holy beams.

I imagine that if the wind huffed and puffed, their collars would bloat like sails. Those sails would carry the priests up and away and gone.

The ceremony itself is a dance and song of our origin story, of stars that fell and grew flesh, of sirens that curse and bless. The dancers twirl through the many decades of the races, while the High Suns sing through the Nine Ahs. Taiko drums sound. Flutes and pipes soar.

A firework of confetti bursts, and streamers fall, and a gong is struck.

The dance has ended. The crowds like an ocean roar.

It has begun.

We start in the plaza. After the plaza are five checkpoints.

The crystal entrance of Tall Titan's largest mall. The tourist canals that lead from the sea sector through to the zoos and parks. The grinding pit in the heart of the industrial zone. The top of the main night market gates. Then back again to the temple gates.

The checkpoints change every decade, but the course has always taken about half an hour to finish. Roaz boasts, of course, that he can close it in twenty minutes.

We're all standing at the starting line, on forty-five platforms several meters off the ground. The drumming has begun. I look over at Naqi's platform to see he's already looking back, and he flashes me a smile.

He signs at me, and I understand it: *may the best khab win.*

My heart aches. I want to laugh, and I want to cry.

A shout resounds throughout the square, and we whistlers wind up our stars.

A second shout resounds through the air, and we mount our anchors.

Silence falls. Silence shrouds everything. I breathe in and out, and the familiar heat of Gaia blooms through me from within. She swallows me whole, bloats and strains to the very seams of me, and the edges of everything I see become tinged by her gold.

I widen my stance. I grit my teeth.

A ram is pulled back before a great gong above us. The ram is released, and it swings in, in—the gong is struck.

With the sound still quaking through my bones, I leap.

I fall.

I fly.

The city is a blur. No one else is before me.

Gaia pumps through my veins, and I hurtle past and past building after building. I know these structures even in the frenzy of my speed, even in the dense visual noise of corners and edges and signs. I know this city better than anyone, better than even Roaz.

The others will be taking the main roads to the entrance of the mall. I will be taking a shortcut.

At the first junction, I flip into a loop and rotate down to the left, into a cluttered side street. It's a cramped thing, full of power lines and bulky building fans that jut out from the walls. I corkscrew past them, weave and bob out of the way and push on and on.

Behind me, I can hear the roar of someone's star. Someone's followed me. That someone is keeping up.

I have no time to worry about them. I fly on.

I see the mall. Past the tree line and the sprawling intersection of the skyway, it looms and gleams, all glass and marble and pristine architectural lines. The rich spend their capsules there at the many high-rising levels, at the many high-end stores. The tourists spend their time there, taking picture after picture.

In the sky above me is a screen mounted on the side of an aircraft. It drifts by slowly. I see myself on it, veil tousled, mask smooth. Behind me is Roaz. He's crouched low against his anchor so that the wind cuts over him, and he is gaining on me.

I'm not going to let that happen again.

I spin and twirl down, down, past the traffic of the air and back toward the ground, where the grand entrance of the mall is wide and waiting.

Briefly, I see a mighty fountain of crystal, its waters arching high. I see men in suits and women in heels and the glisten of polished perfection. I have never been in this space before. I have never been allowed.

I zoom through the mall entrance. To the sides of that entrance, digital posts flash green. That's one checkpoint down.

I flip and loop and crane past the obstacles of the mall—indoor trees and booths and displays—and see hall after hall, twist after turn. I am dizzy, but not from the flight. Panic has gripped me.

I'm lost.

I have never been here before. I don't know where the exit is.

Roaz overtakes me with enough force that I'm knocked to the side by the wind of him, and I roll in the air once, twice, before finding my balance. I grit my teeth and press on after him.

I track after his ichor line. I ride every bump and dip that he carves out. I'm gaining on him but will bide my time. I'll let him lead me out of the mall, first, before pushing ahead.

Escalators. Chandeliers. A wall of mirrors and glass.

I see the exit.

Roaz tucks against his anchor and corkscrews through the archway, and I follow suit. I break back out into the city. Afternoon light blinds for a moment, a moment more, and then my vision clears. I forge on ahead.

The canal is before us. Its waters are deep, and blue-green, and they twinkle like the chandeliers of crystal in the mall. Further down, in the far distance over the water, I see the second pair of checkpoint posts. They're all bright yellow lights, waiting.

Here, on the water, there is nothing in the way.

Here, there is nothing stopping me from overtaking Roaz.

So I look down at Gaia and tug on the cord against my leg.

I open my mind to her, and ask her for more, more. Throttle me far ahead.

Gaia does not speak. She never does. But with an impact like the heartbeat of a titan, ichor beats through me, claps through me, and my vision whites out from it. I gasp but stay in control. I remain firm on my anchor.

Now when I look down at myself, I see that all the edges of me are crusting over with gold. My nails and the sides of my wrists and my elbows are gilded by the dust of ichor.

Then like a whip of flame, I crack forward.

The world becomes smears I cannot comprehend; I'm soaring far too fast to be able to comprehend anything like shapes, like meaning. My skin is full of heat and full of starfire, but it doesn't hurt.

I feel *alive*.

I hurtle past Roaz, over the water, on and on along the canal. The line of my flight, the power of it, pulses waves over the water and over me—stars. I laugh. I'm laughing. I'm hooting and hollering and tossing my arms out wide, because this is what freedom feels like. I am unbound. I am free.

I blow through the posts. They blink green. My second checkpoint.

A dome of trees looms ahead, verdant and lush and dense like the city. It's the parks and the zoos, and I see some of the animals already, grazing by the edge of the trees.

There's a family of giant pandoons—tubby raccoon-like animals three times the size of a man—ambling and rolling, lazy on the grass. Their ears perk at the roar of my approach. They twist and turn and watch.

I'm coming in too fast.

My mind scrambles, alarmed.

Ease back, I tell Gaia. *Pull back, hurry. Leak your power away into yourself. Hurry, hurry.*

And she does—I feel the heat of her ichor sap away from me, and gold peels from my skin. But it's not leaving me fast enough. I told Gaia too late.

There's no stopping the full heat and speed and power of me now as I plow on, on, through the overgrown forests.

I tuck myself closer against the anchor. I prepare for the worst.

Brambles and branches and leaves overhead, around me, everywhere, dense. I swish and tilt and pan this way, that way. It aches, all this twisting and dodging, but if I don't, I'll crack into a tree and break all my limbs. At this speed, my arms and legs would pop clean off.

I zip past an enclosure, I think, and I see it too late—my anchor clips over a line, a metal wire, and that wire snaps. I go spinning.

I slam into a tree—the crash like a ram against my chest so that I'm winded, I can't breathe, and Roaz below me zips by. He's flying nearer to the ground to avoid the branches and the leaves, but that's bringing him straight through the enclosure.

The wire that snapped was holding up a fence, I think. I'm not sure. All I know is that I'm seeing movement of all sorts through the trees and the brush. I see fur, maybe. I see feathers.

Weaving over the water of the canal are the other whistlers. I can see them now. Two, three, more of them have passed through the second checkpoint. I see Naqi with them, I think. They're catching up.

I reorient myself. I shake out my head, hunker down, and continue onward.

The enclosure has fallen open. A herd of ostronis—towering, flightless birds that can outpace even hoverbikes—are bursting from their enclosure and bolting through the trees, and it's chaos, mayhem. The wildness of it all sets my heart pounding.

Flying between the birds is like flying between the roar of waterfalls, like whistling over earthquakes—my thoughts are trampled by the trampling of their feet over earth, through the forests. Fly too high, and I'll get a face full of branches. Fly too low, and I'll be ground into dust.

A flash of silver through the trees. Roaz.

I veer to the right and follow him. I press by the ostronis, past their hefty bodies and long necks, and when the tree line finally thins out, I yank up. I glide high and higher into the sky, blessed sky, and see in the far beyond our next checkpoint—the industrial zone.

It's a jagged profile of cranes, platforms, towers. Warehouses of steel and rust are laid out in grids like panels underneath the sun. Factories of domes and coils impose their shadows over everything, and linking between the factories are belts, still creaking and groaning, full of stone and metal.

I dive. With the wind like a scream against my ears, I level back out and spin into a corkscrew. The weight of the fall throws me forward, like a stone is thrown from a sling.

The third checkpoint is the grinding pit in the center of this zone, in the heart of one of its factories. I've long since lost sight of Roaz, so I can't ride his lines, and I've never bothered to spend much time in this sector before—but it won't matter.

All I need to do is follow the smell of sulfur.

Flying through this broad metalscape, all sounds bounce back to me. The hum of my anchor is a forlorn thing. I am alone in the stretched shadows.

I tilt down and ease back my speed, because I am now entering the mouth of the central factory. The shadow of the gate passes over me, swallows me, and then the dark gives way to something like hellfire.

All over are smelters and furnaces, billowing, roaring, gurgling on melted stone. They congregate around a great space, a vast pit—all swirling, sinking, saw-toothed edges, a graveyard of broken metal bones.

The barbed sounds, layering over and over one another, deafening, must be what losing your mind sounds like.

I see the checkpoint posts. They hover yellow over the center of the pit, blinking, waiting. I suck in a breath and angle forward. I glide close and closer to that ring of furnaces.

Heat like dragon's breath slams into me. I waver, and choke, and jerk back. I can't breathe. Smoke and steam sting over and around me. I cough and cough and cover my mask, and my skin is tight and smarting.

How am I supposed to reach the checkpoint like this? How is anyone going to reach it in this heat?

I don't have time to waste loitering here. Roaz likely already passed through this checkpoint, and the others will be catching up to me any minute.

"Veil!"

My head snaps up. Roaz is above me, lingering by the edge like me. He hasn't flown through yet.

He jerks his head to the side and hollers over the din, "I found a better way across!"

I frown—from the heat, and from my confusion. I don't know if I heard him right.

"This way!"

He yanks his anchor away and cuts behind a cluster of smelters. I linger, but I can't stay where I am, gawking and useless in the heat, and so I twist my anchor to the side. I follow.

I bob and weave through the half dark. I dodge cables and chains and wires. Here, from this new angle by the edge of the pit, there are fewer furnaces and smelters. It is easier to breathe. The air no longer simmers from the heat.

Roaz has already pushed ahead, over the pit, past the machines. He glides slowly, but smoothly, and I bob onto his line and glide along just the same.

He stops. He turns. He shouts back at me and holds out a hand, and I don't hear him, can't hear him—we're hovering directly over the pit, and sounds are a metal violence that screams—but I stop. He's warning me of something.

A groan. I twist to the side. A crane parts through the vapor and slams into me.

Something cracks. My arm, maybe. I don't know. I'm falling, falling; my thoughts are rattled.

I plummet into the pit. I crumple against the metal.

If Roaz hadn't turned and shouted for me to stop, I would have kept gliding along. The crane would've missed me.

The boy wasn't warning me of anything.

He was making sure I would fall.

(That morning in the kitchen, Roaz had turned to me and said, *I'll stop once the holy Veil gets hers.*

And you can bet that I'll make sure she does.)

Pain jars through me. My hands and knees have sliced open from the fall onto the bed of edges—another inch to the right and it would've been my eye, gouged straight through a spike. Pain jars through me again, but not from my cuts.

My omen stain has unfurled and is bristling. I see red.

There's no time, no time for my fury, not while the metal beneath me is shifting and swirling, sinking ever down to be ground and melted away. Above me, someone on an anchor streaks by and does not notice me. Another anchor zips by, and another. Everyone is overtaking me. I'm going to lose.

Or I'm going to die.

I push to my feet, then stumble back down onto my hands. My leg is caught in something. I look back and see my anchor is jammed into the mess of metal, and my leg is still bound to the cord of my star.

"Gaia," I wheeze, and I call for power, power enough to unwedge myself from this trap. Her body swells with light, and ichor floods through the cord and into me, and it hurts. With my stain unsettled as it is, Gaia's presence is all static against my veins.

The anchor groans, creaks, and strains. It doesn't move.

With my split-open hands, I scrabble against all the scraps that are wedging my anchor in. My grip slips from all my blood. There are too many parts and pieces pinning my anchor down, and when I dig one out, two more pile over the space as the metal churns. I'm sinking deeper, now. I can hear the grinding blades beneath me. I can feel the wind of their slice.

I roar. I roll onto my back and slam my feet against the top of the anchor, against the lock. I kick it again, and again. I stomp and stomp. My anchor cracks. Gaia understands, then, what I'm trying to do, and she flares bright, all heat, heat enough to weaken the metal of the anchor around her.

I scream, and kick again.

My anchor snaps in two.

The exposed half of the anchor—the half with Gaia and her

engine-lock—are freed, and I pull back, back, away from the narrowing eye of the pit, even as my scrambling cuts. There's no time.

Loosen from me, I say. And Gaia, with a sigh, loosens her cord from my leg.

Then I do what we are never supposed to do—I place my hand over the engine-lock, where Gaia burns, where water would sizzle into nothing but vapors.

I howl.

Gaia's heat bubbles my skin and cauterizes the cuts of my palm, and it rends at me, peels me raw. It hurts. It hurts. There's no time to hurt.

I grit my teeth and bare them. I grip my wrist to steady my arm. I look up at the checkpoint posts above me and focus there, zero in there. I'll have one shot.

Gaia's power is building. She understands what I want her to do.

Another whistler zooms by, then two more, then three more. It's now or never.

With Gaia's power bloating like far too much water behind too small a dam, and with her pointed toward the metal mound rumbling beneath me, I shout. I shatter the dam.

Power booms.

In a pure beam of light, I arch off the metal mound and out of the pit. Like a missile taking off, I blast through the posts—they blink green—and hurtle through the air. I've used Gaia like a thruster. I have to, without an anchor.

I shatter backward through a window. I fling through the bright of the afternoon. I crash through the tin roof of a warehouse and fall, and fall, and smash through scaffolding and beams, and then the cement ground rushes toward me.

I fling my arms out over my face.

I do not die.

I open my eyes.

Gaia has flooded me with zero gravity an inch—a breath—from the ground, and then she releases me. I thud onto the floor.

Stars. I'm alive. I'm still alive. I made it out of the pit and through the checkpoint, and I'm still alive. My crash resounds through the warehouse, and then silence opens out. I'm alone in the space of this silence, with the sunlight above me, with dust wafting still around me.

It's not good enough.

I strain to my feet. My body feels like the body of a strung-up puppet, all creaky joints and strings that tug every which way, because I can't find my balance. I'm dizzy. Aside from my cuts and my burns, my omen stain throbs. It spills over the whole of my back and even over my front, and it's a good thing my neck is covered. There's no hiding my stain now, not now, not in the pulsing waves of my pain.

I look down at Gaia. I've left her on the ground and am uncorded from her, though she burns on. I can feel the whisper of her presence even now, a presence like incense that clings.

I've two more checkpoints left to fly through, but it's too late now. I've lost. I can't fly like this. It's a miracle I'm even alive. I don't know what to do.

I fist my hands.

Hell and void.

I've lost? I can't fly like this?

I'm pathetic. Utterly. I disgust myself. Don't know what to do? There's only one thing left to do.

There's only one thing I *can* do.

The night markets this afternoon are abuzz with life.

Confetti rains. Banners fly. People like bees bustle and bump along the crowded walkways and balconies. The streets are gridlocked. Colors saturate the eye from fans and masks and flags that wave. There is no rest from the visual feast.

A massive screen hovers on a news-blimp, and it displays in full color and sound the whistlers and their race.

Roaz was first to pass through the second-last checkpoint, followed closely by Naqi, and then others—eight, nine, ten others. The rest follow. Lumi's friend is among the stragglers, finishing off the forty-five.

No. Forty-four.

Where is Lumi, people ask. Where is the Veil, people wonder.

Was she not leading the group along with Roaz? What happened after the pit? With all the smoke and heat, the camera couldn't follow. No one could see what took place.

From the edge of the night market, people have begun shouting.

Like a fire, gasping and screaming spreads.

A rocket hurtles by.

Banners are torn. Flags are loosed. Women cling to their hair and skirts from the force of the wind that follows. Men topple and shout, and like some rail gun of air, a path is blown open above the crowd.

The cameras strain to keep up, but the rocket is a snap—a quick sound, then gone.

It's not a rocket.

People are shouting again, and pointing, and then, like the swell of a wave, they swell with cheering.

It's Lumi. It's me.

I am clinging to a piece of my anchor, and my cord is laced around my arm. Gaia in her engine-lock is carrying me forward with a speed that blurs and bends, and she hauls me up and over the gates of the market and through the checkpoint. The fourth.

There's one more left to go.

I land between the posts at the top of the gate, and from this height, I look out over the plaza.

Flying without an anchor is like boarding down a slope without a board, or like skating over ice without skates. I'm exposed. I'm without control. The only thing I can do is tell Gaia where to go before she flies us into a building, and to hang on, hang on if I want to live, and to win.

I'm in last place.

I look down at my anchor and my hand.

Back in the warehouse, I found what tools I could and bent the top of the anchor so that I had something of a handle to hold on to. I bound my hand to that handle so that I would not slip, and then I spent far too long relearning how to fly.

The heart of Gaia's propulsion is no longer tied to my leg, and my body is no longer anchored to something. There is no foundation for stability. There is no framework for control.

So in that warehouse I flailed and floundered. I crashed into walls. I scraped along the ground. My robes are torn. My body is set rigid, like cement, by aches and bruises.

I'm going to make it to the finish line.

I'm going to make it there even if it kills me.

I turn around. I grip my wrist like that time in the grinding pit and aim Gaia down at the crowds.

"Out of the way!"

The crowds, confused, push back where they can. I aim at that patch of open space and suck in my breath and build up Gaia's power.

Don't stop, I tell her.

Even when I let go, keep pushing, keep throttling us along. Give it everything you've got. We won't make it, otherwise.

Gaia answers by brightening. Her light is like a slice, cutting to look at, but I don't look away, even as the crowds cower and gasp and cover their eyes. I brace my legs against a checkpoint post to hold steady. My arm quakes, but I do not stop. My teeth ring, but I do not stop.

I build the power for two more beats, three more beats.

I let go.

My consciousness blanks.

I pass out, I think, for a breath, for two.

When I come to, I am rending through the air, through the skies, with the world sprawling below me. Gaia has reoriented herself so that she is hauling me behind her, so that the dust of her ichor line cakes over me. I can't tell how fast we're going. All I understand is the roaring in my ears and the roaring in my veins.

Joy.

Gaia is exuberant to be flying like this.

I look down and see that the temple plaza is fast approaching. I see ten or so whistlers before me, spread out, eyes locked ahead. They notice me only after my shadow passes over them, and they gape.

There's another group of ten. They hear the roar of my coming and look over their shoulders, eyes wide. When I blow past them with Gaia, they are buffeted like leaves in the wind.

I see four more whistlers. Beyond them, I see the final

checkpoint—towering posts of gleaming gold with the digital font displaying END over them. Beyond that, I see those that have already passed the finish line.

There's a good twenty there, at least. Maybe more. I may have already lost.

A question taps against my mind. Gaia is asking me what I want.

To win is what I want. To make my wish is what I need.

After everything, everything, I can't afford to lose now.

Gaia speaks.

Are you worthy, she says, *of your wish?*

You know I'm not.

Will you become worthy of your wish?

I don't understand. What does she mean? What is she saying? Something like that, is it even possible?

Gaia doesn't answer. There's no more time left to answer. The four whistlers ahead of us are nearing the goalposts, and there's half a moment left to overtake them. It's now or never.

Something happens.

The world whites out. Shapes in black lines scrawl. One moment I have breath in my lungs, and the next I have nothing, nothing. I feel my existence shuddering. My sight stutters out.

I blink back in, warp back in, nearer to the posts than before. The four whistlers are around me and behind me. Gaia has done something—stars, I don't know. I don't know how any of this is possible.

My binding around the anchor loosens. My grip slips.

I wrench hard against the cord as I fall, and it yanks Gaia off course. She veers to the side and up, and then I break entirely from the cord. I drop.

I tumble.

I skid over the ground and roll through the dust. My mask splinters and cracks.

I roll like this for a long, long while, where up is down and down is up, and maybe I've broken all my bones because pain blares over me.

Finally, finally, the momentum of my rolling slows. It stops. The dust settles.

Silence shrouds.

I don't move, not for a while. If I do, I will learn that all my limbs are no longer attached to me. I twitch. I test the boundaries of my body—my arms are still working. So are my legs.

I push gingerly, gingerly, to my hands. I look up.

I've passed the checkpoint posts. So have the others. The straggling groups are nearing the posts as well and are gliding through.

What happened? Where's Gaia?

Someone helps me to my feet and places their hand on my cheek. Naqi. His hand is on my cheek because my mask has cracked open, and part of my face is revealed. He's hiding it for me.

"My star," I croak.

"It's all right. People saw where she went. They're going after her now."

I swallow. I don't think I can stand for much longer.

"The race. Did I—?"

Naqi's face is solemn. He shakes his head, but it doesn't mean no. He's not sure if I made it. In the chaos of that ending, no one is sure.

I see Roaz. He's standing to the side, eyes wide on me.

Even drained as I am, burned out as I am, my anger simmers. Above us, a screen has begun displaying the names of the twenty-four that passed, the ones that will move on to the second round.

Naqi has his arm cradled around my waist, and I let him hold me up. His hand is still covering the break in my mask, and I let him. We watch the screen. I forget to breathe.

Roaz is first. Naqi came second. Third is a girl named Arba. Fourth is another girl named Ochre.

On and on, the names are listed. Ten, twelve, fourteen names. Twenty names. Twenty-one.

Twenty-second is a girl named Frea.

Twenty-third is a boy named Kry.

Twenty-fourth—does not come. The last row remains empty, taunting, extending the agony of the wait. The screen cuts to a video playback of the final checkpoint posts. I see myself—a wild tousled thing hanging on to the tail of Gaia. I see the other four whistlers.

The video is playing frame by frame, and in one I'm a plume of dust. In another, I'm a burst of light. Another, I'm gone. The next I've reappeared, but I've jumped to the midst of the group, to very nearly the front of them. I didn't imagine it.

Gaia teleported me.

People all around me are murmuring. Is that even possible? Can stars do that?

"It wasn't a port," Naqi says, like he's read my mind. His smile is lit by awe when he says, "Lumi was going so fast, the frames couldn't keep up."

And there, in the final frame, the video zooms in. I see the outstretched fingers of the girl racing against me, and the jagged lines of my broken anchor, and I see the outer line of the posts. Whoever touches that line first wins.

The video rolls on tick by tick, tick by tick.
My anchor and her fingers inch close and closer.
I do not blink, even as my eyes sting.
I do not breathe, even as my lungs sting.
My anchor touches the line first.
Gaia did it.
I've won.

FOURTEEN

It's a blur, after. I pass out more than once, from the pain, from exhaustion.

I'm brought back inside the temple, away from the eyes of those who are forbidden from seeing a Veil's face, and patched up in the infirmary. I've caught scrapes and bruises all over. My knees are split open. My palm is a mottled mess. It's a miracle of Gaia that none of my bones are broken.

I'm given new robes, a new veil and mask. I'm given a new anchor and questioned on what happened.

I fell, is what I say. Got knocked into the pit, is what I say.

I don't mention Roaz.

One of the Suns starsings a song of healing over me, and when the line settles over my skin, it tingles. When I watch the cuts on my skin, I see them knit back together before my eyes.

Naqi arrives with Roaz. They were both enduring interview after interview by the gates of the temple, since Roaz was first place, and Naqi was second.

I wait until the Sun has finished his song. I wait until he leaves. Then I turn to Roaz. He stands with his arms crossed over his broad chest, and his expression is barbed over. Naqi reads the thickness of the air between us, and frowns.

"What's going on?"

I say nothing. I pin my gaze on Roaz and am silent in my stillness. His expression twitches, vexed.

"If you've got something to say, then say it, Veil."

"I've got nothing to say," I tell him. "Not to you."

"Go on and tell the others, then. You don't need my permission."

"That what you want?"

"Does it matter?"

I open my mouth, then, to ask, to demand: Why? Why did you do it? How could you go through with your plan at the pit?

Except I already know the answer. It's the same reason as me and Lumi at the tent, when I let my jealousy choke me blind, when I let my anger string me into its puppet.

I remember Gaia, and what she said. To become worthy.

I close my mouth and shake my head.

Roaz deserves to be disqualified.

But so do I.

"I won't tell."

Roaz stills. Disbelief sinks into him. "What?"

I don't repeat myself, because I don't know if this is what Gaia wants me to do. I don't know if I've made the right choice.

I push past the boys and stride off and away. Naqi doesn't follow me, not right away. I hear him speaking to Roaz, his voice low and soft. I hear Roaz replying, voice thin as breath.

197

We're all given a night and a day of rest. The second stage will take place after.

When night shades in, all the whistlers—even the ones that didn't pass—take to the city. They take to the lights and the drinks and the hot and spicy foods, to the arcades and games and the high of being recognized. People point and gasp and ask for pictures. It's a once-in-a-lifetime experience, and they are out to experience it all.

The acolytes and Suns are given leave to enjoy the night, as well. Pea is beyond herself. She throws her arms around my shoulders and squeezes me tight. She loops her arm with mine and tugs.

"You flew an incredible race," she says. "And now you deserve a break!"

I don't think I deserve anything like that.

So I squeeze Pea's arm and tell her to go instead. *Enjoy yourself*, I say.

I manage a smile, because I've learned how to wear something that looks like one by now, and tell her to enjoy the night for me.

Pea pouts but doesn't argue. I pass her the capsules I have left over from last time, and she trills and promises to buy me a souvenir.

Naqi doesn't go with Pea. He decides to stay in with me.

"Don't stay because of me, khab," I say.

"Bold of you to assume I'm staying for you," he says, smug, so I know that that's exactly why he's staying.

So I tell him about a ramshackle theater by the edge of the old district, one that plays antique films using antique reel cameras, and how there's an upper section in the rafters that we could sit in and hide so that we don't have to pay.

Naqi's smile blooms at the idea of it, though he asks if I'm sure. He knows the Suns prescribed me plenty of sleep for healing.

I say yes, I'm sure, because I sleep better in the noise.

I don't tell him it's because sounds blot out my thoughts. I don't tell him it's because he'll be there, blotting out everything else.

In the dark of the theater, underneath the play of lights from the camera that whirls and beams, I see Esp.

Her silver minidress is made up of layered sequins, and the large squares of them shake like leaves, shimmer like diamonds. Her hair is pixie short and curly and neon blue. She's wearing a half mask of a smiling demon.

I tell Naqi I'm going to get some snacks, and he offers to get them for me, and I tell him I need to use the washroom anyway, so I might as well get the snacks. So he passes me his capsules, and I go—I crawl down from where we're hidden and squeeze past the crowds.

I wind my way outside the theater.

From a distance, I follow Esp as she turns and leads.

She takes us to a side street, then an alley, and in the dark of that alley—before the locked and chained doors of a warehouse—waits a cluster of men and women and children. Omens. These are the Omens I used to run with.

We look at one another, but do not speak.

Their dark eyes flash like polished stones you hurl to hurt.

Esp unlocks the warehouse lock and unwinds the chains. The doors groan as they open. I enter after her. The others enter after me.

Here, the shuffle of our steps echoes. The sounds of the streets fall away, mute into blurred murmurs. The others filter off between the rows of shelves while I'm led past crate after crate and box after box. Some of the boxes are already cracked open, but I don't see what's inside. Their shapes are hazy in the dim.

A hovercar zooms by outside, headlights panning through the dark, and in that brief scan of light I see iron bars, chains, a cluster of dark shapes huddled by a far wall. The light passes. I pull rigid, cold. Every hair on my body pricks in fear.

I saw Omen monsters chained in the dark.

Hulking things. Hunched things. Black as oil and dripping, dripping.

I see them even now, the outlines of them darker than shadow as they shift and breathe inside their cages. Who are these Omens? Where did they come from? Why does Esp have them caged in her warehouse?

Is that what I looked like, when I fully transformed?

Esp is looking at me; I can feel her eyes. So I look back at her and open my mouth to ask, but she cuts me off with, "Save your questions." She says, "It's not for you to know."

I stifle my frown. "When can I know?"

"What happened in the race?" she asks instead.

Esp still doesn't trust me. Even now, after everything, I'm still unworthy.

But maybe she's right not to trust me. I told Gaia, after all, that I'll be making a different wish. And, maybe, a part of Esp senses that I've changed.

I look down. I answer, "Sabotaged."

"By?"

"It doesn't matter. It won't be a problem anymore."

Esp stops. Her silence is steely, like the towering metal shelves fencing us in all around. Far above us, moonlight slants silver through a high window.

"That's not good enough." Her voice chills.

I fist my hands. "What do you want me to do, then?"

Out him? Sabotage him back? Hurt him the way he hurt me?

Esp says, "Change of plans."

I pause.

"It's clear you won't be able to handle the rest of the stages."

I don't understand. "What?"

"Too much is riding on your success. We can't afford another mishap like today, and we can't afford a loss. So we're forgoing the plan. We strike the day of the second round."

What? What is Esp saying? Nothing she's saying is making sense.

Another vehicle outside hovers by, headlights flashing. In that moment of panning lights, I see the shapes inside the boxes and crates.

Guns. Assault rifles. Submachine guns. Mines and grenades.

The light passes. Esp and I are shrouded back in darkness, gilded by silver.

My heart rattles. My voice is a wisp of smoke. "What does this mean?"

Esp does not explain the weapons. She doesn't need to. She's always been a keen edge, a clinical incision. I've always known that her hand knew well the shape of a gun.

She says instead, "What you did to that boy at the pool. You still remember?"

I'm too stiff to nod, but of course I still remember.

Esp continues.

"On the day of the second round, the day of the starsongs,

when everyone is gathered in the plaza—you're going to do there the same thing you did to that boy."

She says, "Sing the line you wrote that night. Curse the people. Stain their skin. Sing them into Omens, all of them, every last one of them."

In the silver of the moonlight, Esp smiles.

It looks the same, exactly the same, as the smile of her demon's mask.

That's what she wants. Monsters. Monsters she's always believed were lurking beneath their unmarred skin.

Monsters that she can kill.

After the movie, on our walk back to the temple, Naqi beside me says, "You know you can tell me anything, right?"

I don't stop walking. "That came out of nowhere."

"I mean: you know you can trust me, right?"

I say nothing.

Naqi looks at me, sighs, and says, "I can tell something is bothering you, okay?"

I narrow my eyes and repeat, "You can tell?"

"Yeah. You're easier to read than you think you are."

"Don't be annoying, khab."

"Lu."

"Drop it," I tell him, and he replies by taking my wrist.

He tugs me to look at him and asks, softly, "What are you afraid of?"

I want to tell him: *You.*

I am afraid of you, for you, of me and the things I could do to you.

But I don't know how to say it without breaking into a thousand pieces. So I say instead: "I'll kiss you if you drop it."

His hand around my wrist twitches. He forgets to move, or to blink, and maybe he forgets to breathe. He looks at me with red creeping over his cheeks and ears, and down his neck. He asks, "What?"

"You heard me." And I say it again, because I want to say it again. "I'll kiss you."

He scowls. He jerks away. He's still red, so red, when he says, "I'm trying to be serious here."

"Who says I'm not?"

Naqi shakes his head and turns away. He walks briskly away from me, shoulders tight. The tips of his ears are still red.

Gaia would be able to do it.

My meek star of before wrote an omen stain that was temporary, one that stung but faded.

Gaia's curse would be permanent.

And if Esp wants monsters, then I could write madness into their skins. Rage. Loss of control. The crowds that gather for the second round would stand there, trapped by one another's bodies, eyes aimed up at the beauty of my line—beautiful because they wouldn't know the things I was writing.

All they would understand was the wind of my flight and the gold of my line, and then their bodies would crack out of shape.

I should have never told Esp what I did at the pool.

The night before the second stage, Naqi crawls into our nest in the tree by the hole in the wall. He tucks beside me on the blankets, the cushions, and doesn't say a single word. He doesn't look at me.

We lie in silence.

"Lu?"

"Mmm."

"Are you happy here?"

I frown, but don't answer. After a while, I say, "This about last night again?"

"I don't know. Maybe."

"Maybe you should cut it out."

"I'm being serious, Lu."

"So am I."

"Please." And Naqi pushes up onto his elbow. He turns to hover over me. "Please."

When I look at him, with the lantern lights hazy behind him, I see that his brows are crumpled, that his eyes are pinched, that the skin around his eyes is puffed. He's about to cry. Naqi is about to cry.

Panic grips me. This isn't fair. This isn't fair.

"Hell and void, Naqi."

"Sorry," he flusters. "I don't know why I'm—it's just, I have a bad feeling. I was meditating with Togarath and . . . I don't know. You're happy here, right? You like the lessons. You love flying. Nobody can fly as fast as you."

And then *he* says, he says: "Let's leave."

I stare. He pushes on. "Let's get away. We can pack our things or whatever we want, and slip out, and sneak onto a transport, out of this city, off this planet. We could go and find my parents. They'd love you. And I bet you'd love them too. They're real funny, did you know?"

"Naqi."

"No. You're not listening. And you're not, not—nothing needs to happen. We don't have to stay down here, looking up. We could be up there instead. We could draw shapes between the stars with our travels."

I reach out. It's an unthinking thing.

I touch Naqi's cheek, and then under his eye, because maybe I could catch his tears if they fell. I want to tell him. I want to tell him everything, but I don't know how.

"Please, Lu."

I shake my head. I pull away. I push to my feet and climb out of our nest, and I pretend I don't hear Naqi calling my name behind me.

FIFTEEN

The day of the second race. It's a day that chills, a day full of wind.

I'll be watching by the edge of the plaza, Esp said.

My people will be waiting, she said.

She didn't say it, but I know they'll be waiting with edges in their hands, with triggers and pins that are ready to be pulled. The white of the plaza stones plus a crowd of people like paints—easy, so easy to splatter open.

A wide stage has been erected in the center of the plaza. The starsongs have already begun.

Lumi's friend is whistling *tekiah'taqa*—trumpet blast. And she strings *yafa* all around that blast so that the sounds mold into beautiful things, moving things, things that uplift.

The whistler she is flying against is a boy with a mole on his cheek, and he whistles *makeem'ainfa*, and from his wide lines, polished sweets burst forth into existence and fall, and the crowd laughs and stretches out their palms to catch and to eat.

The winner is decided by the volume of the cheering they receive.

The boy wins.

I'm up next.

I don't know the name of the girl I'm flying against, and I have no space to care, to think. Naqi is up after me. He's flying against someone whose name I also don't know, and he's sneaking glances at me, again and again. That feeling he had last night lingers even now.

I mount the stage.

The other whistler goes first. She is whistling *mha* and *agnia*, and I'm looking out over the crowd. Esp is there somewhere, standing in some shadow, waiting, watching, watching to see if I will let her down again.

The girl's song ends. I hear applause and cheering—all distant burbled things—and someone is announcing my turn, so I step onto my anchor. I lace up to the cord, and ichor floods.

I fly.

I circle the stage in a lazy loop. I ponder the world from my height. I circle higher, higher, whistle soft and shy, and then I begin.

A smear-circle-smear, four loops, a gap, a perfect swirl.

Arah—expose.

It's easier flying this line the second time around.

Far below me, I see movement. People are parting through the crowds, I think. I see out the corner of my eye people shifting by the stage. Most of the whistlers recognize my line. They understand its meaning, and the meaning that followed.

Avah. Sin. The sin of the Omens.

I twist into another pattern of smears—*H*. I fly a tight loop for *A*. I spin out into another loop, and people are shouting. There's commotion on the stage. A Sun is pushing people out of the way, I think. Some of the whistlers are getting onto their anchors, to dip away and flee maybe, or to whistle up to stop me.

I jerk hard to the left, ride the curve to a point, then swing back into a spark of starfire. *K.*

Avah has been turned into *Kavah*. Wound. Sickness.

And then I fly the line for healing, the same line I've seen Naqi fly time and time again over Roaz, the same line that was flown over me for my bruises and cuts.

Rapha—a circle and three dots, six loops, a looped swirl with a smear.

Expose their wounds and heal them. Expose their sicknesses and cure them.

I dip down and away from my line, and hover, and watch.

The light of my ichor line scatters into dust and light. It falls slow like snow over the crowd, over the gathered thousands. The dust melts into their skins, and then something like a sigh passes over them all.

People are gasping, and laughing, eyes up and bright. They look at each other with wonder. They feel rejuvenated. That ache in their tooth is gone. That pain in their hip is no more. The fatigue of the day and of the sun has slid off them like rain over glass, and they are lighter and brighter for it. They raise their hands and rejoice.

Their cheering for me thunders.

I've won.

I land back on the stage and look over at Naqi, but I can't see him, not right away.

There. He's there. I see him.

His smile on me makes me want to sing.

A speaker squeals, pierces, and the crowds cower from the pain of it. They grip their ears. I grip my ears. When the squealing cuts out, I look up.

Esp is on top of a large booth with a speaker mic held in her hand.

Her hair is full and like lava, dark at the roots and bright at the ends. She's strapped tight in leather, looking ready for war. On her face is half a white mask and half a pair of red lips, and to her side is another woman, someone I've never seen before.

Esp passes that woman the mic, and she takes it.

Trembling, she presses the mic to her lips. Trembling, she presses the button.

"That girl," she says, "is not Lumi Sidik."

Not Lumi Sidik, she says.

The woman is older, dark from the sun, with lines etched over her brows and around her mouth—laugh lines. She's not laughing, not now. Her body is quivering. I think it's fear, until she lifts her hand and points her finger, her finger like an accusation, like the barrel of a gun.

"That girl is an Omen. And she killed my daughter."

Lumi's mother. Lumi's poor farm-colony mother is here, on this planet, in this city, and she knows the truth, all of it. How. How?

Esp is watching me. Her mask is smiling.

"She deceived her way into the same school as my daughter and abused her kindness, and on the day of the Joining, she used her omen to beat her to death, to take her place. She tore my Lumi's veil off her and posed as her, masqueraded as her. All this time, mocking her death, trampling on all that she is. That, right there, is not a Veil. That, right there, is a *monster*."

The crowds are stirring. Confusion brews. Unease simmers.

I'm locked where I am. I need to move. I need to turn away and leave the stage, or I need to open my mouth and deny the woman—I am Lumi. You can't prove otherwise. There are no pictures of me anywhere. No one aside from you has seen Lumi's face.

But people have seen *my* face, Sozo's face.

People from my school. Esp's omens. They're here at the stage or scattered through the crowds, and I've been careful to keep my mask and veil on around those who would know my face, but now. Now—

I don't know why I can't move. I don't know why I can't speak.

I'm strapped beneath the blade of my sins and I'm waiting for it to fall.

Suns have taken hold of me, but their grips are loose, unsure. Esp takes the mic from Lumi's mother and says, "Her left shoulder blade."

She says, "Her omen mark is there, one that she hides, though she can't hide it for long."

Why, why—

Esp.

If ever I had a daughter, she would be like you.

Everything I ever did (my lie in the dead end, my lies at the school, Lumi, Lumi) was for you, for *you.*

I don't notice the state of my omen. By the time I do, it's already frosted like ice over glass, over my shoulder and to my hips, my front. Just a little more, and I know my omen will peek through and out. I can't breathe. I can't breathe.

People have begun to shout.

Get these women out of here, some cry. *They're holding up the show.*

An Omen in the race, some gasp. *How could they allow such a thing?*

A dead girl. A dead Veil. If what this mother said is true, that thing on the stage must really be a monster.

Guardians are wading through the crowd and heading toward the booth, toward Esp and Lumi's mother. Other people have come to my side—Lumi's friend. Naqi.

Naqi positions himself between me and the crowd, like the body of this singular boy could be a shield for me against the whole of the world, and it aches. My heart aches.

Naqi.

Naqi who saw me and stayed, and still I lied to him.

Naqi who knew something was wrong, and still I lied to him.

He begged me to run away with him.

We could've been up there by now, in that broad blackness like beauty, making believe a better life, drawing shapes between the stars with our travels.

Lumi's friend is looking at me with wide wild eyes; all the dots are connecting for her—the way I've acted, the things I've said. My weeks in the temple and how unlike Lumi every one of my acts has been.

"Lumi." Her voice is a string about to snap. "I'm sorry, but, will you—will you let us see your face? No. Me. Just me is fine. Let *me* see your face."

The girl has never seen Lumi's face, but she's seen the faces of those she went to school with. And if what the mother said is true, there would be the possibility of her recognizing mine beneath the mask.

It's not just a possibility.

She's seen my face, Sozo's face.

She's passed me in the halls of our school, sat in the same classrooms. She's seen me at the training pit, alone with my anchor, unkind and hostile. She will know who I am.

The girl stretches her hands toward my veil and—my understanding crashes back over me.

"No." I wrench my arms away from the Suns and jerk back from her. "No."

It's the wrong thing to say. It's the *worst* thing to say.

The girl's expression blanches, and she looks in that moment like a ghost—wide of eyes, slack of mouth, gaze set stormy by the admission found in my no.

"Show us your face, Lumi." Her breath catches. "If that's even your name."

Naqi has turned, and he's frowning.

"Frea." Ah. The girl's name is Frea. I never even bothered learning her name.

He says, "You can't be serious. You're Lumi's friend."

"Exactly." Her voice wobbles. "It's exactly because I'm her friend. I've always found it bizarre—startling, even—how much she changed after the Joining. I always blamed it on something that happened with the Joining star, but this—all of this makes sense, now. Show me your face. *Show me.*"

The Suns are gripping my arms now. The guardians have reached the booth. If Esp and the woman are wrong, then they will be arrested for disrupting the race. If Esp and the woman are right, then I, I—

My veil is pulled back.

My mask is torn off.

I am exposed.

(Someone. Someone.

Can anyone save me?)

Frea rears back and wails. The mother tears at her hair and weeps.

(There's a humming in my ears. Frea's slapped me. My robe is torn open from the back, and it's cold. It's a day that chills, a day full of wind.

They can all see my stain now.

Murderer. Killer. Omen scum.

Put it to death! Death! Death!

My arm is twisted behind my back. I'm knocked onto my knees. Someone fists their hand in my hair and backhands me, and I hear Esp's voice over the speaker, saying: "She's caused nothing all her life but distress and grief. Treated people as things. Thought only of herself, of what she could get out of them."

It's not true. It's not true.

—Is it?

Dispose of her, they cry. Toss her body outside the gates and dig for her no grave.

I'm passed from the stage and away, away, through the surging and seething crowd. I'm no longer a Veil to them, a *girl* to them, just a vessel to be soiled—spit splatters over me, my cheek and my hair. Women hope hurts upon me. Men grab their parts at me and reveal to me the things that will be done to bile like me.

It's what you deserve. It's what you deserve.

It is what I deserve.)

SIXTEEN

They bind me and put me in my old cell, the one I stayed in that
first time in the temple. They won't kill me, not yet, not during the
Decade-Races. The blood of my death would bring only stains and
bad luck, after all.

My jaw is swollen. My cheek is split. In the rocked frenzy of
the crowd, Esp slipped away. The mother, a solitary figure lonely
on her height, wept on.

The High Suns stand before my cell. The guardians fan around
them. All of them ask me questions: *Where is the real Lumi? What
is your real name? What is your relation to that red-headed woman?
Why did you do it?* How *could you do it?*

I tell them nothing.

There's no point now, no point at all.

They confiscate Gaia from me and store her for the moment
in a steel locker in another cell down the trench, because they are
unsure how a star like Gaia could have accepted something like
me. Perhaps the star has been corrupted, somehow. Such a thing
shouldn't be possible.

The High Suns and others are leaving. Yashi is my guard once more, and she takes her place to the side of the grate, and she does not look at me.

The races will continue as normal, though guardians and police will be deployed in searching the city of Tall Titan for the body of Lumi Sidik. A few days after the Decade-Races officially end, I will be executed on the stage in the plaza, before the eyes of all.

I wonder if they will use a bolt gun, the same kind of gun from years ago, against the canvas of that white wall, against the head of that blue-eyed girl.

I see Naqi. He's come to the cells.

Back at the plaza, I kept my eyes down, because seeing Naqi and the faces he might have worn—I would have shattered open.

Now I rise to my feet and climb up the ladder. I press against the grate.

The High Suns have stopped him. They stand stoic before the boy, murmuring. I don't hear what they say. Naqi hangs his head, looks up at me several times, and does not smile.

They don't let us speak. They tell me nothing else. Naqi is led away with a hand on his shoulder, and he looks back at me the entire time. His neck strains against the turn and the distance. His eyes cling like grasping, desperate hands. My cheek sinks into the lines of the grate, and I do not blink. My eyes burn and water, and I do not blink.

I don't dare blink; Naqi's back and neck and needy eyes will be the last things I ever see of him.

In the middle of the night, someone rattles my grate.

I turn, and look up, and see Pea.

Yashi is standing guard to the side, eyes gleaming in the moon-light. She says nothing with her hands, to me or to Pea, so I push up from my bed. I move to the ladder, though I don't climb. I stand there, looking up, waiting.

For a long while, Pea says nothing. She watches me in the dim. Her hands are fisted against her robes.

I remember how she used to touch the back of my hand.

I remember, seated by the edge of my hammock, how she said, *You can talk to me, you know? Whatever is on your mind. Anything. I'll listen.*

So I open my mouth.

I say, croak out, "I'm sorry, Pea."

My voice is a crumpled thing. My heart is a crumpled thing.

"I should have—told you everything. I should have—never been here. I . . . I can't run anymore from the things that I've done, and I'm . . . I'm scared, Pea."

I'm so scared. I'm terrified. Why didn't I die instead of Lumi?

And then Pea opens her mouth.

She says, "Good."

She says, "You should be scared. It's what you deserve. But you talking about it? Thinking you deserve to be comforted? To be helped? It's sick."

Her voice is all coils, coiled, like a snake.

"You've hurt so many people. Lied to so many. Staying scared is the only thing you deserve, nothing else. I don't know your real name; Frea's catatonic and won't speak. But your real name is a curse, and I came to say that we'll all be glad when you're gone."

She turns, and leaves, and melds back into the night.

She's right.

Rama is right.

Of course. That's why it hurts.

It hurts because I keep thinking that maybe, maybe, it's not true—the things they call me, the things they throw. Maybe Esp's words about me are not the etched laws of who I am. And maybe I can be saved. Somehow, someone will look at me and see me and choose to stay, choose to help, because maybe there's still something in me worth saving.

But that's a lie. Of course.

When my omen stain thickens over me, all of me—cracking and growing my bones and teeth and nails—I don't stop it.

I will give myself once and for all to what I was always meant to be, to what I always have been and always will be—a monster.

(I understand the world in clicks.

Click, click, again, again. I hear the whine of a pitch that holds. It keens higher, louder, like a kettle screaming, like something evil stepping close and closer.

I can't see, not really, though I understand shapes and colors. I don't know up from down from in from out, and it's like I'm seated in a storm, blown and tossed. A thunder-like rage crashes over me.

This will be my life now, for the rest of forever. Forever, until someone puts me down.

I've broken out of the cell. The trench is caked white like a flour mill because I've blown through everything, and rubble tumbles over and around me. My hands and knees and feet are like those of an animal, and I ravage through cell after cell, just because I can.

A bright light. I remember I used to know this light.

A large tree. I remember I used to know this tree.

Someone is shouting, or laughing, I don't know—but it's wet and wrong and broken. I hate the sound. I hate it.

So I turn on it and open my jagged maw, and then that someone raises their hands and smears out a smile and says, "Don't shoot."

Oh.

Oh.

Something is wrong. It hurts. Everything hurts. This someone has shot me. He must've. He's shot me clean through.

I never knew words could hurt like bullets.

A sense pops open between my brows, a sense like light dawning.

I feel the beats of a boy's heart inside my chest.

I feel the heat of his blood in my veins.

I hear the roar of a monster and see the diseased hide of one, and then I see that my hands—not my hands, the hands of that boy—are clutched on a star. Pain jars through me, through him. Heat like spikes pierces through the boy's body because of what he's doing with the star, but he does not let go. He reaches up and touches my not-face, my not-cheek, and isn't afraid.

An image flickers behind my eyes: the boy knocking his fist against his chest and kissing it to his forehead.

Ya'tuv mi-eh.

I'm slipping. I'm falling.

My understanding is sapped from me.

The world gives way to dark.)

I come to by the tree underneath the hole in the wall.

My robes are tatters. My omen falls from me like matted fur. I understand two things:

Yashi is here with her hand on her sling, and beside her is an anchor.

Naqi is here with his hand around a star, and he is lying on his back.

His head is in my lap. I don't know how it happened. All I know is that omen stains are creeping over his skin, over Naqi's skin.

His skin has been stained.

The black scabs crawl up his neck and over his mouth, and over his eyes and ears. He doesn't move.

What is this?

What have I done?

I snap my head up to Yashi.

"Yashi," I quake. "What is . . . what did I—?"

She holds up a hand: *Stop.* She looks off into the brush and listens.

People are coming.

Rama went to get help, or people simply heard for themselves the roar and the rage of me, bulldozing through the cells and the trees and Naqi . . . Naqi. If people saw him now, like this, what would they do to him? Lock him up like me, or worse? Stars, stars. What do I do? What have I done?

Yashi is standing before me now, and her movements are clipped, quick. She replaces the star in her sling with the star that Naqi is holding—it's Gaia. Why was he holding Gaia? Wasn't she locked away?

She winds Gaia up and slams her into the lock of the anchor, and then she takes me by my arm and wrenches me to my feet.

She explains nothing, not with grunts, not with her hands. She lifts Naqi up and drapes him over my back and places my hands beneath his thighs to support him. Then she hauls us up the tree, into the cradle of the tree, all with the anchor in tow.

Suns and guardians are breaking through the brush now. They carry with them lanterns and torches and lit stars, the fires harsh and crackling. They know where we are. They've gathered around the roots of the tree.

Yashi thrusts me into the hole toward the edge, and I don't understand. I don't understand anything. Why is Yashi doing this?

She guides the silver cord around my leg and then kisses her forehead gently, gently, against the lock. She closes her eyes and communes. She is speaking to Gaia. When her eyes open once more, she pushes at me and pushes at me until I'm teetering by the edge.

"Yashi." My voice is a shattered thing. "I don't . . . what are you—"

She shakes her head at me: *Don't, don't ask.*

She points at the horizon behind me: *Go, go now.*

A Sun has climbed up the tree and is scrabbling at Yashi's heels, and she gives me no time to think, no choice to think—she shoves me and Naqi off the wall. We fall.

I don't let go of Naqi.

Ichor bleeds through me, and the anchor realigns with the soles of my feet, and then we are flying, I don't know where. Gaia is taking us somewhere, somewhere Yashi disclosed to her.

The sky is thick and gray, and in the distance, thunder growls.

Hunched under the coming sheet of rain, I weep.

SEVENTEEN

The city of Tall Titan is surrounded by hills and mountains like rolling waves, waves of dense jungle. And tucked between a hill and a valley, hidden by curves and dips, is a hospital compound. Gaia lands us in its courtyard.

The rain is all thunderous applause. My vision washes out with it, curtains of gray. Out of that gray come people—men and women in hospital gear—who rush to my side and Naqi's, Naqi, who is still on my back.

They carry us in. All is a blur.

This is the hospital Naqi mentioned that time in the nest, the one that Yashi went to for the removal of her omen-stained tongue.

It's a humble complex, only three floors high with two small wings, a courtyard, a wind-tossed garden. No roads connect through the mountains to the complex. Instead, behind the building, a line of tracks runs straight and sleek. Freight trains rumble over them every once in a while, and the mountains rumble along.

Inside, the fluorescent lights catch in the polish of the halls, looking like wet smudges, and the silence is sterile.

When the doctors look me over, when they examine my body, they tell me that my stain is gone. I don't understand.

I look at my bared back in the mirror. I see the curve of my shoulder blade. It's pale and without blemish, smooth in the absence of scabs. The doctors are telling the truth. My stain is gone. I'm no longer an Omen.

I feel—nothing.

All my life, all my life, I've wanted this, dreamed this.

But the reality of it thuds hollow, falls empty.

The truth of it rings through me and then peters out, away, gone. Nothing is left.

I stand outside an infirmary room. I look in through the window.

Naqi is on the bed inside.

His eyes are wrapped. His hands are taped down with drips. Flakes of dried medicine-oil still cake the insides of his ears, where the nurses and doctors didn't reach far enough to clean. His chest rises up and down with his breaths, shallow breaths.

I don't move any closer. I don't deserve to.

A doctor asks me questions I don't know how to answer, because I was a monster then and knew only monstrous things. But while I was a monster, I felt Naqi. I felt him touch my cheek, and felt his pain. I know now that Naqi traded places with me.

He took Gaia my star and replaced his human senses with my monstrous ones. He took on my omen.

The doctor says it's dampened his sense of touch, though it

seems to be returning slowly, surely, as most of his stains recede slowly, surely—it's a blessing no one understands, though I think I do. The original state of my stain was six or so inches long, two or so inches wide. If Naqi truly took my stain, it would make sense that his would be the same size.

And while the omen caused extensive damage to his eardrums, those stains are also receding. With the doctors' help, his ears should heal with time.

But his eyes. But his eyes.

I don't know why the omen didn't settle over Naqi's back like mine. I don't know why it's chosen to sit over his eyes, instead. It's painted like brushstrokes over his nose and lids, black beneath his bandages.

I see Naqi smiling at me, puffed with pride, saying things like, *Takes skill to walk around perfectly without my eyes*, and I crumple my hands against my own eyes, because I don't deserve to see.

I don't deserve to look at him.

The news on the screen says this:

The Decade-Races have been put on hold indefinitely. The Omen girl has fled. She rampaged out of her confines like the monster she is and abducted Naqi Imka. And the temple guardian Yashi Quay is currently under investigation for her involvement with the escaped Omen.

Authorities have retrieved Lumi Sidik's body. They were given an anonymous tip—likely from the same mysterious woman that tipped Lumi's mother—that led them to a small but kempt shack by the edge of the sea sector.

Her body is intact, in one piece.

When you turn me in, I tell the doctors and nurses, *will you please continue caring for Naqi? Will you please keep him hidden, keep him safe?* And the doctors and nurses say only, *Yashi sent you here. She risked her guardian-hood, her life, to send you to our hidden sanctuary. Therefore, here you will stay.*

I will stay by Naqi's side.

They say it will take a couple of months before his hearing returns. They say it will take a couple of miracles before his sight does.

It doesn't matter, the months, or the miracles. I will care for Naqi.

I will care for Naqi for as long as I am allowed.

The hospital is different from those black market places I've heard about, with the doctors that operate in the dark of night, and the patients that have to hold back their cries.

It is privately funded by several anonymous donors, and hosts only a dozen or so patients, all Omens. Aside from my help in the kitchen or out in the gardens, or fetching supplies in the halls, the doctors and nurses require no capsules from me.

For days, Naqi sleeps.

I keep him clean. I change his bandages. I stand in the corner with my hands gripped tight when the doctors come for checkups. I learn which sets of wrinkles mean Naqi is improving. I learn which smiles are lies.

Gaia no longer responds to me. I whirl her in her whistle-sling, but she doesn't crack awake. I wanted to write a line of healing over Naqi. I decided that, if the healing didn't work, I would trade places with him again—reclaim my stain and take his suffering from him.

Gaia only slumbers on.

I weep against her glass-like skin. She doesn't stir.

On the third night, Naqi eases gently out of sleep. I take his hand. He starts, and says, "Who's there?"

And then he asks again, louder, "Who's there?"

And then he forgets how to breathe. He shouts on frenzied beats and cuffs his ear again and again because he's trying to strike sound back into it. I can't help him. There is nothing I can do. I wind my arms around him to keep him from thrashing. I trap his arms in my hold. My ear is pressed into his chest, and I hear the rhythm of his fear there.

The nurses come at all the noise. They sedate him and check his vitals. Naqi's shouting dims when the medication seeps in. He sags with weight. He lolls against his pillow, and slips back into sleep.

The next time he wakes, I bump lightly against the side of the mattress so he knows someone is there. I touch the backs of his hands before I take them. I perch his hands on top of mine so he can feel my signing.

I sign: *Good morning.*

He doesn't understand, not the first few times. I slow my signing. I exaggerate the motions. He says, slow, unsure, "Good morning?"

I nod, then remember he can't see it.

I sign: *Good.* I sign: *You are safe.* And I have to sign through the words several times again before Naqi understands. He swallows. He squeezes my hand, and maybe that means he's scared. Maybe that means *okay, all right, go on.*

I don't know enough hand signs to explain everything to him, so I flip his hand over and brush open his palm. With my finger, over his life and heart and sun line, I trace out the shapes of starsongs.

You're in Yashi's hospital, and you're safe. You fainted at the temple and were omen stained. The stains have mostly faded. Your hearing will return. They'll do what they can for your eyes.

And then he fumbles for my hands and flips them over and traces out his own lines, over and over my palms.

His first question is this:

Lumi? What about Lumi?

Then he asks with his mouth, "Is she all right?" He asks, "Is she safe?"

Oh.

Naqi can't see. Naqi can't hear.

His hands are the sole windows to his world now, and his hands don't know me.

For a long while, I write nothing. So Naqi fumbles for my hands again and traces: *I don't know her real name, but I'm talking about the girl from the race. The one they locked up. Is she all right? What happened to her?*

Anger pops through me. Guilt follows sharp. Why is Naqi still asking after me, after everything, everything? Why is he so foolish, so naive? Hasn't he hurt enough?

I trace: *She's an Omen. What does it matter?*

Naqi's brows crumple. "It matters. Please."

When I write nothing still, he says again, breathes out, "Please."

So I trace: *She's safe.*

Naqi sighs out a smile. He squeezes my hands again, and this time I know he means gratitude. He asks, "When can I see her?"

I flinch at the word *see* and trace: *You want to see her?*

"Of course."

After everything she did?

Naqi shakes his head but says nothing, so I trace harder: *She did this to you.*

"She didn't do anything to me. I chose this."

I jerk away. He's right. But why? Why would you choose this, Naqi?

He says, "I want to see her."

"Khab," I say, because he can't hear, and I trace: *Aren't you scared?*

"What?"

Aren't you scared she's going to hurt you again?

Naqi only smiles. "She's never hurt me," he says, lies, because doesn't he remember? That night in our nest, he was hurt enough to cry. That time in the dust, he was hurt enough to bleed. Why doesn't he remember?

I trace: *I'll see what I can do.*

"Thank you," Naqi says. "Hey," he adds. "What's your name?"

I don't answer. I'm numb.

When we were bonded through the sense transfer, I felt him hurt. I felt him hurt because of me. And though he says he chose this, that it isn't my fault, he won't be saying the same things days from now, weeks from now, when the reality of the finality of his hurts settles in, settles like the stain over his skin.

He will come to hate me.

I know it.

So with guilt like a spice over my tongue, over my skin—with heat enough to sting my eyes wet—I take his hands. I work our fingers through the letters of a name he does not know and am reminded how I am a liar.

Ever since that time under the people like stars, I've always known how to lie.

S, O, Z, O.

Sozo.

I tell him: *My name is Sozo.*

EIGHTEEN

My new lie is that I am an old friend of Yashi's, one she taught signing and starsongs to, and so I have been assigned as caretaker over Naqi.

The boy doesn't question it. The doctors and nurses can't sign or write starsongs, so they can't refute it. I don't tell them, anyway, what it is I'm doing.

It's cruel, my lying. I know. I've lied enough for two lifetimes or three. I know. But fears rattle on in my rib cage. Most of those fears look the same: Naqi turns to me, and his expression twists, and he says, *I regret giving up my senses for you. I regret you.*

Another fear, smaller, burrowed deep and deeper, sees Naqi turning to me and smiling and saying, *Ya'tuv mi-eh.*

And I can't.

I can't.

I would rather that he regret me than accept me after everything I've done.

In the hospital cafeteria, as I eat, news from Tall Titan crackles from an old radio.

The people are enraged—at Lumi's death, at Naqi's abduction, at my disappearance. Injustice after injustice. So mobs have taken to assaulting Omens on the streets, or raiding known Omen hide-outs, and the Omens retaliate with tooth and nail and scavenged weapons. Despite police presence, looting and violence break out like hives throughout the city.

I can imagine it, the sounds of it all like firecrackers.

The food in my mouth no longer tastes like anything.

When I return to Naqi's room, I hear the shattering of glass.

Naqi reached for the water on his bedside table and missed. The cup fell and shattered, but Naqi did not hear it, so he stepped unknowing into the sting of glass when he swung his feet down from the bed.

His foot is up on his knee when I see him. He's hissing. The glass is sunk into his flesh, and he touches it like it is a hot thing. He picks and picks, but his blood is slippery. He picks and picks, but he can't see how small the glass is. He can't see how deep it is. He can't see.

I step over to him. I reach to help, but then he's swearing, and I stop.

He fists a hand in his bedding. His fingers smear red where he clenches. He turns and covers his mouth, hides his face, but he can't hide the shaking of his shoulders. He can't hide his bandages that patch dark with tears. He crumples into himself, lower, lower, so his lap swallows his sobs. I'm not supposed to see this.

I step away. I exit the room. In the hall, with the door closed behind me, I lose my strength. I'm on the floor. The wall is cold and hard on my spine, and I wonder when, when?

When will the blade fall?

When will I burn?

He doesn't cry when he knows I'm around. He smiles. He signs things like: *Gosh, you're looking quite nice today, Sozo. Did you get a new haircut? You sound like you're about to get a cold, Sozo. You should be careful.*

And I have to tell him to stop being silly, and to slow down, because there's only so many signs I understand.

He asks me about me—about Lumi—every day. When is she coming? Have I talked to her? Seen her? I've told Naqi by now that she was the one who flew him to the hospital, and that she left soon after, because maybe she's a coward.

"What's there to be afraid of?" Naqi laughs. "I'm just a blind, deaf boy."

This blind, deaf boy frightens me more than any monster ever did.

The week comes to a close. I fall into a routine.

In the mornings, I help Naqi with what he needs, and then I work in the kitchen or garden. In the afternoons, after lunch, I bring Naqi to a seat out in the courtyard, underneath the shade of a tree.

He sits there. He lounges there. He smiles when he feels the breeze over his skin. I go to the back of the hospital, where my star and anchor are kept in a shack. I stare at Gaia. That's all I do. She still won't wake, no matter what I do.

"Why," I ask her, "did you let Naqi do what he did?"

She doesn't answer.

"Why," I ask, "won't you answer me?"

Still there is silence.

I pace into the shack and lift Gaia above my head, and I think about hurling her down the mountain, or throwing her against the ground, again and again, until she shatters. I'm angry, so angry. Why would she let Naqi hurt himself? Why won't she let me take the omen back?

I don't toss her. I never do. I set her down and leave the shack and return to Naqi. Against his protests, I help him back to his room.

Tonight, out in the foyer, the news on the screen is consumed by fire. The shaky video is of looming beasts, three times the size of a man, with fur like prickly shadows. Their teeth are serrated knives, and their eyes flash red. The headline reads:

ACT OF TERROR. TEMPLE ATTACKED BY OMEN MONSTERS.

I don't understand what's happening.

For nights, I've pondered over Esp and the things she did at the plaza, and on some level, I understand why she did them.

Eye for an eye.

She betrayed me after I betrayed her.

She'd commanded me to draw the stain on everyone's skin, and instead the opposite happened. She saw me smiling on that stage, basking in the glory of my line, and she said enough.

Sozo must be punished.

And now, with this news of terror flashing on the screen, I know how she was able to cut me loose so easily.

If I acted according to plan, it would have been war.

If I didn't act according to plan, still it would have been war.

In Esp's mind, there's never been and never will be another way.

Her guns and bombs were for this moment. In secret, in the shadow of her warehouse, she has been training her Omens to turn into hulking monsters, things that would rail against the temple walls with wild abandon.

If I was able to break through cement wall after cement wall, what could her monsters do?

The newswoman says that the temple walls and gates have yet to be breached, but the number of Omen monsters seems only to be increasing. Guardians and authorities are doing what they can, and are holding strong, but for how long?

The leader of the monsters goes by no name, and the only thing known about her is her demand: that all who have oppressed Omens must suffer and die.

Those who have betrayed her must suffer and die.

Anyone who has ever wished harm upon Omens will get what is coming to them, for she is a reckoning, a retribution, one the guilty will never be allowed to escape.

Naqi's parents send him a transmission.

The hospital reached out to them through an encrypted message, to mask the location of the hospital, and received an encrypted message in return.

I sit Naqi in front of the holo of the data-packet, and touch-sign everything I can to him. I palm-trace the remaining words I do not know.

They say: "Naqi, darling, sweetheart. Honey, we love you. We love you so much. We're coming to see you as soon as we can. By the time you receive this transmission, we should already be on our way. Hold out for a little while longer, honey. We love you so much, and you've been so brave, been through so much, but you're so strong, *ko-ang*, darling, sweetling."

And then they're crying. I've never seen a man weep. The mother wipes and wipes at her face. Even through the holo, their cheeks shine.

I don't know the different signs for *darling, sweetheart, honey, sweetling*. And I don't know what *ko-ang* is. I don't ask. So for all the endearments, I replace them by pressing three specific fingers—the position of love—over Naqi's heart, because I think the meaning is the same.

Every time they say Naqi, darling, they are saying Naqi, we love you.

Naqi, sweetheart. Naqi, we love you.

Naqi is crying too. He fumbles three fingers over my heart and taps them there, again and again, like maybe his fingers are telegraph keys, and he's tapping out the code for love, to be carried from his heart through mine, to be pulsed like radio waves through the vast dark of the galaxy.

The temple gates have been broken. The carnage plays live over the feeds.

Bodies like torn flags litter the steps. The entrance is all crumpled ruin. Smoke rises black and in billows, and out of that blackness rise the hunched backs of monsters.

The first monster I ever saw was still like a girl, just feral, all teeth and nails. These monsters are nothing like girls, like boys—their limbs are no longer stitched together. It's like some-one has taken their bodies and cracked them open and apart and filled in the gaps and breaks with tumors that pulse, with filth that writhes. They are creatures playing at humans.

I see the arms and legs of one—the arms and legs of a man. They dangle useless in the air because the rest of his body has bloated into something like a giant leech, all oil and cracking scabs. I see one with their rib cage cracked open, walking on those bones, like a centipede with its many legs.

Is this what I looked like, when I turned?

Is this what I really am?

All the monsters tower. All their hides are like steel. Blasts of ichor from whistle-slings are to them like puffs of wind, and it's a wonder the guardians and authorities have held out for this long against abominations like these.

I see Esp. She's stepping into the temple.

The newscaster rattles on and on from somewhere off-site, saying that the woman has taken the temple and the people inside as hostages. One wrong move, or a move she doesn't like, and she'll kill those hostages one by one by one.

Brother Marat is still in there. Sister Ena is still in there.

Yashi is there, and Frea, and Roaz, Rama.

Slowly, surely, understanding dawns.

It's not like Esp to take hostages, to hold back from pulling the trigger when her mark is in her sights. So she's holding back because she needs them—the whistlers, the racers, the ones who could survive the titan's eye.

Esp is still planning on making her wish.

A cry shatters through the hall. I startle, and jerk to my feet. Naqi. That was Naqi's voice.

I bolt toward his room. Naqi is being held down by two nurses. He's thrashing. He clutches the bandages over his eyes while his omen stain bleeds out of those bandages, down his cheeks, down his neck.

His omen is getting worse.

Why, why?

No one knows why. No one has answers. I'm useless here.

Something has to be done.

I turn from the room and make my way down the hall, down the steps, behind the building. I enter the shack and take up my star, Gaia in her whistle-sling, then return to the courtyard, where there is plenty of space for a star to be swung.

And like that, by the tree Naqi sits at, smiles at in the breeze, I swing my sling—on and on, slowly at first, with an ease like warming up, and then harsh, curt, firm. I clap the full edge of gravity over Gaia's skin, and when she still does not wake, I wind back down. I repeat the process. I start slow, then snap fast. I start loose, then snap tight, muscles tensing and teeth gritting.

On and on, I do this.

On and on, I work and work to swing Gaia awake.

The sky above me was dusking when I started.

The sky above me now is cloaked violet-gray, static-gray.

Hours have passed. I am still swinging.

Nurses, dozens of them, have come to where I am in the court-yard and asked me to come back inside, to take a break, to get some water and sit for a while, I've done this for long enough, and it's already dark, and Naqi needs you, doesn't he? So come back inside.

Come back inside.

I don't answer them. I don't answer any of them.

Naqi needs me. I know. He needs me to take the stain back from him, to take away the pains that were meant for me, and I can only do that if Gaia is awake to transfer our senses, and so I have to do this. I have to be here, twisting and whirling, for as long as it takes, for as long as it takes.

My hands are bleeding. The swinging cord frictions my skin away and makes me bleed, but it doesn't matter.

Naqi is hurting so much more.

Yet the stars above me are coming out, and the city of Tall Titan—small in the distance—is winking full of lights, and Gaia is still not waking. Gaia will not return to me, or answer me, or heed me, and I will do this until my hands chafe into dust, and then I will swing with my teeth if I have to, but, but—

The cord slips and clips hard into my finger, clips into it wrong, and I yelp, and drop her. I falter. I sink to my knees. Gaia rolls in the dirt before me. My hands scrabble at dust.

I bring those hands up to my eyes, and keen.

My wail, even to my ears, is a ghastly, ghostly thing.

I want to help Naqi. I want to save him. I want to run away with him, and make believe with him in the stars, and I want to hit him and call him khab, and then I want to kiss him. But I don't deserve to. I don't deserve to.

Why did he save me?

Why can't I save him?

Omen stains, omen scabs, sins that turn us into monsters. Esp and her lumbering beasts and all the hate given that brought them there, to the temple. They're monsters now, yes, but no one sets out to be a monster. I gave in to one because I thought it was all I deserved.

I want it to end. I want it all to end. I want no more, no more. Please. Please.

Gaia taps against my mind.

I don't hear her, not at first—the pulse of my sorrow is something that drowns. But she taps again, and again, like a bird against a windowpane, and I stop. I jerk my head up.

Gaia in the dust is bright awake, wide with light, so very like the sun. Her warmth brims like hope. Her presence against my mind is like an old friend.

She says nothing. She doesn't need to, not anymore. I understand her, just as she understands me, me on my knees, me in the dust, me buried beneath the hide of a monster.

I know what I have to do, to save Naqi, to save them all.

It's time, she says.

I agree.

This, finally, is how the blade falls.

This, finally, is how I burn.

NINETEEN

I don't have much time, so I don't waste any.

I carve over the city of Tall Titan, a falling star against the night sky, a comet that hurtles toward our hole in the wall. I expand Gaia's power so that I blow through the gap like a bullet, so that I am not slowed by stone and bark and memories.

I'm a gust through the gardens, all light and wind. I flurry past the training pit and the work tents toward the main chancel of the temple, the temple bordered in by monsters.

Though the doorway is the size of an aircraft tunnel, the three monsters there nearly plug its entirety, and they see me coming— me a roar of flame, an arrow of light. I don't slow. I don't stop. I'm aiming for that singular gap above their heads.

When the monsters raise their claws for me, I corkscrew a hole through their claws. I come out on the other side, shaking off oil and blood, and take in the scene inside the chancel.

The acolytes are all kneeling on the floor, hands bound behind their backs. The whistlers are bound in another group, facing the acolytes.

Esp strides between them, tall, dark. Her hair is sleek and long and like starlight, and her lips have been painted indigo. She's wearing no mask, because she no longer needs to. She is done with hiding.

Stationed all around the chancel are men and women—Omens who haven't yet turned—with guns in their hands.

Roaz is on his anchor, and he is about to leap into the titan's eye.

I was right.

Esp is going to use the racers—someone she can coerce, threaten, someone who could survive the portal regardless of whether they won the previous stages or not—and then take the wish they capture, take it for herself, for her own gain.

Roaz sees me. They all do.

I see Rama, and Sister Ena. I do not see Yashi or Frea. Esp turns to me and watches me, and I see, for the first time in a long time, the shape of her scar.

Like someone's taken a hook and sunk it into the corner of her lips and tugged, her omen is a lumpy path of congested flesh. It's got the red rawness of a burn-scar that worms over her cheek and up into her hair, and for the first time in all my life, I realize—

Esp has never been beautiful.

Not because of her scar. Not because of her omen.

Because of her eyes.

She takes out a gun, cocks it, and she's aiming it toward an acolyte kneeling by her feet—Rama, blotchy-skinned and smeared in tears—because she's telling me that she'll shoot if I come any closer, and I do what Gaia did at the end of the first race.

Lights warp and bend around me.

I blink.

I reappear.

I've charged through and snapped past Esp, knocking her gun aside, but I don't stop. I don't go for the others, not the acolytes or the whistlers, not the men and women who are now raising their guns at me or the monsters that are now screeching and rumbling and crowding close.

I blink again, toward the wishing well.

Roaz, eyes wide and wild, jerks out of the way and, with a snarl, dives into the portal.

I don't close my eyes.

I want to see everything: the sands, the dark, the storm that follows.

I let Gaia sing through my bones and my veins. I dive into the eye.

Silence roars.

Ancient cathedrals of cloud.

Mighty pillars of lightning.

Absolute power rolls by me and by me, around me like the thick robes of a god, of gods, and I am but a speck in the titan's eye, caught in the folds of its royal curtains, curtains stitched from nebulae. I've entered the belly of a beast.

So this is what myths are made of.

Sound crashes back over me.

Thunder roars, then cracks. Lightning flashes.

I'm teetering on my anchor, crouched low against its body. I'm flowing along a current of wind—the breath of sirens—even though wind here is an impossibility. Through the curtain of the storm, I can see the vast beyond of outer space, of the universe, of every star within it.

I can still breathe and am still alive; it must be Gaia's doing.

Far before me, like a wind-tossed bird in a storm, Roaz struggles and glides.

I go to him.

I ride the impossible current through the storm, and with static electricity prickling over my skin, and with a howling around me like women in mourning, I reach him.

Here the wind is much stronger. I open my mouth and shout, "Roaz, Roaz!"

He twists toward me and bares his teeth, and he shouts words at me that the wind takes away, but in flashes like lightning, I hear all his thoughts. I hear him the way stars are heard.

Get away, you monster.

This is all your fault.

It's your fault so many people have died—guardians, Suns. It's your fault we're so scared. Your fault Rama is so scared. Did you see her? How tearful she was? If she dies, I will never forgive you. If she dies, I will kill you myself.

I understand, then. This is how Esp twisted Roaz's arm. This is why he is here, in the storm, seeking out a wishing star for the sake of Esp. No. Not for her sake.

For Rama's sake.

The wind lashes out.

The howling of women twists into giggling, cackling, layered and malicious, and then Roaz and I are tossed from each other and hurled from the current.

I spin and tumble and batter through the flesh of the storm, through its clouds full of static, and—

There's solid ground beneath me.

I open my eyes and see my own reflection—pale and strained, mouth open on breaths. The stone is black tourmaline, polished to be like a mirror, and it's just like the inner sanctum of the kori tower. How is this possible?

I push to my feet slowly, slowly. All my movements echo.

I see the kori tower. There are no stars in any of the sirens' hands.

A girl steps out from behind the tower, a little girl, a girl with bright blue eyes.

I know her. She's the one I let die by that white, white wall.

She doesn't blink. Her eyes, like the eyes of a corpse, are rigid and open. The top of her forehead is caved in, though the skin there is unbroken, unmarred. She opens her mouth and says, *Your lie killed me.*

So now I will kill you.

She lurches for me.

Bare feet flash against stone. White nails carve through air. The girl pummels into me and sinks her teeth into me, and I'm twice her size—I've grown and aged while she's stayed a dead girl—but I have no strength in me to fight this, to fight her.

I topple to the ground and shove at her, but her grip is inhuman. I twist about to scrabble to my feet, but then her fingers are in my hair, and she is yanking, and then she is looming over me.

In her hand is a bolt gun.

I can't die here.

I elbow her, hard, in the gut. I knock her off her feet and step on her wrist and wrench the gun out of her hand. I take aim against her dead blue eyes and hook my finger around the trigger.

I don't pull it.

I can't. I won't.

I've already killed her once. I won't kill her again.

As much as she rightfully hates me and rightfully rails against me, I won't hate and rail in return.

I toss the gun aside.

And then I fall, I'm falling.

I'm back on my anchor. Gaia is shining within her engine-lock. I'm hovering again between the folds of the storm, bumping against static and riding the current, and there's no black stone or tower in sight. There is no little girl.

There was never any little girl.

Brother Marat said the titan's eye would test my very soul.

There, darting like a hummingbird, is a star.

Gold drips from its nebulous form like honey. Every move and twitch and dance rings out like a chime and like the giggling of children. It bounces through the air like a stone skips over the surface of water. It swims through the cosmic clouds like a koi.

It's a wishing star.

That's the star Roaz came here for.

That's the star *I* came here for.

I charge ahead.

The chase begins.

Wind roars over me like fire. Unseen sirens laugh and howl. I hunt after the wishing star as it skips down a path, one of rolling storms, then another of jagged lightning, and I dip and dive and drive after it, around curves and bends and impossibilities.

It looks to me to be galloping, sometimes. A golden deer. A mythical creature, unfurling for the thrill of the chase.

I see Roaz. He's slumped against his anchor, though his eyes still flash. He sees the same wishing star as me, but he's falling behind. He can't quite keep up, not against the braying of the storm or the heat of lightning that strikes around us.

I can taste the star's tail.

The stardust is a spice on my tongue.

I stretch out my hand, and strain forward my fingers, and the tip of my nail scrapes through the edge of its liquid body—

I'm somewhere else again.

I'm in the garden of the Temple of Celestial Ichor, at the foot of my ancient tree, our ancient tree.

The wall is white, like the bark, like the grass, like the sky above.

The tree is dead; its branches are bare. Nothing else stands in the garden around the tree, only the blinding stretch of eternity. When I move again, everything echoes.

Rama and Esp are here. They are on either side of me.

Esp says, *Everything you do is selfish.*

It's clear from the things you've done that you think only of yourself, of what you can get out of others—Lumi is an accessory you used then disposed of. I am an accessory you used then disposed of. You followed me until it no longer suited you.

And Rama says, *You tried to use me too. Tried to get me to feel sorry for you, to let you go, to free you from your cage. That's all you've ever done all your life. Lie and manipulate and abuse. I thought we were friends—but all you thought was how you could get away with it.*

Naqi is here. He's here too. I can't. I can't do this.

He's sitting up in the tree. His legs swing from the branches. He looks down at me and smiles and says, *For my kindness, you paid me lies. For my softness, you paid me hurts. I will never see again. I will never see again because of you.*

All I wanted in return was kindness, softness, truth.

But a viper can't know these things.

Why, why?

Why didn't I die at birth?

Why did my knees receive me?

Everything they're saying—it's true. It's true. All of it.

It doesn't matter what my reasons were. I killed Lumi, and I used her name and veil. I betrayed Esp, even though she had spent so much of her efforts on me. I used Rama, I did—I wanted in her a friend who would sympathize, and I didn't think about her, how she would feel, how she would hurt.

I am what Naqi says I am—a viper.

Something in me pulses.

Gaia. Gaia.

Hrah, she pulses. *Sha*, she beats. *Sav, Sahd, Tahv, Rahv.*

She's pulsing out the Nine Ahs in me, to me. But why? What does it matter now? What does any of it matter?

Anvah. Enkrah.

Ahavah.

I see.

So that's it. So that's why.

I never knew. I never understood. But now I do. Now my eyes are opened.

"You're right," I say, to no one, to everyone. "Everything I've done is selfish."

"You're right," I say, "that I've lied, and abused, and nothing excuses what I've done. I'm ashamed, and I am sorry, and even if my back is unblemished, nothing will ever change the fact that I'm an Omen. You're right. Thank you. Thank you. For breaking me down, breaking me open, allowing me to see—"

I must be going mad; I'm laughing. Through my tears, my

laughter crackles. A great weight has been unchained around me, from me, and I am unshackled.

I am free.

I lift my head and say, "Naqi never wanted anything for the things he did. He gave me kindness, he gave me softness, because of Ahavah."

Ahavah—to seek someone's well-being without expecting anything in return.

His trading with me was his Ahavah.

His *ya'tuv mi-eh* is his Ahavah.

I may be an Omen, but I am loved.

I was looking for someone who stayed, and he did.

He did.

The world falls away. Esp and Rama and the tree fades away, and Naqi, smiling, shimmers into mist.

I am standing before a great horizon.

There are mountains of ice in the distance. A plane stretches before me, of cloud, or of snow, swirling, shining. In the center of it all is a mighty torrent of fire-water, of ice-flame, pouring in waterfalls from a star like a moon, the size of a moon, set high in the night sky.

The wishing star is there.

It bobs before the torrent. Its light quivers like a candle's.

Gaia is gone. So is my anchor. So, I walk.

I tread through the plane of snow and of cloud and move forward, forward. It's not cold. I don't tire. The wishing star doesn't flee from me.

And then the star wobbles into a shape. The closer I step, the crisper the shape.

The star has taken the form of a girl.

The star has taken the form of Lumi.

"Hello," she says, and her voice resounds.

I watch her, and watch her, and can say nothing at all.

She laughs.

Lumi is wearing no mask, no veil. She is just a girl, a girl with eyes that twinkle and hair that curls. She looks like a siren would look, if they were nothing but kind.

"It's really good to see you again."

". . . How?"

"Well, for starters"—Lumi laughs again—"none of this is exactly real."

I quiet. I'm reminded of Lumi's mother, then, of that lonesome woman weeping on the booth. I'm reminded of Lumi's friend, who tore at my falsehoods and wept.

"I'm sorry," I breathe.

"I know," she says.

"I can never atone."

"I know," she says.

Then she stretches out her hand, palm up, and waits for me to take it. I don't. I don't take it. I say instead, "The wish Esp and I wanted to make, in the beginning—it was an evil wish. We wanted to turn anyone who wasn't an Omen into a monster."

Lumi says nothing.

I continue, "Then I changed my mind, and changed my wish to the thing I know best: hiding, lying. I wanted to wish our stains away so that no one would ever be able to tell who had done wrong."

Lumi smiles, then.

"But now," she says, "you've sorted things out."

"I want to stop Esp."

"But you want more than just that."

Yes. I do. My want resounds.

Living liquid light bubbles out of the seat of Lumi's palm, and this time, this time—with a sun cresting over the horizon and the star-moon above us rumbling, cracking open, giving birth to light, more light—I take Lumi's hand.

I claim my wish.

I understand the world in patches. The light of my wish dazes.

I've reemerged out of the titan's eye and am hovering on the power of my wishing star.

I see Roaz. He's on the floor of the chancel with his anchor beside him, and Rama is kneeling over him, and he is alive, breathing, well.

I see the monsters in the chancel, and many of their hides are sloughing off and away to reveal women and men, girls and boys. Some tear instead at themselves with claws and teeth until there is nothing left to tear at, until they are dead, unmoving.

I see Esp. She tosses her arm over her eyes at the light of it all and fires blindly, blindly, at me and at me until she is out of bullets. The light swallows them up, burns them all to dust. And then she turns her nails on herself. She screeches. She writhes. The scar on her face is bursting open like a fly-filled corpse, popping open at the seams. She rakes at her hair and yanks it off.

Her hair underneath the wig is patchy, wispy, like weeds.

The omen stains there are bubbled and frothy, like scum.

She stumbles away. She knocks into Roaz's anchor and paws at it, and then she reaches for the star inside the engine-lock. It's another weapon that she could use. An ichor blast. A sling of metal.

She grips the star in her hand.

With a ping like vibrating glass, the whole of her bursts into flames.

If she screams, I don't hear it; starfire is gurgling out of her mouth.

When she dies, her flesh charring black, I don't look away.

TWENTY

This was my wish:

To change the nature of omens.

Every Omen who understands their guilt and is regretful will be healed. Any Omen who harbors no guilt and no remorse won't be healed.

Esp might have felt guilt once, when she was a girl like me. But the Esp I grew up with was blind to the idea, callous to the thought. All she wanted was to hurt.

So the omen gave her what she wanted. She hurt and hurt until the end.

This is what happens after:

Gaia and my anchor are lost to the portal, though I don't think about them as being lost. They're home.

Many Omens lose their stains, though they don't regain the things they lost to their stains, like their arms or legs, their sight, their minds. My wish didn't cure everything.

A week is spent clearing out rubble, ruins, and debris. The

temple is slowly, surely, put back to rights. A citywide funeral is held in honor of the deceased—the guardians and authorities who gave their lives against the frenzied monsters, the acolytes and Suns and unfortunate bystanders. Even Omens. It's a first for Tall Titan.

Brother Marat also died in the attack, protecting the whistlers. They mention him especially in the eulogy, saying that he was kind and wise and strong, even to the end, and I remember the time he laid his old hand on the top of my head, and know he must've been.

I try not to cry.

Yashi is alive, and so is Sister Ena. Rama and Roaz and Frea are fine. We don't speak to one another at the funeral, partly because no one knows how exactly to treat me. No one knows what I am anymore.

In the past, those who won wishes became something like stars themselves, icons, celebrities, heroes.

But how could an Omen be a star? How could an Omen become a hero?

The only one who interacts with me is Yashi. She weaves her hands at me and asks about Naqi, and I tell her that he's being looked after at the hospital, and my wish should have taken his stain away, too, though I don't know about his wounds.

But I can't go myself to check. I don't think people would allow me to take off. Not now.

She says, *You'll see him soon.* She says, *I'll visit him with you, after everything.*

Debate happens around what should be done with me.

I was Omen, one that colluded with Esp, and I ended the life of a Veil.

But I am also a champion of the Decade-Races, one whose wish brought an end to the Omen threat. I've forever changed the nature of stains. Things, from now on, will never be the same.

Ten years is what they decide on, in the end.

That is my verdict.

For ten years, I am to be exiled from the city of Tall Titan, and three of those years will be served on the farm-colony of the Eurydice moon. My service order there, my community restitution, is to work the fields without pay.

My stationing was something Lumi's mother herself asked for. I don't know why. Maybe she knows how much it'll hurt me, seeing her.

My remaining seven years are to be spent on other moons and colonies, doing compulsory unpaid work, or if I am paid, it will be meager, laughable. I will be put to cleaning or sorting or whatever else the authorities deem best.

And then after my years are served, I can return to Tall Titan.

I can return to Naqi.

The only thing I ask for as champion is this:

Don't send me out until Naqi is healed and well. And they grant it to me.

By the time I'm released from the hearings and the courtrooms and the mess of the city, by the time I can finally return to the hospital with Yashi, a woman and a man are by Naqi's side, and they are weeping.

It's his mother and father.

They cradle over and around Naqi like petals that have not yet budded, that will not bud, because how precious is the thing they have between them.

The boy's eyes have been unbandaged. There is no stain over his eyes and nose anymore, only a faint iridescent shimmer when he tilts his head this way and that. His eyes, when he opens them, are a pale blue.

The stain has taken his sight for good.

In the hallway, through the window of the room, I watch them, though not for long. Their faces are overflowing with love, love, love, and it's not something I have permission to see.

So I turn and leave. I give them their space.

In the middle of the hall with the sunlight streaking, as I am overlooking the courtyard, Naqi's mother and father find me, and the mother says, "Sozo? It is Sozo, right?"

I turn to them and draw in a breath, and nod. My face and name are all over the news these days, so they'd know now that I'm not just Sozo the caretaker but Sozo the Omen girl.

The mother . . . smiles, though it's a hard thing for her to pull on.

"Hello," she says. "Yashi has been translating for our son, and he's told us so much."

I swallow hard, and nod again.

The father sets a hand on the mother's shoulder and says, "You've been his eyes and ears in his time of need. Thank you."

The mother says, "And ko-ang speaks of you so highly. He says you were great friends in the temple."

"So he knows?"

I wanted to tell him myself, that the Sozo he met through his hands is the Lumi he befriended in the temple, that it's me. *It's me. I never once left your side.*

The mother and father look at each other, and then they shake their heads.

"We haven't told him that the Lumi he talks about is you," he says. "Rather, we were thinking it . . . may be better, if he didn't know."

I don't understand.

My frown is my question.

The mother answers. "We've talked to Yashi as well and asked her not to tell. We've told him that no one knows the Omen girl's name—your name—but have said the truth otherwise, that she won the race and made a wish, and helped put a stop to all that madness."

"Just," the father continues, "his mother and I think it would be better for him, easier for him, if the friendship was left on that note. He's—very fragile, right now. And you're leaving soon, for so very long. It would hurt him more than necessary, to say goodbye."

"So," the mother says. "So."

And then the father steps up to me. He squeezes my shoulder, and it doesn't hurt, not really, but looking at his contrite smile does, because I understand.

They're afraid of me. They're ashamed of me.

I was the one that hurt their son, and those hurts will never heal. I am everything a parent would fear for their child, a bad influence, an evil influence. And though Naqi tells them about me as Lumi, they would know me as Sozo from the news, the news that continues to malign me as the Omen I was, or am.

255

Hundreds of years of prejudice isn't going to dissolve because of my wish.

To his parents, Naqi must come off as someone who has been manipulated.

I blink and blink and blink. If I don't, the tears will fall.

"Darling," the mother says, and she's by my side. She touches my other shoulder. She touches it with the tips of her fingers, like I am an old, dusty, dirty thing. She says, "You've done so much for our son's sake, and we know you care for him. And because you care for him, you'd do what's best by him."

"This is for you, too, Sozo," the father continues. "Instead of dragging things out and prolonging the pain, you end things now. And you've such terrible experiences in the city, such harrowing memories. The sooner you leave, the sooner you can heal."

I hang my head. My eyes are weighed heavy.

They want me to leave without a goodbye. Cut things off without a word.

Am I strong enough for something like that?

When I speak again, it comes out as a hush. "Until he gets his hearing back."

"What?"

I straighten. I repeat, "Until he gets his hearing back. I'm staying until then."

The mother and father look at each other again. They frown.

"I won't tell him," I say. "Because that's what you want. I don't know how you'll handle him after, when his hearing returns and he learns the news of my name for himself. But until then, I'll remain Sozo the caregiver, not Sozo the Omen girl who made the wish. And then after his hearing returns to him, I'll leave."

The parents are still frowning, because they don't like it, because they don't trust me, so I puff a laugh. There's no mirth to it, only edges.

"Don't worry," I say. "I've been lying all my life. One more will be easy to bear."

"What kinds of things would I need to bring," I say to Yashi, "for when I leave?"

She signs something else instead, something about parents.

"Have the parents talked to me?" I venture.

Yashi nods, and I say, "Yeah."

And?

"And they told me everything."

And you agreed to it?

"Mostly," I say. "I won't tell Naqi who I am."

Yashi shakes and shakes her head, because she doesn't agree with any of this. She signs fast and clipped, and I don't know half of what she means, but she's angry. I see Naqi's name. Something about hurts. Something about lies.

"Yashi," I say. "My question."

She throws up her arms. She blows out a breath. I look at her and say nothing, do nothing, until she sighs again and signs: *I don't know, Sozo.*

She signs: *Just pack what you need. The essentials. Take with you what you can't live without.*

I dig out a small backpack. I fold into its belly three sets of clothes, a towel, a toothbrush and toothpaste, and a small bag of essentials. I slide an empty wallet under the towel, and then I pat the remaining emptiness inside the backpack.

I zip the whole thing closed. I will finish packing as Naqi heals.

Naqi asks me where I've been, because I've been gone for a good week at least, and I tell him it's a secret, so he laughs and waggles his brows and says, "Bet you snuck off to meet someone you like."

And I tell him not to be silly. I lie again by telling him that I wouldn't have gone for so long for something so very insignificant, for the sake of a boy.

I learn the things Naqi likes to smell, like roasted chestnuts and water on hot concrete, of all things.

So I dig up an abandoned grill from the hospital shack. I roll it out underneath Naqi's window. In the mornings before he wakes, I step outside to roast chestnuts, and I keep the hood pulled back, so the aroma carries into Naqi's room.

For our afternoon walks, I walk him to his tree in the court-yard and take off his sandals, and then I hose down his feet and the sunbaked ground around him. He cackles and wiggles his toes, and slaps his feet in the water, and takes in large pulls of breath.

Every night, he sits by his window. His parents have told him that not-Lumi has been exiled from the city for the things she's done, and that's why he should stop asking about her, after her, because she's long gone.

So he sits by the window, quiet in the night breeze, seeing nothing at all. He no longer asks about me.

The first week.

I remember the things Naqi likes to taste, like coffin bread, ice cream burritos. I learn he has a special fondness for red bean pastries, especially the ones shaped like fish.

So for lunch and dinner, I leave him his favorites on his platter beside his cafeteria foods. I watch him work through his soups and breads, and then he bumps his hand against my treats because he doesn't expect them there. I watch him peel back the wrappings. He sniffs. He nibbles, cautious, and then smiles. Sometimes he laughs.

The second week.

I learn the things Naqi likes to touch, like dice and wool sweaters, and so I find a dozen dice for him to play with. He lays his cheek against the table and tosses the dice again, again, just to feel the bumps, the jumps in vibration.

I dig up wool sweaters and wash them every morning. That way, when I pull them out of the dryer, Naqi can hold the warm cashmere in his hands. He nuzzles the warmth and breathes in, and smiles.

He doesn't like touching food. He doesn't like chalk and glue, because it dries up or sticks up his hands.

But he likes my hands, even though they're rough, or sweaty

sometimes. He lays his hands open, palm up, and waits for me to lay mine over his. And that's all we do. He tilts his head toward the window, because I think he can still see shades of light, and then he settles in our silence. He settles under my warmth.

The third week.

Naqi's hearing comes to him like water you can't shake out, clogging the ears, but day by day, the water drains. He takes to talking to himself, like a mad old thing, but the burble of his voice arrests him, fascinates him. So I don't stop him.

The doctors say, at the rate he is healing, his hearing may very well return by the end of next week, the end of the fifth week.

That is how much time I'll have left with him.

That is how much time I'll be allowed by his side.

The sky casts gray near the end of the fifth week.

Lighting scrawls on the horizon, looking like cracks on abused porcelain, and the storm clouds in billows of gray and deep purple roll across the mountains like a hungry thing, swallowing, greedy.

Soon that porcelain storm will shatter over the city, over the hospital.

And a few days before the storm breaks, Naqi's hearing opens entirely.

He's on his feet, jumping, laughing. He jumps to hear the sounds of his feet thumping against the floor. He laughs because he cannot contain it.

The hospital gives him a metal cane that extends and retracts, and he taps out a map of his world with it. He takes to walking down the halls by himself—with me trailing silently behind him—to learn how corners sound, how thin walls sound, how big and small rooms sound.

He tells me: "When there's a corner, the echo of my stick's rubber end thunks out like a fan." Or, "Sometimes you can feel sound, like a hand. You feel how far it goes or what it touches."

"You're a fast learner," I say, and I've pitched my voice lower, just in case he recognizes it. And if I speak with too much fondness, Naqi says nothing about it.

He laughs. "It's hard. But it's fun, like a puzzle."

Only Naqi could say something like that.

I learn that he likes the erhu—a two-stringed bowed instrument—and it surprises me, because an erhu sounds to me like a woman who is weeping. But he sits by the radio and listens to erhu music, or to any music at all, until his hips are sore, until his legs are all pins and needles. He twists left and right through the different stations just to hear the static.

He befriends all the nurses and make believes ranks for them based on how strong their finger snap is. He laughs and holds his breath when I drop a coin on the floor. He likes how it wobbles on a rotation, round and round, fast and faster, until it flattens into silence.

He likes the sound of birds. He likes the sound of thunder.

He says the sound of thunder is the sound of storm-monsters yawning, and the closer the storm rolls to the hospital, the longer Naqi spends with his arms pillowed in his open window, leaning, listening.

The next day, Naqi's mother sees my small backpack of clothes and essentials and coos about buying me more clothes, better essentials. She touches my shoulder with the whole of her hand and frets. When I tell her I don't need anything else, she asks if I am sure, and I say, "Yes," because in secret, I am already bloated with things.

In secret, I have packed things no one can take away from me.

For breakfast, I have dried mangoes and bananas. I have leek pie and a rice roll, and a tall glass of soy milk. This will be my last meal in the hospital. This will be my last meal in the region of Tall Titan for a long, long while.

After breakfast, I check the transport schedule. The train is already stopped behind the hospital. In twenty-three minutes, it will pull away and head back through the mountains, down to the city and through its many many districts, to stop at the shuttle station. The proper authorities will be waiting for me there.

Yashi offered to fly me over to the station—it's quicker, easier—but I told her I wanted to be alone. I told her that I wanted to wind through the denseness of Tall Titan one last time.

I return to Naqi's room.

He is sleeping still, because it's barely mid-morning, and Naqi is still not a morning person. I place nothing for him on his bedside table, because I know. His parents would see it and toss it away. A gift from someone like me would only be a stain.

I move to his bed. I nudge his palm up and over.

In the seat of his palm, I trace a sentence over and over again. I write it into his skin, into the heat of him. This invisible thing is the only thing I can leave to him, the only thing no one can take.

And then, with something leaden between my shoulders and

leaden in my chest, I move to the door. I don't look back. If I look back, I think I will turn into a pillar of static and dust. If I open my mouth to say goodbye, nothing but thunder will come out.

Naqi is waiting for me by the train tracks, underneath the transit shelter.

It's only been a few minutes, a few minutes of me grabbing my bag from the locker room, of me saying goodbye to Yashi, of me making my slow way down the stairs and to the tracks. But Naqi is here underneath the shelter, and the storm is above us. And the storm is breaking.

He's tilted his face up at the coming rain. His cane is gripped between his hands. There is a backpack slung over his shoulder, and he hears me coming and turns and smiles.

"Hi."

I don't know what to say. Naqi laughs and says, "Don't know what to say?"

He taps his way to me, where I am standing by the edge of the shelter. The rain falls around us. He holds out his hand to shake and says, "I'll make this easy for you."

He says, "Hi. I'm Naqi Imka. Your turn."

My words cork in my throat.

"Your turn," he nudges.

I open my mouth and let out a sound. Naqi laughs again.

He says, "Don't cry."

"I'm not crying."

"Stop that." He clutches my hand. "No more of that. No more lying."

"Can't," I say, and I close my eyes. "It's what I've done all my life."

"That was before," he says, and though I can't see him, I can hear his smile. "This is now. It's a brand-new start for you."

"You make it sound easy."

"Because it can be."

I open my eyes and shake my head. "Why are you here?" I ask.

"Oh," Naqi says. "You went blind too?" And he thumps his cane against the ground and hefts his backpack higher.

I scowl. "You're not going anywhere."

"Without my toothbrush, I know. Don't worry. I'll get one at the station."

"Naqi."

"Sozo."

My breath is blown from me. He's called me by my name many times by now, many many times. But now, in this moment, there are no more veils between us. There is no one here telling me to lie, to hide.

Naqi knows my name. Naqi knows me.

"How long," I ask, "have you known?"

Naqi answers by reaching up and tapping his fingers against his brow.

Khab. It's the hand sign for *khab*.

Oh.

I'm such a fool.

That time I caught him crying, I had signed to him and told him not to be silly. But I don't know the hand sign for *silly*. I only know the hand sign for *fool*, the one we made up together: *khab*.

"And," Naqi continues, "Yashi's signing rhythm goes all stuttery when she lies. And . . ."

This time, he beams. "The food. The snacks. Almost everything were things we had together."

All this time, he knew. All this time, and he played along.

"Why . . . why didn't you say something?"

He stops, then. I don't expect it. His face looks like something breaking. "Why didn't *you*?"

He says, "Even after I asked for you again and again. For the longest time, I thought . . ." and he stops. He doesn't finish his sentence.

His eyes weave here and there, like they are tracking smoke twisting up and up in the air, but he cannot see. He is only trying not to cry.

I turn my hand. I link my fingers with his clutching ones, and it is my turn to say, "Don't cry."

"I'll cry if I want to."

"Graduating from khab to crybaby?"

"You know it," he says, and smiles. He reaches for my cheek, and it takes him too long to find it, so I take his hovering, searching hand. I press it warm against my cheek. I forget to peel my hand away, because touching him is habit.

The rain pitters, patters, falls like applause. The drops bounce against our feet. Thunder purrs above my head and expands inside my chest, vast, so vast, and I think: *Ah, if only there were room in my backpack for this.*

"I can't believe," Naqi says, and he pulls away to scrub his sleeve over his eyes, "that you were going to leave without a goodbye."

"I can't believe you were going to follow me."

"Were? I still am."

"So they can add kidnapping to my crimes?"

"Yeah. It'll be romantic. We'll be elopers."

Stars. I'm laughing. The sound is wet and broken. I blink and blink, and my eyes sting. Then a horn is beeping and smoke is puffing and the earth begins to rumble. The train's engine is revving up.

Naqi stops.

"Sozo," he says, panicked.

I can't stand it. I want to tell him, tell him everything, the things I learned in the titan's eye, about him, about his Ahavah—but there is no time. So I take his hand. I fold it into a fist. I knock it against my chest, and then I kiss it to my forehead.

Ya'tuv mi-eh.

Naqi stops again.

"Zo."

I can't stand it. My chest is about to burst. I let go. The train has already started to move, but slowly, slowly, and I step out from under the shelter and haul myself up one of the train's ladders, onto the outer walkway.

"Sozo?" Naqi is unmoored. He drops his pack. "Sozo!" He twists toward the sound of the train and turns his head here and there at where he thinks I might be.

I drop my own pack on the walkway and lean over the railing, and the railing creaks. Naqi hears it. He taps into the rain and toward the sound and calls, "When will you get to the colony?"

The rain falls and falls over my head. "Couple of days."

"Do you have enough capsules?"

"Yeah."

"Zo." He steps into puddles. He drops his cane. He fumbles against the metal coat of the train, and I reach down to take his hands. "I told you to stop lying."

"I'm not lying," I say. "It's a service order. There'll be officials there. I won't be on my own."

Naqi's words clatter from him when he says, "I haven't even . . . I didn't even have time to . . . Sozo, I have so much I . . . did you pack enough? Do you have everything you need?"

"Yeah," I say. "The essentials. The things I can't live without."

"Sozo," he says, and I know he does not believe me, but I have. I've packed what I need. For five weeks straight, I have packed what I need.

The smell of roasted chestnuts is what I need. The smell of sunbaked concrete is what I need. When I am hungry, red bean pastries are what I need. The smooth faces of dice in my pockets are what I need. Soft sweaters and warm sweaters, they are what I need. I know now that I cannot live without the sound of erhu on the radio, or birds in the air, or thunder on the horizon.

I don't know how I've managed to pack it all; I never knew I would have space enough inside me to hold something like this— pitch-black senses and pale-blue eyes—something like a home.

Naqi says, "You are not allowed to *not* send me transmissions."

"Okay."

"Sozo."

And then I say: "Kiss me when I'm back."

"What?" Naqi grips at me. "What?"

"Kiss me," I repeat. "Like a promise."

"Are you . . . are you telling me to wait for you? Like . . . like a bride or something?"

"Yes."

"That's . . . Sozo. You're . . ."

I do it again. I fold his hand into a fist. I lean down and down and kiss my forehead against that fist.

And then his hand is wrenched from mine because the train is going too fast. I'm the one unmoored, flung far, like a kite with its string cut. Naqi is a wet smear of white in the rain. I think, maybe, I hear him shouting.

The train rolls along the curving track, and I look back at Naqi the entire time. My neck strains against the turn and the distance. My eyes cling like grasping, desperate hands, and I do not blink. My eyes burn and water, and I do not blink.

Him, blurry in the rain, is something I must also keep.

ACKNOWLEDGMENTS

The Omen Girl is very much a mirror.

My language frustrations as an immigrant became my fascination with language barriers. My memories of Taiwanese night markets—of the smells, the food, the lights and sounds, the *heat*—became the city of Tall Titan. The magic of Ghibli's Miyazaki, whose films filled my childhood with wonder, became the wind and wings of the story.

Sozo and the Omens and their stains are me when I was at my lowest.

Having gone through a kind of cataclysm in my life, and being thoroughly convinced that I was unlovable, unworthy, and a monster—the only thing that saved me was my own Naqi.

My sincerest hope for readers is that, when they find their own Naqi, they will invite them in.

You are worthy, even when you don't feel it. You are loved, even when you feel you don't deserve it.

And to all who stayed by my side, thank you.

My agent, Kesia, my knight in shining armor. You are a sword and a shield and a comfort in dark times. Thank you to Wattpad and PRH for believing in this story. Thank you to Fiona, my editor, and to Matthew, my first editor from a lifetime ago. You helped unearth the bones of this story.

To my husband, Alvin. You have cared for me and loved me so tenderly all these years. This story and I would not be here without you. To my baby girl. I hope to read this story to you one day. I hope you can be proud of me.

And last but greatest of all, to my God. Thank you for saving me and for loving me, and for the promises you keep. You are with me always, to the end of the age.

To You be all the glory.

Yueh Yang

ABOUT THE AUTHOR

Yueh Yang is a Canadian immigrant born to a Korean mother and a Taiwanese father. Moving as a child from the small summer island of Taiwan to the vast winter wonderland of Canada set in her a love and awe for the beauty of different worlds. Her works are a colorful blend of science fiction and fantasy and often explore the premise of barriers, be it language or otherwise. She is a piano teacher by day and an avid consumer of all things movies and anime by night. She lives in Toronto.

READING GROUP GUIDE

1. What was your favorite part of the book? Why?

2. At the beginning of the book, Sozo isn't particularly likeable or even sympathetic. How does she change over the course of the novel? Do you believe that she really has changed? What do you think is the main reason behind her changes?

3. Esp wants Sozo to win the wish for her own reasons. She plans to inflict suffering on people who have abused Omens in the past. Can you sympathize with her at all? Do you think she has a point, or do you think her motives don't excuse her actions?

4. Do you like Naqi? Could you be friends with him? What is his most endearing trait? What is his most annoying one?

5. Roaz dislikes Sozo/Lumi immediately. Why do think that is? And do you think his feel-ings toward her have changed by the end of the book?

6. Starsong is an important part of the Decades Race competition. The first time Sozo flies against Roaz, they both start to write starsongs:

   > *[Roaz is] writing rahka again, fire, but this time he's connecting that fire to a shape*—shakhal, *lion..*

   > *I don't know what he's planning, but I can tell he's deliberately writing his lines over mine, peaking the*

swirl of his S to cut through my words, disrupting
their meaning.

I . . . arrive behind Roaz's line. I corkscrew and
swoop and cut right through his ichor drag so that
his lion is severed.

7. Then I connect my line to taqa—a great sound, a blast. I'm going to write into existence the roar of a lion, a roar like thunder enough to fill the skies."

8. What would you write if you could?

9. If you could take part in the Decades Race and capture a wishing star, what would you wish for? Why? (Remember, it can be something personal or something "bigger.")

10. If you could bond with a star, what kind of star would you want? In the novel, the star of Nim is described as headstrong and willful, but loyal. Nayha's star is full of hope. To-garath's star is vivacious, playful, and brilliant. Gaia's star is full of vast power. What kind of personality would you want your star to have?

11. Sozo's star, Gaia, forces her to confront her deepest fears. Do you think you could do that? Would you be willing to do it if the reward was a wish?

12. Do you think Sozo's punishment at the end of the book is fair? Is it too little or too much?

13. What do you think will happen when Sozo and Naqi are reunited? Will they even be reunited?

14. Author Yueh Yang creates a rich and fully imagined world. What was your favorite part? What, if anything, would you like to see if you could visit Tall Titan?